undying DEVOTION

devotion series

PERSEPHONE AUTUMN

UNDYING DEVOTION

devotion series

PERSEPHONE AUTUMN

BETWEEN WORDS PUBLISHING LLC

Undying Devotion

ISBN: 978-1-951477-04-2 (Ebook)

ISBN: 978-1-951477-05-9 (Paperback)

Editor: Ellie McLove | My Brother's Editor

Proofreader: Rosa Sharon | My Brother's Editor

Cover Design: Abigail Davies | Pink Elephant Designs

BOOKS BY PERSEPHONE AUTUMN

Devotion Series

Distorted Devotion

Undying Devotion

Beloved Devotion

Darkest Devotion

Sweetest Devotion

Bay Area Duet Series

Click Duet

Through the Lens

Time Exposure

Inked Duet

Fine Line

Love Buzz

Insomniac Duet

Restless Night

A Love So Bright

Artist Duet

Blank Canvas

Abstract Passion

Novellas

Reese

Penny

Lake Lavender Series

Depths Awakened

One Night Forsaken

Every Thought Taken

Stone Bay Series

Broken Sky — Prequel

Standalone Romance Novels

Sweet Tooth

Transcendental

Poetry Collections

Ink Veins

Broken Metronome

Slipping From Existence

PUBLISHED UNDER P. AUTUMN

Standalone Non-Romance Novels

By Dawn

Is it awkward to dedicate a book to yourself?
Whatevs…
This is to past me. The woman who discovered herself and lost people along the way. The woman who stood strong and owned who she is. And the woman who learned it's okay to be dark and twisted and naughty.

PROLOGUE

RICK

LIQUID SEX BLEEDS from the speakers in the club. Every inch of Apex packed with slick, bare skin, ready to ring in the new year. This year's turn out is much higher than previous years. Although Apex is invitation or members only, the club has never had a crowd of this magnitude in the five years I have worked here.

As I weave my way through the club, I check in with our regular clients. Since we invited several one-timers tonight, it is imperative our regular clientele enjoys the evening with the same level of comfort as usual. As I approach one of the large, circular couches, I stop and take in the three couples spread across the oxblood leather.

A middle-aged man stands at one end, his entire body exposed to the voyeurs, while a woman half his age rests on all fours atop the couch and sucks his cock like it is her last meal. At her backside, a younger man plows into her pussy while tugging on the chains attached to both her nipples like horse reins.

Off to the side, a third man lays lengthwise with his calves dangling off the curved edge. One woman straddles his hips and rides his cock while another does the same atop his face. The two women kiss, fondle, and occasionally suck the other's breasts, all while being pleasured by him.

Such a magnificent sight. Not quite enough to get me hard, but enough to knock me a notch above flaccid.

After enjoying one last moment of watching them, I walk off and continue my route through the club and touch base with the staff working tonight. Apex has several rules laid in place for staff. One of those rules allows employees to join in on the festivities within the club, but only under strict guidelines. With tonight being one of our busiest nights of the year, the guidelines were reiterated before we opened the doors.

All acts must be consensual for both parties. No ifs, ands, or buts.

You are an employee of the club, on the clock, and expected to work. So, if at any time you are needed, you must step away. Period.

Meeting clients outside our four walls is permitted, but caution must be exercised. They are paying clientele. If things go south with the arrangement outside the club, it is up to the employee to right the wrong. No exceptions.

To date, we have had zero issues with the policy.

"Hey Tink," I holler over the music as I approach the bar. "Doing alright?"

"Yeah. But fuck if it's not busy as shit tonight."

Tink started at Apex in February. Although she has worked several major holiday events since she started, New Year's Eve always draws the largest crowd. She may be bombarded with the never-ending drink orders, but she will be thanking the gods later.

"True. Just wait until you count your tips. You'll beg for every night to be New Year's Eve," I tell her.

Tink throws me a half smile as she pours a line of shots. "You're probably right."

"Anything I can do to help?"

She shakes her head. "Nah, I'm good. Just keep 'em buying, boss."

I nod and settle on the barstool near the wall. At least once per shift, I park here and scan the club. Since the bar takes up a chunk of this corner, I have a great vantage point for most of the club. Everything in Apex is open. With no closed-off rooms. No displays to shadow people in corners. The dim lighting may provide a sense of security to several of the patrons, but I have worked here long enough to see everything around me like a predator in the night.

Just as I finish my visual circuit of the club, I stop when I spot a young brunette at the opposite end of the bar. Her face unfamiliar, but one I would remember without question.

I remain rooted on my stool and observe her a few

minutes. Clad in a form-fitted red lace dress, her skin visible beneath the intricate pattern, I notice flesh-colored pasties on her nipples. *Wonder what lies hidden beneath the bar, between her legs.* Her wavy, russet hair frames her round face and black-rimmed glasses and falls inches beneath her shoulders. In a studious way, she is fucking adorable.

After a minute, I wave Tink over. "What's her story?" I ask, jutting my chin toward the woman. The brunette has yet to talk to anyone near her and it fascinates me. *She* fascinates me.

Tink chuckles as if privy to top secret information. Or perhaps at my curiosity. "As far as I can tell, it's her first time here. And she came alone. Tried sparking a conversation with her, but she didn't seem keen on talking."

I nod. "Thanks. She seems a bit out of her element. I'll check on her in a minute."

Tink walks off to pour another drink and mumbles, "I'm sure you will."

Another minute or two passes, and no one approaches her. I abandon my stool and head toward the brunette who holds my interest captive. With each step forward, heat tugs at my cock. Something about this woman stirs at the animal inside me. An animal that begs to come out and play more often than I allow.

When I reach her, I lean in close, rest my hand on her forearm, and drag in the smell of her. A soft floral perfume tickles my nose while a jolt sparks beneath my hand on her skin. A power grid straight to my groin.

"Hey, gorgeous. I'm Rick, manager of Apex. Wanted to introduce myself as I haven't seen you in here before."

She peers down at my hand a second, then lifts her gaze to meet mine. A pair of steel blue tornados shielded by her glasses. Naughty teacher and dirty librarian fantasies zap through my mind, one after another.

Fuck.

"Christy," she says in a whimsical tone. "Tonight's my first time." After a beat, she adds, "Here. My first time here." As if I thought otherwise.

"Welcome. You alone?"

Not that it was out of character, but most women didn't come to Apex unescorted. Christy is safe here, but it wouldn't be difficult to be whisked off by an undesirable. Every once in a while, they slip in unnoticed.

After a sip of her raspberry cosmopolitan, she nods. As I suspected.

"Finish your drink. Then I'll show you around," I tell her. Not necessarily a command, but a strong suggestion. Something tells me she isn't opposed to such demands.

Christy locks eyes with me for one, two, three breaths. Her stormy eyes brimming with questions. The moment her gaze drops to my mouth and she swallows, I have my answer. But like a proper gentleman, I wait for verbal acceptance.

Without preamble, she throws back the remainder of her drink. "Ready when you are."

Quite telling. Color me intrigued.

Stepping away from her stool, I offer her my elbow.

She hooks her arm in mine and I weave us through the crowd. Inside Apex, there is no way to gradually introduce someone to the scene. Some couples are more vanilla than others, but there is no escape from the fact Apex is what it is. A sex club. An elite underground sex club. Not just anyone can get in here, so I wonder how she managed.

"Christy, who invited you to Apex?" Management, staff, and VIP clientele are the only individuals capable of inviting non-members.

"This is going to sound ridiculous," she says with a giggle. *Fuck me running.* Her giggle stirs my cock from its slumber. "A woman I work with invited me. We hung out and went shopping," she pauses and makes this adorable goofy face, "and I wanted to go into the lingerie store. She asked if I planned to wear it for someone, and I said no. That sometimes I liked to put on sexy lingerie, take photos of myself, and post them in a chat room. I never show my face, though."

My expression stoic, I ask, "So you enjoy being watched?" If she says yes, I may just come in my pants.

"Yes and no." Close enough. "I've only ever been 'watched' online through posted images. Never a live feed. And never in person. I'm a bit nervous being here."

"Why the nerves? Everyone is here for similar reasons. And there are rules inside these walls. Strict rules." She has no need for fear. Not here. No one does.

"Performance anxiety, I suppose? What if some

weirdo pushes himself onto me and things happen I don't want?"

"That will never happen here," I state firmly.

Christy nods. "Glad to hear." Her free hand goes to her hair and she twirls a lock around a finger. "I guess I'm just nervous to do something new."

I stop us in front of a large, round leather ottoman. Four people perform together. A man on his back at the base fucks the woman above him in the pussy. On his knees behind the pair is a man claiming her ass. Standing before her is a third man, who continually pounds his cock down her throat. The four of them have a rhythm all their own. As a voyeur, it is comparable to watching sexual poetry in the flesh.

Out of the corner of my eye, I gaze at Christy to catch her reaction. Part of me is surprised and another not so much.

Christy inches forward, eyes fixated on the act. Her tongue darts out and swipes her bottom lip before she swallows hard. Arm still hooked with mine, her muscles contract as she leans a little closer. Hungry for more. And I want to give her more. So much more.

We stand and watch the group another minute before I speak up. "Come with me."

When she takes a breath, I realize how statuesque her body stood beside me while watching. After she snaps out of her haze, she nods and I walk us away from the four-some. Attached to my side like she belongs there, she inhales sharply halfway across the club floor. If I didn't know any better, I would say she is working to regulate her breathing, undetected. But even through the buzz from her body to mine and the heavy bass of the music vibrating the floor, I pick up on every single detail. Call it a gift.

We reach the roped-off VIP area and step inside. Everything within VIP is visible to the entire club, but only select members have permission to walk past the red velvet ropes. And only a set number of invitations are given. Within VIP, it is less crowded and less invasive. More space to breathe while you enjoy the club. Although all patrons can see you, no one ogles. Call it exposed privacy.

I walk us to a vacant couch and sit us down. Beside me, Christy peers around. Not only is VIP somewhat secluded, it also bodes "accessories." Toys. Implements. Various surfaces, furniture, and swings. Every molecule inside me screams to ask what she thinks of it all. But I hold my composure and wait for her to speak up.

And I don't wait long. Less than a minute passes after we sit and she asks, "Why did you bring me in here?"

She doesn't face me but instead stares at a woman who rides one man's cock and sucks another's. Christy appears more curious than taken aback. This delights me more than imaginable.

I trace her arm, bicep to fingertips, and she shifts her attention to me. "Because it's less chaotic in VIP. From what I can tell, this scene is new to you. I'd rather you not be overwhelmed on your first visit."

After a moment, she squares her shoulders and sits taller. "You speak as if I'll return. What makes you so confident?"

"Everything about you begs for more. The way you lean in to absorb what you see. Your fevered skin and rapid breathing. How you clutch me closer when you're turned on."

"Hmm," she mumbles. "Well, I'd have to be invited or become a member to return. And seeing as I'm not able to become a member—"

"You're a member. Just a matter of semantics. But I'll handle it before you leave."

Her stormy blue eyes spin like a hurricane and I get lost at sea. Taking a risk, I continue tracing my fingers along her body. From her hand onto her knee, I inch my way up her bare thigh. Her lips part as her chest rises and falls in rapid succession. *Has she never been touched like this?*

I stop my trek to heaven and ask, "No offense, but are you a virgin?"

Eyes wide, she verbally slaps me. "What?! No! Why would you ask me that?"

"Wasn't trying to upset you. But your reaction to my touch is indicative."

Christy rolls her eyes. "Well, I'm not a virgin. Sorry to disappoint," she huffs. "Maybe no one has ever let me feel things during sex."

This confuses me for a second. Does she mean no one has touched her except for sticking their dick in her? Or that she has never experienced foreplay? Or, worst of all, has she never orgasmed from sex?

"Care to elaborate?"

With another huff, she says, "Most of the people I've had sex with did what was best for them and didn't reciprocate."

I reach up with my free hand and tip her chin up, locking her gaze with mine. "That will never happen with me."

She sucks in a breath. "How can you be so sure?"

"Because I'm not a prick. Your pleasure is my pleasure." An absolute truth. I lean my face closer to hers as my fingers slowly graze her thigh. With my lips an inch above hers, I whisper, "Can I kiss you?"

My fingers skim the edge of her lacy dress, just at the junction of her thighs. If I moved north another half an inch, I would graze her nude lace panties. Without a doubt, they would be drenched.

"Yes," she whispers, eyes locked on mine.

I crash my lips to hers and she opens up for me—her lips and legs. In a heartbeat, I stroke her tongue with mine and slide my hand the rest of the way up her thigh. Both sets of lips hot and slick and eager for my touch.

Continuing to fuck her mouth with mine, I trace my fingers up and down her lace panties, coating my fingers with her juices. After the third swipe down, she rocks her hips forward in invitation.

I groan against her lips before pushing her panties to the side. Before another second passes, the slick heat between her thighs coats my fingertips. My middle finger circles her clit once, twice, and then dips between her folds. Fuck. So hot and wet and eager for me. I slip my finger out and play with her clit a moment.

Within minutes, her red lacy dress inches higher and higher up her body. Legs spread wide for me, she beckons and I slip off the couch, sit on my haunches on the floor between her thighs, and worship her pussy with my mouth. After she comes with my mouth on her, I tug the red lace off her body and lay her down. She rubs her hands up and down her body a second before she starts playing with her clit.

As quickly as humanly possible, I strip my clothes and grab a condom from my pants. After I roll the condom on, I kneel down between her legs and slam inside her. She cries out beneath me as I rear back and slam forward again. Her breasts bounce and I glance down to see the pasties still in place. I rip them both away and she cries out again, her cunt wetter.

I lift one of her legs to rest it on my shoulder as I lean forward, plow into her, and suck her nipples. Her hands fist my hair and yank me down to her lips. The way we kiss and fuck is vicious and insane and I never want it to end.

Her breathing shifts into high-pitched cries as her walls clamp down and milk my cock. Un-fucking-believable. I have always been in control during sex, but Christy rips the control away and I come before I can stop myself.

I collapse on top of her and she wraps all four limbs

around me. Previous partners are no comparison to the woman below me. There is a purity about her—a virginity to this life—that magnetizes her to me. It is undeniable, and I ache for more. Of her and what we could be together.

"So," I heave. "When can I see you again?"

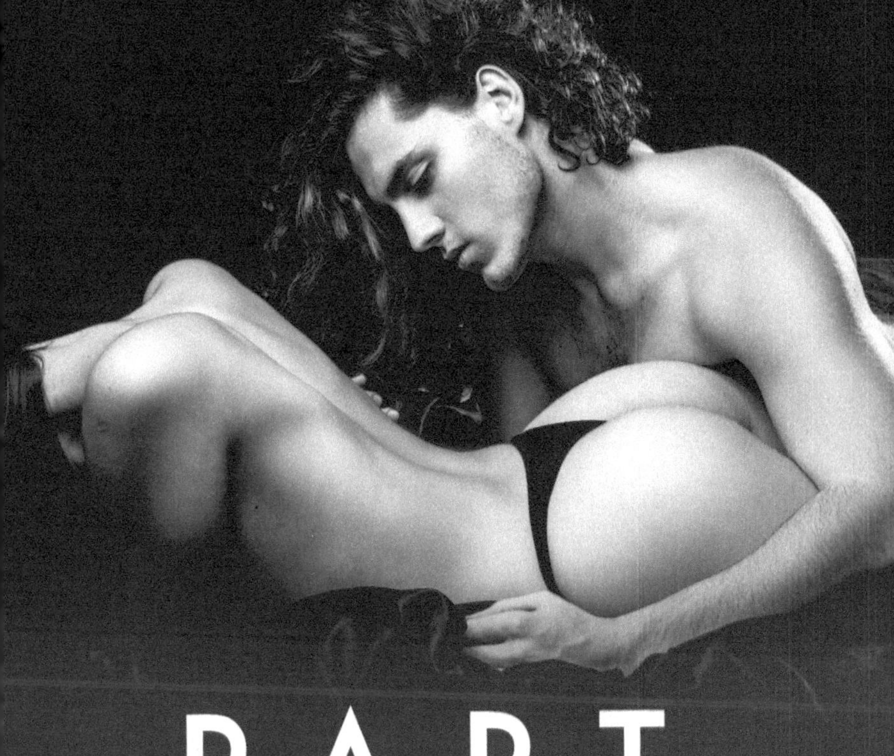

PART
one

ONE

CHRISTY

June—Four years later

"I UNDERSTAND why you're moving, but does it have to be across the freaking country, bitch?" I whine to my best friend, Sarah.

Less than two months ago, one of our coworkers—who shall remain nameless—attacked and molested Sarah. For months, he had sent her anonymous gifts and notes. And we will truly never know how long he had been stalking her. Maybe since the day she started at Hammond Life. A shiver rolls down my spine at the notion.

Rick and I have been exposed to a lot of people in our lifestyle. Most of them respectful and respectable. If someone ever did to us what happened to Sarah, I'm not sure I would have it in me to be so vulnerable with others again.

"It sucks to move so far away," Sarah says as she hugs

me. "But I need to get as much distance between me and Georgia as possible. I can't breathe here anymore."

I nod. I get where she is coming from. If I were in her shoes, Rick and I would have left as soon as possible too. But over two thousand miles away… not so sure about that.

"Bitch, I feel like I'll never see you again." *God*, why the hell am I such an emotional baby today? Maybe it is my godforsaken hormones.

"Are you kidding me? Of course we'll see each other again. You're my best friend. That doesn't end because I'm moving."

Point made. But I can't seem to help myself. With Sarah and Jackson—her boyfriend—moving away, it feels as if I'm losing a chunk of my family. My family is small enough as is, I can't lose any more of it.

"Yeah, you're right," I say. "Rick and I will have to plan a trip out to see you guys after you're settled." I peer over at Rick, who is helping Jackson haul larger pieces of furniture from the house to a moving truck outside. He pops a half-smile and winks at me.

Damn, I love him.

"Plus, we'll talk on the phone all the time. No chance in hell you're escaping me." Sarah laughs and I join in. I was so lucky to have a friend like Sarah. Unfortunately, I haven't been able to share all aspects of my life with her. In context, not physically. That ship sailed a while ago.

We finish packing the contents of her kitchen cabinets, then move on to the spare bedroom. It serves as an office and guest room. There isn't much in the room to pack other than the desk contents and two overflowing bookshelves worth of books.

The rest of the packing goes by quick and their house is an empty shell before nightfall. Sarah and Jackson plan on staying with Liz and Tiffany tonight, after their going-away party, and driving out in the morning. As gracious as Liz was to offer hosting the party, I suggested it be at my and Rick's place. That way, if Sarah and Jackson were ready to call it a night, the party wouldn't keep them up. Liz agreed without hesitation.

Liz—my other best friend—recently started dating Tiffany. Tiffany is super sweet and clicks with all of us, like we have known her years instead of months. Before Sarah met Jackson, I suspected Sarah and Liz had a fling going because I caught them making out. More than once. But the topic was never broached by any of us. Oftentimes, I contemplated bringing up Rick and my lifestyle with them, just to have it out in the open, but there was never a time that felt right. So, I kept it bottled up.

The guys join us in the vacant living room and Rick traces his fingers down my spine before gripping my hip and drawing me into his side. Every time he touches me, a new star burns in the night sky.

"Let's all grab dinner, then head to the party," Rick says.

I press the side button on my cell and check the time. Three hours until the festivities begin. It won't be as lux as Liz's parties, but it will be a good time. "Sounds good."

Glancing between Sarah and Jackson, I toss out, "It's your last night here. Where do you want to go?"

They stare at each other a minute, smile, then say, "Barbecue." In sync, like Liz and I did to mess with Sarah months ago. Memories…

"Barbecue it is," I say, laughing.

"Besides you guys, I am really going to miss the food here," Sarah says from the passenger seat. The guys behind us—Rick driving the moving truck with Jackson's car in tow, and Jackson driving Sarah's car. Which is an interesting sight—a six-foot one, muscular man behind the wheel of a Beetle. Definitely worth a laugh.

"Well at least I get priority over the food," I say, giggling. "You're my best bitch. You know that, right?"

Sarah nods, her eyes welling. "Yeah."

A few minutes later, we park outside our place. We have about an hour before everyone arrives, but I know Liz will be here any minute. Her inner party planner wouldn't have it any other way.

We shuffle inside and start setting up the snacks and drinks. I barely have the cups on the kitchen island before Liz and Tiffany arrive. So freaking predictable. Liz goes to Sarah first, picks her up off the ground, and squeezes the life out of her. Swear to god Liz holds her for an eternity.

Did she forget the rest of us were in the room? Her girl-friend included.

I throw my arms wide open and clear my throat. "Am I invisible, bitch?"

Liz and Sarah laugh hysterically before Liz sets Sarah down, they run at me, and tackle me to the ground. "You know we love you," Liz says. "Sarah just gets extra hugs tonight. Don't be jealous."

"Yeah, yeah," I tease.

When I glance over at Rick, a smolder darkens his liquid honey eyes. In an instant, my thighs dampen and lungs heave. An invisible, impulsive chemistry has always existed between us. A bond so powerful, words do it no justice. I reach up and run my fingers over the thin, silver collar around my neck. To an onlooker, the shiny silver is just a unique necklace. Solid with a hinge on one side and a lock on the other. Snug, but not a choker. A small loop on the front most would think is for pendants. But is far from it.

Rick's eyes drop to my throat—my collar—and a wicked gleam shines on his face. The kind that soaks my panties. He clasps his right thumb with his left fingers and toys with the thick, black band. My lips part centimeters and I breathe a little heavier. Simple gestures between us sometimes spark the hottest flames.

Two-and-a-half years ago, just before Rick and I moved in together, he gifted me the collar. In return, I gave him the ring. An effortless exchange, but it meant so much more to us. We were nowhere near ready for marriage—if I'm honest, we still aren't—but the two tokens were representative of our bond to each other. An unbreakable bond.

"Did you hear me?" Liz asks.

I shake my head. "Sorry. What?"

"There's someone at the door. Want me to get it?"

"Sure. We should just put a sign up that says come on in," I joke.

An hour later, our apartment overflows with bodies and the party is in full swing. I haven't seen Rick in a while, but I sense him nearby. His proximity always pops up on my radar. Even the night we met. Rick's soul was a beacon calling out to me.

The music changes—Liz, of course, in charge of music —and my body vibrates to the beat. Before I scan the room, a familiar pair of arms wrap around my waist as his body presses flush against my back. "Hey, gorgeous."

"Mmm, hey." Rick skims his hands up and down my torso, openly fondling me. "Where've you been?" I groan.

"Did you miss me?" he asks before licking the shell of my ear.

"Always," I murmur, grinding my ass against his groin.

"Patience, gorgeous. When the party ends, the real fun begins."

I spin around and stare at him a moment. "Really? Who?" I whisper-ask as if someone will hear our conversation over the music.

Rick hauls my body back to his, slips a leg between mine, and grinds against me to the music. I lace my fingers behind his neck and dance with him. He won't answer me immediately, this much I know. Dragging out the anticipation is part of the pleasure.

When the song ends, he kisses me. He sucks my bottom lip before nipping it and kissing his way to my ear. "Tim and Jill are here," he says.

I moan loud enough for Rick to hear, but no one else over the music. We have only been with Tim and Jill one other time, but it was phenomenal. And suddenly, as eager as I am to spend time with my friends, I want the party to end. Rick senses my mood shift and chuckles.

As if I voiced my desires aloud, several people start leaving. Twenty minutes later, Sarah and Jackson approach me and Rick and say their goodbyes. A lengthy process, but hugs and promises to stay in touch are exchanged. When Sarah, Jackson, Liz, and Tiffany walk out the door, the only people left in the room with us are Tim and Jill.

A scorching fire brushes over my lips as Rick kisses me with unrestrained fervor, his fingers slowly peeling my clothes away. Behind me, Jill and Tim grope one another in similar fashion. Both men still fully dressed. Standing exposed before him, I sigh as Rick strokes his fingertip side to side just above the junction of my thighs with his eyes locked on mine. A dark amber mixes with his honey eyes the more he brushes against my skin. Pausing for a micro blip of time, he draws a line with his finger up my midline, starting at my shaved mound and stopping at my collar. When he reaches the cool metal, he hooks a finger under the silver and tugs me to him.

"Remember who you belong to, gorgeous."

"Always," I tell him.

"Remember who I belong to."

"Yes," I breathe.

He releases me and I spin around to face Jill. Face to face, we are all hands and fingers. Touching and teasing and kissing. A woman's skin is much softer and delicate, and the smooth flesh under my fingertips drives me to explore her terrain. Meanwhile, her fingers drift down, down, down and tease my pussy folds as I pinch her nipples.

Jill has bite-size breasts. Maybe somewhere between an A cup and a B. Not too much, but enough to play with. Unlike my full Cs, which annoy me at times, Jill has the luxury of going braless as often as she pleases.

Her lips break away from the skin above my collarbone and she leans forward to whisper in my ear. "Enjoy fucking my husband again." And then she dips her finger once, twice inside me before walking over to Rick with the taste of me on her tongue.

Tim steps up to me, his t-shirt and khaki shorts securely in place. He traces a line along my jaw with a finger before tipping my chin up and kissing down the curve of my throat. His lips on my sensitive skin amplifying the fire Jill ignited between my legs.

Rick and I have strict rules when with other people. In this life, our rules set boundaries and keep the lines from blurring. The rules are black and white, but there is always space for gray.

First and foremost, no kissing on the mouth. Ever. The act an intimacy only we share. Second, no talking during the act other than guidance, praise, or permission. The reason behind our lifestyle isn't to form intimate connections with other people. It is lust and hunger and a desire to fuck. Plain and simple. Intimacy is saved for when we are alone. Third, if someone does something we don't enjoy, it stops immediately. No ifs, ands, or buts. And last but certainly not least, Rick and I always remain in the same room during every act. Not that we distrust one another, but more so we can enjoy ourselves and protect one another. Baring yourself completely to another person puts you in a vulnerable position. Safety is vital.

After everything that happened with Sarah and her stalker over the last six months, Rick and I tightened our rules and enforced them with everyone who we allowed to step foot into our sex play. If couples were uncomfortable or unable to abide by our rules, we bid them farewell. Nowadays, there is no such thing as being overprotective. Honestly, you never know who is batshit crazy anymore.

Tim kisses along my collarbone as his fingertips dance down my arms, leaving a buzz in their wake, and land on my hips. I reach forward and pop the button open on his shorts, slowly pushing down the zipper. After the slider trails down the teeth to the stopper, his shorts slip down his thick glutes and thump on the hardwood. Beneath, Tim flashes his commando status with pride, and, for a second, part of me wonders if Rick set up tonight with Tim and Jill before the party. Tim seems awfully prepared. And I can't recall if he was bare last time. Not that it matters.

I wrap my hand around his cock and glide up once, twice, before I fondle his balls in my grip and drop to my knees. Behind me, Jill sucks Rick's cock like a gold medalist. Rick fists her hair tight and pumps into her with unmatched vigor.

Tim strips his shirt and tosses it to the side as I suck one of his balls into my mouth and play with it while I stroke him. I pop it out of my mouth and lick the underside of his cock, root to tip, before taking it all in my mouth. The head of his cock hits the back of my throat and I relax my muscles as I bob my head up and down.

Jill's ass brushes against mine, neither of us stops sucking the other man's dick, and I reach between my legs and feel for her pussy. The moment I touch her wet lips, she moans. *So fucking wet.* I slip a finger inside her and she rides me a beat while she face fucks Rick.

In no time, Jill comes on my finger. Her juices coat and run down my finger and onto my hand. Once she drifts back to earth, we stop sucking the guys and climb on the bed. With Jill on her back, head at the edge of the bed, I mount her, press my core against her lips, then lick the length of her slit and suck her taut clit. Breaking my mouth away, I dip two fingers in her cunt as Rick steps up and grabs my hair.

"Suck me, gorgeous," he purrs.

With Rick on my tongue, my fingers inside Jill, and Jill's mouth on my clit, my body goes into stimulus overload. Or so I thought. That is until Tim clutches both my ass cheeks and spreads them wide. *What happens next?* My silent question answered when Tim licks from my clit to the clenched opening between my ass cheeks and circles the tight hole over and over.

My eyes roll back in my head and I forget how to breathe for a split second. White heat lights up every atom in my body. Too much and not enough, all at the same time. Not sure when or how it happened, but somehow I became the center of attention in our foursome. For some reason, everyone wants to contribute to my pleasure. And I won't complain while it happens.

"Such a tight little hole," Tim says behind me as he continues to swirl his tongue over the puckered flesh between my cheeks. "Can I fuck you here?" He lifts his mouth, presses a finger to the center, and pushes in slightly. I gasp around Rick's cock and push back into the pressure.

"Yes," I moan.

Rick tips my chin up before I take his cock again, his eyes intently studying mine to be certain this is what *I* want. The seconds that pass feel timeless. I nod and so does he. Part of our unspoken language. Not just in the bedroom. It came natural to us and formed the night we met, growing stronger with time. Rick knows my boundaries—just as I know his—and when to check in.

Tim coats my rim with my arousal before he dips his cock in my pussy once, twice. *Fuck, he is big.* "Just relax your muscles," Tim says as he grips my hips firmly. A second later, he is there. Cock pressing forward as the hole contracts against the pressure. Jill swipes my clit in small, slow circles, running her finger over my folds every other revolution. In front of me, Rick cups my face in his palm as he strokes my cheek. Rick is what soothes me enough to grant Tim access. No one settles or spikes my heartbeat like Rick.

Once Tim pushes forward, I gasp at the rush of sensation coursing throughout my body. Lust and pain and immense pleasure. A slight burning around the edges until a dollop of moisture coats his skin. He slides out slowly to the crown, then glides back in. Rick's eyes locked with mine, I see an insatiable hunger ignite them. I suck up and down his length for three strokes, peek up at him, and silently tell him to fuck Jill.

A curt nod and Rick retrieves Jill out from under me. He flips her on her stomach and yanks her ass into the air. I refuse to look away as he strokes himself before rolling a condom on and teasing Jill's pussy with the head of his cock. A second later, he thrusts forward and she screams.

Tim bends over me, wraps one arm around my hips and the other at my breasts. He plunges into my ass over and over as he swipes his fingers over my clit. "So fucking wet," he groans. I whimper as he circles my clit again and again, then inserts two fingers inside me.

Jill cries out, her orgasm hitting her quick. But I know Rick isn't done. He can go forever before release. He dips between her thighs and laps at her juices, building her up again with his fingers and tongue. Before I've reached my first orgasm with Tim, Rick has given Jill two and a sense of deprivation washes over me.

Sensing my temperament, Rick abandons Jill for a moment and finagles himself beneath me. Tim stops for a beat, realizing what's happening, and gives Rick a moment. Once situated beneath me, Rick tears off the condom and slips inside my cunt.

A slow rhythm starts. Rick in, Tim out. Tim in, Rick out. Like a seesaw, back and forth. I relax my weight on Rick and he wraps his arms around me before he grabs my ass cheeks and spreads them farther apart.

Rick and Tim work my body like a well-oiled machine as every molecule in my body climbs higher, higher, higher. The hunger and fire raging inside me is intense and addictive and intoxicating. I groan into Rick's neck before I bite his shoulder.

"Feel it all, gorgeous," he whispers in my ear. "Do you know how unbelievably stunning you are right now? Letting someone fuck that tight little ass of yours, and me fucking this pussy. *My pussy.*"

I groan louder. When Rick talks dirty, it dumps gasoline on the bonfire low in my belly.

"You know what would make this hotter, gorgeous? Fucking you while watching this over and over again."

"Yes," I cry out.

Jill, who sits near the pillows finger fucking herself while watching the three of us, gets up and grabs Rick's phone. He unlocks it and opens the camera for her. "If you're okay with it," Rick says to Jill and Tim. "We can set it on the dresser and record. Unless you don't want your face in it."

"Don't care," Tim grunts out. He is so close—the thickening of his cock tells me so—but holds out for my orgasm.

Jill gets the phone set up on the dresser after hitting record and returns to the bed. As Rick and Tim continue to fuck me, she straddles Rick's face and I suck her breasts. Jill rides Rick's face like she's at a rodeo and soon the pitch of her cries changes. She's close again. Rick slips his hand between us and plays with my clit.

Balls slap my skin, cocks piston in and out, Rick circles faster and harder with his fingers. It builds so quick, and I clamp down hard on Jill's nipple. She orgasms on Rick's face as I explode around Rick and he comes inside me. Before a scream escapes my lips, Tim detonates. Both men pulsing inside my body as I visibly vibrate from my orgasm.

"Holy shit," I gasp. "Fucking intense." My voice garbled and skin tingling.

Jill dismounts from Rick's face and I kiss him, tasting her salty tang on his tongue. Slowly, Tim pulls out of me, but Rick and I don't separate. He remains inside me and semi-hard as we kiss the hell out of each other. Right now, I hope Jill and Tim get dressed and leave.

A zipper grates beside us. Feet shuffle on the wood. Rick and I remain connected in every possible way. A moment later, the front door clicks and it is just the two of us.

I sit up, plant my hands on his pecs, and start rocking my hips over him. "Tim not do it for you, gorgeous?"

Back and forth. Back and forth. "Not like you," I tell him as I bring my hands to my breasts and pinch my nipples.

Rick grabs my hips as he hardens inside me. "Tell me what you want, gorgeous."

I bite my lip, grinding down on him. "Fuck my ass."

He reaches around and plays with my hole. "You sure, kitten? You sure it's not tired?" he coos.

I love it when he calls me kitten. That is when I know he holds full control and I am at his beck and call. "I'm sure, Daddy. Fuck my pretty little ass."

He pinches one of my nipples and twists. "Only after you come on daddy's cock pretty kitten." Rick lays back and I press my hands against his chest and ride him until I scream out in pleasure. Then he flips me on my back, grabs a vibrator from the drawer under our bed, turns it on and inserts it in my pussy, and guides himself in my tight hole.

"So tight, kitten." A moment later, my legs are over his

shoulders and he's hovering an inch above me, fucking my ass hard.

"Oh, god," I moan. Within seconds, he has me feeling a thousand times more than what Tim did. "I need to come, daddy."

He clutches my shoulders and fucks me harder, faster. With my whines and his grunts, it will be soon. "I'm there, kitten. Let go, gorgeous."

Hot seed floods my ass as I explode around the vibrator. Rick leans back, yanks it out, and runs his fingers up and down my soaked slit. "Who does this belong to, kitten?"

"You, daddy."

"Remember that."

"Always."

TWO

I WAKE to Christy's bare flesh draped over my body. Leaning my head away, I stare and get lost at the sight of her. *Fuck, she is unbelievable.* How in the hell did I get so lucky? How did I nail down the perfect woman? I am one lucky son of a bitch, that is how. The first night she walked into Apex, it could have been my night off. She could have met someone else. Or left alone after finishing her drink.

But it didn't happen that way. Thank fuck.

The night my eyes landed on Christy, it was as if a lighthouse lamp lit up and pointed her out to me. Before her, I had been with my share of beautiful creatures, and done countless acts with faceless women and men. But Christy is different for me. Although she is still quite tame in the grand scheme of things, she has an unavoidable radiance I refuse to ignore.

She is a beacon. *My beacon.*

"Quit it," she mumbles and giggles in her sleep. I scan over her face—lips perked up slightly, strands of hair lay haphazardly over her eye, along the side of her nose, and drop off her chin. Even asleep, she is perfection. Wonder what she is dreaming about? Hopefully something involving us.

I wrap my arms a little tighter around her and hold her close. Her all too familiar fragrance pierces my nose and I inhale deep. Peonies and amber and all Christy.

On the first night, I had been skeptical. My radar had failed me in the past and led me down paths I hope to never see again. Sitting at the bar, Christy sipped her drink—so innocent and timid. Her red lace dress screamed for attention while her body language stated the polar opposite. Lucky for me, my radar didn't malfunction with her and I followed Christy's lead. Every day since that moment, she has surprised me time and again. Last night included.

I have tested the water with Christy several times. There were still so many things I wanted to do with her. Claiming her ass being one of them. It sat on a long list with items slowly being tick-marked. My hesitation to try some of them stems from her lack of experience. But after last night, my level of hesitation is slowly going out with the tide.

Tim may have dipped his cock in before me, but he doesn't have what it takes to get my girl off. And that tells me Christy is, and always will be, mine. As I am hers. Sure, we fuck other couples and have a good time. But no one gets my dick harder or makes me come like a god the way Christy does.

After kissing the crown of her head, I strategically slip out from under her and off the bed. Slipping on a pair of boxers, I shut the bedroom door and head to the kitchen. My girl deserves a big breakfast after last night's festivities.

Just as I set the last strip of bacon on a paper towel, the familiar shuffle-thump of Christy's morning strut enters the kitchen. Before I have the chance to spin and face her, her hands hit my hips and skim around my front side, scratching their way to my pecs. I close my eyes as they roll back into my head. Her touch generates a low-lying hum in my veins I would die without. A jolt of life.

"Mmm, smells so good in here," she mumbles against my back before pressing a kiss between my shoulder blades.

"Bacon, eggs, and blueberry pancakes." I grip her hands, lift them, then turn to face her. "Coffee?" I ask the question, although I already know the answer. But why pass up the opportunity to mess with her.

"Is that even a legitimate question?" She rolls her eyes. "Coffee. Please." Christy pads out of the kitchen. "Gotta brush my teeth. Be right back."

If there is one truth in this life, it is that I know my girl. Her routine. The fact that she isn't, and never will be, a morning person until at least eight ounces of coffee is in her system. How she loves her eggs cooked—over medium, so she can poke the yolk and slather it on the egg white. Sometimes she likes to dunk her toast in the yolk, but it varies by day. And how undying her love is for me.

Love… it was never a territorial line I wished to cross. But, within months of meeting Christy, my desensitized heart thumped again. Even in my youth, I had never "loved" anyone other than family. But even the familial love slipped away. Christy knew I only spoke with my parents two or three times a year, during the holidays, but I never told her an in-depth reason why. Not that I don't want to. I do. And one day I will, but I still can't bring myself to say the words. When the time is right, it will pour out of me.

Christy has hinted to me about her family here and there, but just breadcrumbs. And I refuse to pry. Our bond travels boundaries I never imagined possible. When she is ready to let go of her pain, she will. And she will deliver it to me—the guardian of her heart. But I admire her strength and courage. Not everyone rises easily from the ashes. It takes guts and resilience and fire. Qualities my girl harnesses like a goddess.

Just as I pour maple syrup on the pancakes, she swoops in next to me and dives for the coffeepot, filling her mug to the brim. Three, two, one… "Ahhh," she sighs with the mug to her lips after her first gulp. "Thank you." She pushes up on her toes and I lean down and kiss her.

"You're welcome, gorgeous."

I carry our plates to the table and we plop down and eat. When she hits the bottom of her coffee, I automatically get up and grab the pot and bring it to her with the cream and sugar caddy. Her smile beams so full of life, I breathe a little faster. Every day it amazes me how one woman is capable of owning my heart for eternity.

When our plates are empty, I broach a topic I am certain won't sit well with her. "Gorgeous?"

She swallows the gulp of coffee in her mouth. "Yeah?"

"There's no good time to talk about this, but we need to talk about how we're going to handle other couples going forward." Christy tilts her head and furrows her brow. God, she is adorable as fuck. "After what happened with Sarah, I want to be sure we're being as safe as possible."

Understanding settles in her stormy eyes and she nods. "I wondered about that," she says, twirling a lock of hair.

"Going forward, I'd like to look into anyone entering our bedroom. Or us entering theirs. Even people we've been with. We can't be too safe."

"Agreed. What can I do?"

I reach for her hand and take it in mine. For two breaths, I stare at our joined hands and relish in the love I have for this woman. "Let me know if anything off-putting comes up. Tell me who catches your eye. It'd be nice to see new people, but I don't want us unprepared." Stroking small circles on her palm, I bring her hand to my lips and kiss the center. "What happened to Sarah… that *will not* happen to you."

For a beat, a solemn expression flits across her face. But as quickly as it appears, it vanishes. "You'll keep me safe. Never doubted that for a minute."

I kiss her palm again. "Enough with the heavy conversation. What would you like to do today?" And when her face lights up, I have done my job. Fuck, I love her.

After a two-hour walk through the aquarium and some lunch, we head home. With the day half gone, I head straight for the bedroom and get ready for work. Although Apex doesn't open until eight at night, there is prep to be done. Helping restock the bar. Sanitizing the entire venue. Checking all implements and equipment for safety reasons. We also have a small menu of appetizers, so minor kitchen prep has to be finished.

Usually, I arrive around six in the evening and leave between two-thirty and three in the morning. It's a long day, especially now when the northerners aren't here. But I love my job. By no means is it glamorous—to people who care about glamour—but I am in my element and it never feels like work.

Besides, I would have never met Christy if not for Apex.

I slide up the knot on my merlot red tie and fold down the black collar of my dress shirt. Honestly, the only dress code at work is to be presentable and polished. A button-down and no tie would be completely acceptable, but it comes off too casual for me.

As I put my keys, wallet, and phone in my pockets, Christy walks into the room and whistles.

"Well, hot damn," she rasps. "I love it when you wear black and red." Another thing I know about my girl—the clothes she loves me in. She walks up to me and runs a hand down my tie, tugging it when she reaches the end.

"Careful, gorgeous." She bats her lashes at me. "Coming in tonight?" I ask.

"Yeah. Might see if Liz and Tiffany want to grab dinner first. I'll be in after."

I gaze into her stormy eyes, grab a lock of her hair, and play with it. "Whatever you want. Just let me know." She nods.

Since we helped Jackson and Sarah pack up their place yesterday, my girl hasn't been her usual bubbly self. Hopefully, her sadness will fade with time. Christy and Sarah are much closer than Christy and Liz. Their friendship started more than a year prior. And in that time, Christy and Sarah formed a sisterly bond. Once Sarah and Jackson reach California, and Christy talks with her more often, she will perk right up.

At least I hope she does.

THREE

CHRISTY

LIZ AND TIFFANY agree to meet up for dinner. Thank god.

Today seems like a never-ending trek of loss and gloom. Sarah hasn't been gone twenty-four hours yet and it is as if someone stole a chunk of my family—and my heart—from me. The little bit of family I have left.

Generally, I resonate on the polar opposite of doom and misery. But with Sarah physically absent in our circle, I find it harder and harder to smile already. The misery won't last forever, but last time I lost family, I had friends ready to lift me up. People on the sidelines who jumped in and rescued me. Now, everyone has higher priorities in life besides making mopey little Christy feel better.

This fucking sucks.

I meet Liz and Tiffany at a small Italian restaurant not far from Apex. Another secret. All of my current friends believe Rick works in a restaurant/bar. Honestly, it is the easiest way to explain his weird work hours without sharing he manages a sex club. Anytime Sarah or Liz suggested we "go to Rick's restaurant" for dinner, I always made an excuse.

Just had dinner there last night.

Rick says they're swamped tonight.

Someone called in sick and he's super busy.

Blah, blah, blah.

Don't get me wrong, I love the life Rick and I enjoy together. Couldn't imagine our relationship any other way. Sometimes, though, it would be nice to share that piece of myself with the people closest to me. To let those people who hold a piece of my heart know the real me. The me that hides who she is outside of specific walls.

But the repercussions of the last time I revealed the real me still scar me today. And I am nowhere near ready to travel down that road again. I refuse to lose anyone else I love because of who I am.

Sitting at a table for four, I twirl my fork and create craters in my napkin with the tines. So intently shredding the napkin, I startle when Liz and Tiffany walk up to the table and sit down across from me. Why the hell am I so spacey? And jumpy? So freaking annoying.

"Hey, girl," Liz says as she studies my face. "You alright?"

I plaster on my big girl smile and answer, "Of course. Just bored waiting for you guys to get here." My cheeks sting from my over-exaggerated smile.

Liz and Tiffany scoot farther into the red vinyl booth, the springs creaking under their weight. Hell, the worn booths would squeak with a thirty-pound toddler sitting on them. But this place is the best Italian restaurant in the area and no one cares how dated the décor is.

Before any of us gets in another word, the server approaches the table, rattles off the specials for the evening, and takes their drink orders. Less than a minute later, she steps off and promises to be back with drinks, fresh bread, and garlic-herb dipping oil.

The table is layered in a blanket of awkward silence as they both stare at the menu. Me? I have been here ten minutes and decided what I wanted nine minutes ago. So, I dig my napkin crater deeper and zone out. Nothing worse than staring at someone without reason. No need for me to make things more uncomfortable.

After the server drops off their drinks and the bread, she takes our orders and disappears again. Maybe she senses the strain on my heart and, by proxy, with Liz. With Sarah gone, Liz is the only close friend I have in my inner circle. But she has Tiffany, and they spend most of their time doing things together... without anyone else. Which is understandable in their newish relationship.

"You sure you're alright?" Liz asks.

I peer up at her from my Swiss cheese napkin and nod. "Sure. Why wouldn't I be?"

"Don't know. But I've never seen you so..."

"Glum," Tiffany chimes in.

Flipping fantastic. Am I really that transparent? Obviously, I wear my heart on my sleeve. Somehow, I need to reign that shit in quick. Last thing I need is to be doted on as the sad one in the group.

"Yes," Tiffany says.

"What?" I ask, unsure of what Tiffany is agreeing with.

Tiffany shakes her head. "You just asked if you were that transparent. And I said yes."

"Shit. Didn't mean to say that out loud."

Tiffany reaches across the table and sets her hand, palm side down, in front of me. "It's okay to be sad because one of your best friends moved away. You, Sarah, and Liz are like sisters. Honestly, it'd be weirder if you weren't sad. But don't bottle it up, okay? Let people know why you're down."

Not that I wanted Tiffany to be my therapist right now, but her insight helped. She had only been a part of our circle for a short time, so she knew the least about us all. An unbiased view. Which turned out to be a bonus in the current situation.

"I will, and thank you. Losing people is challenging for me. Especially those who are close."

"Losing people shouldn't be easy for anyone, sweetie," Tiffany says. For some reason, her term of endearment sits oddly with me. Maybe she is trying to pacify me. Whatever. I really don't have the energy to care right now.

With my brain a monsoon of thoughts, it is a wonder I can function at all. Thankfully, I am saved from potential word vomit when the server brings our meals. Over the next twenty minutes, we eat in silence. Liz slurps her spaghetti, as she always has, and Tiffany cuts her eggplant parmesan with precision. I expect nothing less.

Once we pay our tabs, we walk out together and part ways to head to our respective cars, but not before Liz gives me a huge hug. A hug that swallows me whole and tries to make up for the hugs I won't get from Sarah anytime soon. I wish I had a fraction of her enthusiasm right now. But she remains strong through all this because Tiffany stands to her right. How would Liz be if she came alone tonight? Would she be as miserable as me? After a quick hug with Tiffany, and promises to meet up soon, we go our separate ways.

Secure in my car, I fish out my phone and call Rick. I let him know I'm leaving the restaurant and headed to Apex. Occasionally, the constant checking in irritates the hell out of me. But we do it for a good reason. The same reason Sarah left. Because you never know what could happen between point A and B.

"Drive safe, gorgeous. See you soon."

Ten minutes later, I walk through the door at Apex and smile at the bouncer. "Evening, Ray. Been a good night?"

Ray is a burly, beefy teddy bear. The first time I met him, he scared the bejesus out of me. He towers a foot taller than my five-foot-five and has biceps bigger than my thighs. I was an ant beside him, and his combat boots could squash me in point-five seconds. But he also had the most charming smile and gave the best hugs. Everyone who worked inside these walls was family. It was impossible not to be. With the level of intimacy, safety, and trust required, how could a familial bond not form?

I may not work inside the walls of Apex, but everyone who did considered me family too. So, when Ray bends down, lifts me up, and gives me a hug—my feet dangling a foot off the floor—there is zero awkwardness between us. If anything, Ray is like the older, bigger brother I never had.

"Not too bad, Ms. Christy. You here to see boss man?"

"Yeah. Had dinner with some friends, and it ended sooner than expected."

I step away from Ray as we say our goodbyes. At least his booming nature brought a half-smile to my face. Apex seems quieter than usual tonight, but a decent crowd fills the walls. Weaving my way through a few groups, I sidle up to the bar and try to spot Rick. After a quick scan of the crowd, I land on him twenty feet away. He talks with a couple who look to be in their late forties/early fifties. A moment later, he glances toward the bar and nods for me to go to VIP.

Ordering a drink, I take it and head over to VIP and wait for Rick. When I first started coming to Apex, it was strange to sit in here and just observe. I thought, *Do these people think I'm a perv or prude because I watch more than partici-pate?* But over time, the worry fell away. I learned several people played voyeur now and again. Especially when bored with their day-to-day lifestyle.

Minutes later, Rick sits down beside me and presses a kiss to my lips. "Sorry you had to wait, gorgeous. New couple." New couples in the club always got the grand tour and were taught the rules and expected behaviors on night one. If they visited other clubs prior to Apex, my guess is the rules would be similar. But I honestly had no idea.

"No biggie. I was enjoying the view while I waited."

He scoops up my hand and brings my knuckles to his lips, kissing each one in turn. "How was dinner with Liz and Tiffany?"

I hunch my spine and huff. Silent a moment, I don't want to say I didn't enjoy spending time with them, but it was lackluster without Sarah. "Alright. Kinda blah, actually. We exchanged maybe five sentences with each other."

More kisses peppered across my knuckles. "I'm sorry, gorgeous. It's probably going to be off for a little while. But it'll get better. Promise."

I nod. God, I hope his words hold truth. Not having people I care about close by splinters my heart. For a few minutes, we sit on the couch. Me sipping my drink, and Rick with his arm draped over my shoulders and rubbing circles on my upper bicep. Such a soothing motion.

Rick runs his nose from the crown of my head to my ear, inhaling deep. "It's slow tonight, and I can take a break while you're here. It's been a while since we've put on a show." He pulls my earlobe between his lips and sucks. Soon, he kisses his way down my neck and I tip my head to the side to give him better access.

White hot heat sears my skin where he kisses me. It travels along my collarbone, from my shoulder to sternum and down between my breasts. Rick slides his hand up my thigh from my knee and my legs automatically open for him.

After many of our first nights together, I learned to love dresses more. With Rick, anytime we were together was an open invitation for intimacy. At home, in the club, out to dinner, or the movie theater. No matter where we went, I prepped for possibility. In my opinion, a girl can never be over prepared.

The tips of his fingers graze my folds and he hums in delight. "Naughty, naughty, kitten." I groan at my pet name. A name used only in this lifestyle. Only between us. "Did you forget to put panties on? Or did you leave them off on purpose?"

He dips the tip of his finger inside and I rock my hips. "On purpose, daddy. Knew it would please you."

Up and down. Circle, circle. Up, down, dip. I rock my hips again and he clucks his tongue at me. "Patience. First things first. Let's get more comfortable, shall we?"

My ribcage expands and contracts faster and faster. "Yes, please."

One by one, Rick unbuttons the front of my red dress. Not quite a sundress, yet not formal—somewhere in between. It hugs my curves and exposes just enough flesh to be flashy, but not trashy. When all the buttons are open, Rick exposes my bare skin to the world.

"Well, well, well. Looks like you forwent the bra as well. I'm not sure if I should punish or praise you, kitten."

Arousal slicks the skin between my thighs and I gyrate

my hips as I run my hands up my body and caress my hips and belly and breasts. "Whatever daddy thinks is best."

A few couples in VIP watch us. And let's be honest here, most people stop to watch us. Not that Rick and I do anything as vivid and intense as others, but we have a bond. Our connection is like no other couple's in the room. Anyone can have sex in a room full of strangers. But exposing yourself, being one-hundred percent vulnerable, physically as well as emotionally, is not something you see all the time.

When our eyes connect, a hurricane swirls between us. Everything around us is obliterated. It is him, and me, and nothing in between.

Rick rises between my legs and begins unbuttoning his shirt, draping it over the back of the couch once he finishes. A moment later, his pants follow suit. Beneath his clothes, he is commando. Running my hands up his quads, I follow my line of sight and trace his body with my fingers. Flawless and pristine and not a lick of hair above his knees.

At his nipples, I twist a second before clawing my way down his abdomen. He hisses, "Careful, kitten." It sounds like a warning, but he craves the sting of my nails in his skin.

So, I apologize by leaning forward and kissing the tip of his cock. It jerks under my lips, so I do it again. And again. Until a moment later, I take him between my lips, swirl my tongue around the crown, and suck the head. Rick strokes my hair and whispers words of praise. His encouragement pushes me and I take him further into my mouth and throat. Before I realize it, my fingers slip between my legs and I circle my clit.

Before my body reaches the precipice, Rick breaks us apart. "Lay back, kitten."

I do as he says, spreading out against the wide, cool leather. As he studies me from head to toe, he strokes his cock. Enamored by the act, I miss it when he stops and invites two men to join us. When they step up to us, Rick whispers in their ears and they both nod in agreement. Rick has never had intercourse with another man—as far as I know—but I have watched him kiss and touch other men. So the moment he releases his cock and runs a hand down both their chests and grips their cocks, not an ounce of shock registers in my brain. If anything, my clit throbs harder.

The first man—a thin, clean-cut blond with the whole "boy next door" appeal—steps around to my legs. Number two—a stalky, professional-looking brute with rich brown hair—walks toward my head. Rick stays anchored at my mid-section in admiration. As if they have done it a million times, the two men begin. One squats down, licks his way up my legs until his tongue laps at my folds. Two lowers himself slightly and dips his cock between my lips—I give him a slow tease of licks only on the head. I suck the crown of Two's cock like a lollipop, occasionally releasing it and watching it bounce above my lips before taking it again. Before long, One fucks me while Rick and Two stroke themselves and watch.

After One gives me an orgasm, Two takes his place and flips me over, jerks my hips up, and fucks me until I scream. Once they have had their fun with me, Rick sends them away and makes love to me, sweet and slow for all to see. Moments like these are the ones I lock up for safekeeping. When Rick treasures and worships me like a priceless artifact.

Once we are both spent, the length of his bare body lays unmoving atop mine. His chocolate-rimmed honey eyes lock with mine as he plays with my hair. "I love you, gorgeous. You never cease to amaze me."

A symphony plucks my heartstrings. "I love you, too." Out of left field, tears well in my eyes and a lump forms in my throat. I do my best to hide the emotion choking me, but it won't work. Rick is my own personal emotion detector.

His eyes dart between mine as he drops my hair. When his fingers paint a line along my cheekbone, I close my eyes and the traitor tears leak out. Soft and warm, Rick presses a delicate kiss on my lips. "What's wrong, gorgeous?"

My tears feel juvenile. The remnants of a sad, pathetic girl. But if I don't tell Rick what is on my mind, he will be glued to my side until I do. Only, I don't want to be teased. Picked on like a small child who feels betrayed. Better yet, I don't want him upset.

"It's stupid, really," I say, shaking my head slightly.

He kisses me again. "I doubt anything in your beautiful head is stupid."

I roll my eyes and chuckle. "Not so sure about that statement," I joke. After a deep breath and another reassuring glimpse from him, I voice my thoughts. "I was kinda thinking..." *Please don't think I'm stupid. Please don't hate me.* "That maybe we could move."

FOUR

RICK

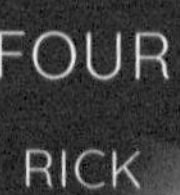

Of all the things that could possibly come out of Christy's mouth, her telling me she wants us to move was the farthest from the list. What the hell.

I jerk my face away from hers and study every fine detail of her face. Her eyes simmer like a storm on the horizon. Lips tucked between her teeth. A timid tremble at her chin. Not only is she serious, but fear threads through her veins.

Dropping back down, I hover an inch above her face. I stroke her cheek and relish in the way her eyes roll back and close briefly before I kiss her. "You don't need to be afraid, gorgeous. I'll keep you safe. Swear on my life."

Another tear falls from her eye and it is a knife in the gut. She nods and says, "In my heart, I know you'll never let anyone hurt me." Breaking eye contact and staring off into the distance—away from me—she sniffles.

Something niggles my thoughts, and it dawns on me.

What if this has nothing to do with Christy feeling unsafe? I automatically assume her safety is what bothers her. But now, I am not so sure. When I stroke her cheek again, her stormy blues come back to me. "Tell me," I whisper.

"God, I feel like such a fucking idiot," she says, inhaling deeply. Her eyes dart between mine as she wages war with herself on whether or not to continue. "I want to move because it feels like my family just left."

If that is not a slap to the face, I don't know what the hell else would be. I bolt off of her and redress without giving her another glance. Un-fucking-believable. What the hell am I? A piece of shit on the side of the road.

Less than a minute later, I'm fully dressed, walking out of VIP and toward the bar. I need a goddamn drink. When I approach the bar, Tink gives me a once over and doesn't say a word. She pours me a whiskey and walks off to talk to other patrons. Funny how well she, and the other staff, know me.

I down the drink and close my eyes as warmth coats my throat and stomach. When I open my eyes, Christy stands inches away from me. Stark. Ass. Naked. Leaning into her, I hiss, "Put your goddamn clothes on."

She rolls her eyes, and for the first time I don't find it adorable. "Why?" she asks, clipped.

"Why? You're joking, right?" She has got to be fucking kidding me. "Because you're walking around the goddamn club like a snack."

Christy flings her arms wide open and crosses her ankles. Now she is intentionally making a scene. And it's pissing me off. "Rick… this is a club where people literally come in to remove their clothes and fuck other people. As if anyone gives a damn whether or not I've got clothes on."

As I scan the crowd, not only has the typical chatter died, but almost every pair of eyes is watching us. *Fuck, fuck, fuck.* I force her arms down to her sides and lean into her, whispering in her ear. "Put your fucking clothes on. Every set of eyes is on you right now. Go home. When I'm off work, we will talk about this."

When I pull away, I study her face a moment. A rosy flush blooms on her cheeks and her eyes are puffy, red, and on the verge of tears. *Goddamnit.* I hate that she is hurting. That she feels like Sarah leaving equals losing someone she loves. But I'm a selfish bastard, and it feels as if she ran over me with a semi.

She may be hurting, but what she said slashed me to shreds.

After a few ragged breaths, she spins around, marches back to VIP, and puts her dress back on. The club remains silent. Well, as silent as a club can be with music oozing from the speakers. Once she zips up her dress, she steps out of VIP with her head high and shoulders back. Every set of eyes locks onto Christy as she storms past me, flips me her middle finger, and walks out.

My heart is a tattered mess on the floor as everyone resumes chatting or whatever they were doing before the whole display. Why can't I breathe? I stumble back and fall onto the stool behind me. We have never fought. Not once. And I have a feeling we are nowhere near finished.

"You alright?" Tink asks.

I hang my head and shake it side to side. "No. Far from okay."

"Tell me to butt out if I'm overstepping. What happened?"

Honestly, I don't want to talk about this with anyone except Christy. But I'm stuck here for at least another five hours. Five hours of nothing except trying to figure out how to fix whatever snapped. "No offense, Tink, but I should talk to her before anyone else."

"No worries. I get it. But we're all here if you need us."

I nod, hand her my glass, and wander off. Only five more hours. It will be over in no time. At least that is what I keep telling myself.

When I walk through the front door, the first thing that grabs my attention is how bright it is inside. Every light in our apartment appears to be flipped on. The second thing I notice is Christy in the middle of the living room, sitting on an oversized pillow, rocking back and forth with her head tucked between her chest and knees. Although her face is hidden from view, her whimpers tell me all I need to know.

I walk over and squat down in front of her. When I

reach out and lay my hand on her shoulder, she jumps. Not just a little. Practically out of her skin.

"Ah! Don't scare me like that," she says, pointing a finger at me.

I sink onto the floor in front of her, ignore the wild look in her eyes, and wipe away the trail of tears on her cheeks. "Sorry, gorgeous. Thought you heard me come in." Wrapping my arms around her, I drag her into my lap and hold her tight against my chest.

We sit like this for a moment. Her tears stain the front of my shirt as her hands clutch the cotton. As much as I don't want to disturb this blip of heaven, we need to talk about what happened earlier. The only way the whole situation will resolve itself is by us opening up and talking about it.

Hesitantly, I break us apart, slip a finger under her chin, and bring her swollen gaze to mine. "I know you're upset, but we need to talk about what happened at the club tonight." Every word a gentle promise that I will do whatever to make this better for her. For us.

Puffy, bloodshot eyes dart between mine in question. How long has she been crying? Hours? After a few seconds, she nods and we move to sit on the couch. It pains me to do or say anything that would hurt her, but it isn't realistic to uproot our lives every time someone else's life changes. That isn't how life operates.

"I need you to talk to me, gorgeous. Tell me what you're thinking and I'll wait until you're done to answer."

She swipes the tears from under her eyes and tucks a

few disobedient hairs behind her ears. When she appears to have regained her composure, she starts. "I know she's only been physically gone for a day, but Sarah leaving feels like I lost a loved one. Family has always been a rough subject for me. And when Sarah became family, I never thought something like this would happen. That I'd lose her."

When she doesn't say anything for a minute as she stares down at her fumbling hands, I assume it is fair game for me to speak. "Hey. Sarah has been in your life for a couple years now, so I understand why you're upset. But we can't just pack up our lives and move across the country because our friends moved away. You'll still talk to her all the time. See her on trips. She's not gone forever."

Christy sniffles beside me. "It's not the same," she whispers. The crack in her voice is a splinter in my heart. No matter what I say right now, it will all fall to shit. Is there a right answer?

"I know it isn't, but it's the hand we're dealt."

Beside me, Christy shakes. It starts as this practically undetectable tremor and evolves to an earthquake. And then she bolts upright. "No," she screams. Not just a simple increase in volume. More on the level so the heavens can hear the authority and disparity in her voice.

"No?" I ask. Honestly, I'm not sure what else to say or ask.

"No. I'm sick and tired of being the one left behind. *It's okay, Christy. Everything will be fine.*" Her tone mocking, but of who I'm uncertain. "Well it's not *fine*. Why does everyone else get to be happy, except poor little Christy?"

I have no idea what the fuck is happening with her right now. This side of her is completely foreign. Where the hell do I begin? "What the hell does that mean?" It is the only sane question to ask. Because I have no goddamn idea right now.

"What does that mean?" she asks. "It means that I always draw the short end of the stick when it comes to love."

What in the actual fuck? Since the day I met Christy, all I have ever done is love her. I may not have classified it as love in the beginning, but that is exactly what it was. And now she is suggesting she has no one to love or to love her in return. If I don't calm the fuck down, my fist might rip through the drywall any minute.

"Care to elaborate? Because if I'm understanding you correctly, you just insinuated no one loves you. And that's fucking bullshit." It is almost four in the morning and the volume of our conversation is reaching levels loud enough to wake our neighbors. I wouldn't be shocked if someone pounds on the walls or front door soon.

"Well, right now, it feels like I'm standing in the middle of a dark forest without a light. In the cold. All alone."

"Wow. So your best friend moves away. She's gone less than twenty-four hours. And no one else is good enough for you. Thanks," I yell. "Thanks for throwing me in the trash."

Her eyes bulge as recognition hits her. But it is too fucking late. She may be upset or distraught over her friend moving away, but she handled the whole situation wrong. Beyond wrong. I should be her strength. The one person she leans on. Who she tells all her secrets to and believes will never leave her side. But she has contaminated that. Laced it with poison. And force fed it down my throat.

She steps toward me and I step back. For the first time ever, I don't want her touch. Nor do I want to be swayed by the potency of our bond. A bond which I thought could never be tampered with. "No." I put my hand up, then point to the bedroom. "Go to bed. I can't do this right now."

Another step toward me, and I back up farther. Her eyes beg me to forgive her. With every ounce of me, I wish it could be so simple. But she didn't just hurt me. She cut out my heart with a spoon, dropped it in the earth, and stomped on it for good measure. It will take time before I heal from her wounds.

Tears rip from her eyes like an avalanche. She walks backward from me, eyes glued to mine, chin trembling as she mouths, *I'm sorry. I love you.*

When our bedroom door shuts, I breathe for the first time in minutes. Dragging a deep breath in through my nose, I exhale the anguish and heartache she just inflicted upon me. For a split-second, I almost lost my shit in front of her. Now that she is tucked away in our bed, I close my eyes and relish in the quiet. If one thing holds true, I never want to see Christy as I did moments ago. Once she realized what she had said, once I threw it back at her, her stormy eyes said it all. That she made a mistake. A huge fucking mistake.

I head to the spare bedroom, shut the door, and drop onto the bed. Half a minute later, I bring my hands to my face and cry into my palms. My heart shrivels and beats cold in my chest. Fuck this hurts. No matter what, I plan to do whatever it takes to make things between us better.

But how the hell do I fix this?

Four days have passed since our fight. Four days and we haven't spoken a single word to each other. No morning interaction. No texts during the day. Nothing. When I come home from work, she is locked away in our bedroom with the lights out. When I wake in the morning, early on the off chance I will catch her, she is already gone for the day.

Not a single sound in the apartment. No kisses or hugs goodbye. No notes on the fridge.

Nothing.

I miss her so fucking much. A light has been extinguished between us and I haven't the first clue how to reignite it. Tonight, I plan to make this right. If not right, definitely better than what it is now. There is no way we can continue living like this. No matter how hard she tries to hide it, I hear her muffled tears when I come home. Neither one of us is sleeping well, if at all, and it ends tonight.

While she finishes her workday, I head out to run errands. After a quick workout at the gym, I stop at the grocery store and pick up ingredients for dinner. On the drive home, I pass Christy's favorite florist shop and turn around.

Generally, flowers and chocolates have never been something I showered on Christy. I am more a man of passion and actions and words. Not to say I have never purchased flowers or gifts for her, but it isn't on the normal rotation in the affection department. Maybe if I had seen my father do such things for my mother, I would be more apt to pass it on. Maybe if I'd had the opportunity to see Harriett as a young woman, my outlook might also be different. But neither of those things happened, so the point is moot.

After I spend my life savings in the florist shop, I drive home. On my to-do list today... whatever it takes to get my girl back. Dinner and flowers seems like the perfect way to start.

"Ms. Nolan? Did you hear me?"

I shake my head and snap out of my foggy state to see Marco standing on the opposite side of my desk. Arms crossed in front of his chest. Head cocked to the side. A blend of scowl and sympathy stretch across his face.

At the sight, I slump farther into my chair. "Sorry. What?"

This week has sucked at work. Between Sarah being gone and the absence of Rick, I haven't been able to think straight, let alone function. My eyes are tired, sore, and swollen from several nights of crying. God, I am so sick and tired of the endless tears. Why can't I be one of those people who suffers from dry eyes? Now would be the perfect time to have such a problem. Unfortunately, my tear ducts seem to have a never-ending supply of sadness.

"I asked if you were doing okay. But you answered without saying a word. Why don't you go home, take tomorrow off, and have a long weekend to recover from whatever has you down."

Sincerity laces Marco's voice as his arms unlatch and he shoves his hands deep in his pockets. The offer to take time off warms my heart and has my eyes stinging. I blink rapidly to keep yet another round of tears at bay. *I will not cry at work. Especially in front of my boss.* As much as I would love to leave, half the work day remains and I have a mile-long list of shit to get done. Shit that I have ignored for far too long during my emotional stupor.

"Let me finish some stuff today. I'll take you up on tomorrow, though."

A gentle smile lifts the corners of Marco's lips. "You miss her. We all do. If you're as close as I think you are, you'll see her again. Don't doubt that, Christy."

And just like that, the dam bursts wide open. I nod and click the mouse, pretending to do something produc-tive on my computer. "Yeah, I know," I mumble over the emotion lodged in my throat. After a beat of silence, Marco nods, steps out of my cubicle and walks back to his office.

The moment he is out of sight, I close my eyes and take a deep breath. *Just get through the rest of the day.* Surrounding me, fingers tap keyboards like wildfire. A cacophony of chatter swirls around as if I am in the center of a tornado. I open up the instant messaging application on my computer and shoot a quick message to Liz.

Christy: You eat yet?

Liz: No. Want to grab a bite downstairs?
Christy: I'll be ready in a minute.

Liz meets me at the elevator two minutes later and we ride down to Carol's Deli in silence. For a deli who caters mainly to the workers of Hammond Life, the place is always packed. We order our food and locate a table near the window. For a moment, we sit and stare out the window. People shuffle along the sidewalk—some enter the building, others just pass by. Although I don't look in her direction, I *feel* Liz's eyes on me. How she senses my unusual disposition. My less than perky self. And I don't think she is quite sure how to handle me.

"I miss her," I say, diving straight into the deep end as I face her.

Liz reaches across the table and sets her hand over mine. "Me, too. But I get why she had to move. If I were in her shoes, I would've left sooner."

I tilt my head to the side and study Liz for a moment. Her screaming red hair recently dyed black. "Really?" Not sure why I ask her this, but Liz doesn't peg me as someone to run away from danger. If anything, Liz seems the type to get in danger's face and shove them in the chest.

"Why do you sound so shocked? I may be badass, but I wouldn't want to stay in the same town and be reminded of some guy who did horrible things to me."

When she puts it in that context, I see where she's

coming from. "I hadn't thought about it like that, but I guess you're right."

She squeezes my hand and I glance up at her. "There's no right or wrong here, Christy. But we should respect that Sarah struggled to smile every day after all that bullshit happened. It's not fair to her for us to be selfish. I miss her like crazy, like you, but I'm not going to tell her that. It would just add an unfair layer of guilt. Right now, she needs to figure out how to start all over again. And that's hard enough, especially in a new city."

Staring down at where Liz's hand still rests on mine, I mull over her words. On so many levels, Liz is spot on. My urgent desire to move away all stems from a selfish urge to keep Sarah physically close. But, in the process, I forgot about what everyone else needs. Rick, especially. I skipped over his feelings and only considered my own. On my solo path to what should have been happiness, I created a major rift between us. A rift that has splintered my heart more with each passing day. A rift I need to settle and heal.

I hang my head, refusing to cry at my idiocy. No more tears. My body can't handle it. "Thanks, bitch," I mutter. "Only you tell me like it is and I actually listen. Now I have to make things better with Rick."

"Hey." Liz jostles my hand. "What happened with you and Rick?"

Shaking my head because I am the biggest idiot to walk the earth, I tell her, "Four nights ago, I told Rick I wanted to move. Less than a day after Sarah left, and I told him that. Needless to say, it didn't go over well. We had a huge fight." I pause a moment and gaze into Liz's hazel eyes, once again on the verge of crying. "We've never fought before, Liz. And it's all my fault. All because I couldn't handle losing Sarah."

"But we haven't lost her," she says.

And for the first time since Sarah left, I understand this now. But after all the bullshit with my own flesh and blood family, it hurts to have someone I care about slip away.

"I know. It just felt like it. In some ways, it still does. Probably will for a while."

"Once she settles in, you know she's going to invite us all out there. It may not be anytime soon, but we'll get to hug her again." Liz smiles and a small weight lifts from my heart. This is the most we have talked since she and Tiffany became serious. "On another note… It's great to hear you call me bitch again. I started to wonder if you only reserved that for when Sarah was here."

I laugh loud enough to turn several heads in our direction. And for the first time in a week, I smile. A true, genuine smile. Oftentimes, I get teased for tossing my favorite word around like a whore at a free-for-all. *Bitch.* Don't remember the first time I used it so casually, but Sarah and Liz called it my signature. I just laughed and called them bitches. Little do they know, I *only* use it with them.

"Sorry I haven't been myself, bitch. Promise to bring her back to life. On one condition, though."

Liz tilts her head and narrows her eyes, intrigued. "And what's that?"

"That I don't lose you to Tiffany." Liz's eyes soften and she squeezes my hand harder. "Seriously. My family did some fucked up shit to me and I can't lose the only family I have now."

A tender expression crosses her face. "You won't lose me, girl. And if it feels like I'm slipping away, set me straight. Okay?"

"Yeah, okay."

I walk through the front door just after six and stop in my tracks. Walking up, everything looked dark behind the blinds on the windows. So, when I step inside to candle light, hundreds of peonies, and the aroma of herbs floating in the air, I'm taken aback.

Doesn't Rick work tonight?

Slowly, I walk from the foyer to the kitchen. At the stove, his back to me, Rick stirs a large pot of something on the burner. He doesn't turn to face me. Just keeps stirring whatever he is cooking. Best guess, he didn't hear me come in because I didn't announce myself. Usually, there is no need to because he is at work when I get home.

For a moment, I lean against the doorjamb and watch him. Clad in a snug black shirt and a pair of khaki cargo shorts, his feet are bare. Rick has many qualities that are beyond attractive. Not only is he physically good looking —long, almost black hair slung to one side, buzzed from the ears down; so tall he towers over me like a tree when I stand barefoot; lines and bulges of sinew in all the right places—he also lures me in with his mind. So incredibly smart with a wicked and talented tongue.

He checks his watch, then wipes his hand on the towel slung over his shoulder. Probably wondering when I will get home. Like a spy, I stand silently off to the side and wait for him to spot me. Before I finish the thought, he spins around and startles when he sees me ogling him.

Slow and steady, he saunters toward me. A lion hunting his prey. When he stands less than a foot away, he reaches out and strokes a finger along my cheek and jawline. Without hesitation, I close my eyes and breathe him in. Leather and bergamot and sandalwood flutter up my nose and settle my soul. I sigh as my shoulders cave forward. God, I have missed him. Us. This.

"Didn't hear you come in, gorgeous," he whispers as his lips ghost mine. I shudder beneath him and his lips curve into a smile against my skin.

"Usually pretty quiet when I get home. Plus, I wanted to see what you were up to."

When I open my eyes, the hunger swirling in his knocks the breath from my lungs. He plucks a lock of my hair and plays with it between his fingers. So intimate and tender.

"I've been so lost without you this week."

I study the lines of his face a moment, making note of the shadows beneath his eyes and how much his usual buzzed beard has grown out. He looks as exhausted as I feel.

Inching forward, I kiss him. Soft and sweet. "Missed you, too," I breathe. He presses his lips to mine again and my world seems more even keeled. He breaks the kiss far too soon and walks back to the stove. The instant he steps away, I crave his warmth and the rough touch of his skin on mine. So, I push off the wall, walk up to his backside, and wrap my hands around his waist. "Need help?"

He peers over his shoulder at me and winks. "I got this. Go get comfortable. Dinner should be ready in a few."

I kiss him between the shoulder blades, happy to finally be close to him again, then head for the bedroom. When I flip the light on, a massive sea of pink hits me.

Scattered on the dresser, bed, and every available surface in our bedroom is countless peony flowers. My favorite flower. To say he spent a pretty penny on flowers would be delicate. The number of flowers in here and throughout the apartment, he spent hundreds. For someone who isn't big on flowers and candies and clichés —neither of us are, to be honest—he sure went out of his way to do something special for me.

Stepping farther into the room, I pluck one of the flowers off the bed and bring it to my nose. Such a subtle fragrance. As I gaze at all the pillowy, blush-colored bulbs, warmth blossoms in my heart. There is nothing this man wouldn't do for me. No bounds he wouldn't push to keep me happy and by his side. The splinters in my heart slowly suture back together, and a wholeness only Rick provides settles deep in my bones.

After I slip on one of Rick's t-shirts and a pair of boxer shorts, I walk out and see him waiting at the dining table. Methodically, he glances up and down my body. A wicked gleam lights his face, and it is all the praise I need.

While we enjoy the pesto fusilli, salad, and garlic bread he prepared, we talk about our days. How work has sucked for me. His trip to the florist—who thought him insane for buying a hundred plus of the same flower. He still won't disclose how much he spent. Not that it matters.

When we finish, he takes our dishes to the sink before we settle on the couch. The elephant in the room standing tall and proud and eager for us to speak.

"I'm sorry," I say, staring at my clasped, sweaty hands in my lap.

Rick slips his fingers beneath my chin and tips my head back as he holds me prisoner with his gaze. "Don't be sorry for telling me how you feel, gorgeous. If anything, I should be apologizing to you. It was out of place for me to talk to you like I did. I will never raise my voice like that again." He slowly leans forward and presses a kiss to my lips.

I nod. "You weren't the only one fired up, but I don't ever want us like that again. This week has been the worst. Not sure if I ever fell asleep without you in our bed."

He plays with the ends of my hair. "Me either. I never want another night without you in my arms. And I never want us to fight. Ever." I agree with him before he continues. "And I've done some thinking. I'm making no promises, but I will look into other opportunities that might allow us to move. If that's what you really want."

My eyes bug out behind my glasses. "Are you serious?"

"I wouldn't bring it up if I weren't. But I need to ask you something first."

The room swirls around me with excitement. "Okay."

"Please tell me about your parents." His honey eyes dart between my steely blues. "It's a touchy subject for you, but I need to understand it better. As open as we are about us, we've never shared that side of ourselves. And I respect your desire to keep it tucked away, because there are reasons we never see my family either."

Rick and I have been together four-and-a-half years and neither one of us has brought up our families. And neither of us questioned the other regarding our silence. In some relationships, your significant other may find this quite odd. But because we obviously both had issues with some or all of our family members, it isn't in our nature to ask or pester.

And I want to share this part of my life with Rick. Be completely transparent with him. But fear has crippled me over the years. Fear of losing more people I love. If something happened to Rick or us, and we couldn't be together... the world would become a dark hole.

But in my heart, deep down in the depths of my marrow, I know I can tell Rick about this. And when I finish, he will still be here. With me. Keeping me safe and guarding my heart as he has since the first day we met. I inhale deeply and settle every nerve in my body.

"When I was sixteen," I start. "I lost my virginity to a guy named James. We weren't dating. In fact, I met him at work. He was older than me. Too old to have sex with a sixteen-year-old."

Rick holds up his hand and I stop for a moment. "Do you know how old he was?"

I nod. "James was twenty-eight at the time." Rick growls beside me, but I ignore it and continue my story. "Anyway, we worked together, but he was in a different department of the store. Every once in a while, our paths crossed. And from time to time, we'd sit together and eat on break. He was a nice guy, easy to talk with. Over time, my attraction toward him grew. After all, I was sixteen and my hormones were all over the place." I roll my eyes for dramatic effect and Rick laughs. "One day, during our break, he broached the subject of sex. Part of me shrunk away from the topic, while another part of me screamed to learn more. Most of the girls from school had already lost their virginity and bragged about how amazing sex was. But, for some reason, no one seemed interested in sweet, little Christy."

Rick smiles at me briefly. "That's because they didn't know how amazing you truly are."

I wave him off and continue. "So, when James took an

interest and wanted to talk about sex, I talked. Within a few short minutes, I spilled the beans about still being a virgin. But that didn't perturb him. If anything, his fascination with me grew stronger. He asked, *'How is a beautiful girl like you still a virgin?'* All I could do was shrug. You can't help how things pan out. We continued these talks for weeks. Most of the time, it was me asking him questions."

"So how did it go from an innocent conversation to you having sex with him?" Rick asks. He means no disrespect; I sense it in his tone. More or less, he is fascinated by how I volunteered to sleep with a man almost twice my age.

"One day, while we sat in the break room, he asked if any of the guys at school caught my eye. Completely honest with him, I said no, but someone outside school had. No lie, at the time, I was enamored by him. He was the first guy to take an interest in me. A man. His attention boosted my self-esteem like no one else had ever done. So, when he asked who I was interested in, I told him. But he wasn't fazed by my attraction to him. Not excited or put down. James simply smiled and told me he was attracted to me also. From that day forward, our conversations were quieter. Our legs or hands brushed against each other time and again. For two weeks, we had the most intense version of foreplay."

A half-smile kicks up the left side of Rick's mouth. "Indeed. But how did no one else see you together? Surely other people took breaks at the same time."

"The store had a break room and a small cafe. Most of the employees ate in the cafe, so we only had company on occasion."

Rick waves his hand. "Continue."

He leans on his palm as his elbow presses into the back of the couch. Gazing at me with such admiration and awe. The more I share with him, the lighter my heart feels over the past. But we haven't gotten to the root of the matter yet, and my pulse hammers in my chest as I continue.

"After weeks of flirting and secret touching and conversations about sex, I was tired of talking. I wanted to know what all my girlfriends had been raving about. Plus, I figured saving your virginity was just my religious parents' way of keeping me *pure* for whoever they wanted me to marry. I was ready to give it up, though. Ready to see what all the whispering was about. So, I told James I wanted to have sex with him. At first, he hesitated. Not sure if it was the age thing, but I quickly reminded him the age of consent in the state of Georgia was sixteen. Once I stated that little fact, the relief on his face was visible for miles. Soon after, we started making plans. Arranged sex. Super intimate, right? But I didn't care."

I pause a moment and take a sip of wine. Rick is fully invested in listening to my story, waiting to see how my relationship with James leads back to my parents. It surprises me he hasn't put the pieces together yet. Maybe he has, but he's reserving his assumption so I will share my story.

"We figured out a day when my shift ended early and James was off work. I lied to my parents and said I was going to a friend's house after work and that I would stay the night there. They were none the wiser. When my shift ended, James picked me up and we went back to his place."

My stomach twists in a knot and a light sheen pricks my lightly fevered skin. Although it was a lifetime ago, my heart beats viciously against my ribcage. But I keep reminding myself this was years ago. Years before Rick and I knew one another. And he would never think less of me because of a choice I made when I was sixteen. It isn't his nature.

"At first, it was like two friends hanging out. We sat on the couch, ate snacks and watched television. He flipped through the channels until he landed on a pay-per-view movie. Essentially, soft core porn, but I didn't know that's what it was at the time. After he paid for the movie, we sat back and watched. Half an hour later, his hand skimmed up and down the inside of my thigh. Another ten minutes in and we started kissing. When the first sex scene popped up on the screen, he hiked my shirt up and yanked my pants down. In less than an hour of the movie starting, I learned what it felt like to have a man inside me. Learned how incredible sex was and what I'd been missing. We had sex for hours that night. The next day, I struggled to get out of his bed and could barely walk. When I returned home, my parents asked why I was limping and I blamed it on too much exercise. Sixteen-year-old girls are obsessed with their figure and it seemed like a good enough excuse."

Beside me, Rick bends at the waist, clutches his stomach, and laughs hysterically. Without a moment's hesitation, I join in. Reliving that last part is worth every painful chuckle stemming from my diaphragm. God, I was such an idiot back then. But as I mull over the whole scenario, my parents were pretty naïve. How in the hell did they believe my fib about too much exercise? They must have never thought their daughter would ever lie to them. Or… maybe they really believed it at the time. It doesn't matter now.

"It was a half truth," I say. "But after that day, James and I hooked up several times. Through him, I learned sex wasn't just about sticking a dick in a hole. It was, and is, an art. A talent that develops and improves with time and routine practice. Something you wet your lips with, but didn't devour immediately. Because of him, I craved sex more than love. He taught me that sex and love could co-exist or be separate entities. I never loved James, but my infatuation for him was strong. And that's when the slip up happened. One Saturday morning before work, I packed a duffel bag like I had for the last several weeks. My mom walked in my room and asked who I was staying with after work. Instead of telling her I was sleeping over at Jenika's house like I had every other time, I said James. I prayed she didn't hear me right, but within seconds I had my answer. She stormed out of the room, hollering for my father.

Nothing like a Marine to shape up a disobedient child, right?"

Rick brushes his knuckles up and down my bicep, soothing me. As if he knows what is coming. Although the situation has long since passed, just thinking of the way my parents handled the whole thing, and how they treated me, boils my blood.

"Needless to say, I lost my job because I'd been grounded to my room and my parents called my work and said I would not be returning. They confiscated my cell phone and drove me to and from school each day. My life became a prison sentence. *No little girl of mine will be a whore on the streets.'* That's what my father told me. After a week, I asked a girl at school who'd worked with me if she could deliver a note to James. He and I were far from serious, but I wanted him to know I was okay. She agreed. What I didn't expect after the note delivery was for James to show up unannounced at my house. He and my father got into a pissing match on the porch. I witnessed the whole event from the living room window. My father's sole mission was to triumph over James because *he was my dad.* While James actually spoke up *for* me and never said a selfless thing. James was the first person outside of my family to care about me. But he was also the reason my parents kicked me out of the house."

Rick jerks his head back, eyes wide as a haze of red slowly creeps up his neck and onto his ticking jaw. "Are you fucking kidding?" If looks could kill, Rick would have killed my parents in a heartbeat.

He may not have known me all those years ago, but he still jumps to my defense regarding the scenario. His devotion to my happiness makes my heart stutter and my breath catch. I shake my head. "No."

"If I ever meet your parents, I'll personally let them know what kind of trash they are." I don't doubt Rick or his promise for a second. Given the chance, he would defend me to the death.

"Honestly, I never want to see them again. After they kicked me out, I stayed with James for a while. But over time, it wasn't hard to figure out we would never be more than just sex. And I wanted more. He was generous, wouldn't let me pay rent, so I saved every penny for as long as I could. After the first year, we became more roommates than lovers. When the second year passed and I graduated high school, we were simply friends who lived together. He saw other women; I dated a couple guys. No big shake. Matter of fact, we were still living together that first night I was in Apex."

"Really?" Rick asks, jealousy dilating his eyes and dancing on his tongue. "Do you still talk with him?"

"He checks in every six months or so, making sure I'm okay. Other than that, we don't talk."

What happened between James and I was a lifetime ago. When I met Rick, I was twenty-four and James was in his mid-thirties. A lot had changed since I first met him at sixteen. For a time, James was my only trustworthy friend, more like family. Keeping in touch with him over the years only seems fair, after everything he did for me.

Rick nods with a loose fist pressed to the corner of his mouth. Intrigue swirls in his eyes and I fall victim to the hypnotizing sight. "Dare I say I'd like to meet him?"

His interest snaps me back to reality and I laugh. "You sure about that?"

What would it be like to have James and Rick in the same room? The man I willingly surrendered my virginity to next to the man I love and share sexual partners with. Hmm, I sense a struggle for power in the future. What a chest pounding, snarl inducing match that would be. Although James and I haven't been anything other than friends for more than a decade, I easily picture him sizing up Rick and running down an invisible checklist to see if he is worthy. It makes me smile.

"Yeah, gorgeous." His tone softens. "I'd love to meet the man who rescued you from hell. And thank him."

That's a one-eighty from where I thought this was going. "Thank him?"

He nods and drops his hand from his cheek. "For not wanting to keep you. Because then you wouldn't be mine."

A bevy of doves takes flight in my belly, soars up, up, up, and steals my breath. When did Rick become so swoon-worthy? "If you're serious, I'll ask." Face straight, eyes locked on mine, Rick nods as he reaches forward, grabs a lock of my hair, and plays with it. "Okay then," I say. This whole conversation has been equally exhausting and relieving. "So, now do you get why losing people hits me a little hard?"

Rick closes the space between us and presses his lips

to mine briefly. "I do. And now I'm willing to compromise."

"Compromise?" What is he talking about?

"Yeah, gorgeous. I'm willing to see what job options are available in California."

I jump off the couch and throw myself onto his lap, peppering him with kisses. Although we don't say the words often, in my heart, Rick will always be mine and I will always be his. Our bond is electric and instantaneous and persistent. There will never be another person who jolts me to life the way Rick does. And there isn't a single thing he wouldn't do for me, or I him.

I CAN COUNT on one hand how many times in my life I let my nerves get the best of me. Tonight is one of them.

Nothing about Chad intimidates me—physical or demeanor. But before heading into work, I shot him a text and asked if he could meet me at the club. Every time a boss hears those words, it is the same as your girlfriend saying *we need to talk*.

So, when I walk through the front door at quarter to six, it doesn't surprise me when I spot Chad behind the bar helping Tink restock. Something I normally do. As my shoes clack against the hard floor and announce my arrival, Chad peers up from the cutting board and calls me over to the bar, telling Tink to take a break. Hesitant to leave, she studies the pair of us for a minute. When neither Chad nor I say a word, she tosses her towel down, walks out from behind the bar, and heads to the back.

Once Tink leaves and the back room door closes, the

nervous energy encapsulating me doubles. "What'd you want to discuss?" Chad asks, not beating around the bush.

Hands stuffed in my pants pockets, I hold his gaze. "Some stuff happened to a friend of mine recently and it has my girl a little spooked."

Chad stops slicing limes, sets the knife down, and comes around the bar. Pulling out a stool beside me, he pats my shoulder. "Sorry to hear, man."

"Thanks." I nod and prepare myself for what I haven't said yet. *This is just Chad, get ahold of yourself.* "Since then, she's got her heart set on us moving. Out of state." Chad's brows shoot up to his hairline. Glad I am not the only one surprised by such a notion. "Yeah. But I told her it all depended on both of us securing jobs. Can't move unless that happens."

Chad twists on his stool and faces me head on. "So, where do I fit into the equation?"

"Right, so I was wondering if you had any connections in Cali? Nowhere specific out there." It is a longshot, but Chad is the only person I know to ask. It's not like businesses such as this put help wanted ads in newspapers and online job search engines.

He swipes his index finger over his lips a moment. "I'll make some calls. See what I can find out and let you know."

"Thanks, man. Appreciate it."

"Sure thing. Least I could do." He rises from the stool and slides it back in line with the other untouched stools.

"Be back after opening. Let me know if we need anything while I'm out."

I nod and thank him again. Once Chad leaves, Tink walks back over and asks what just happened. Now is not the time to divulge the fact I may leave, so I tell her I needed a word with Chad, but everything is fine. Management stuff. Tink pinches her eyes in a tight line and stares at me, trying to suck the unknown out of my head. When I don't budge, she gives up and we go about our usual pre-opening setup, and the time passes without notice.

Just after ten o'clock, Chad returns and loiters with the clientele. Not too often, but on occasion, Chad indulges with the patrons. Tonight happens to be one of those times. After an hour of play, he unties a woman from a table, kisses a man as if he'll never kiss anyone again, and heads my direction. In all his glory.

For his age, Chad is attractive as hell. Mid-forties. Silky chocolate skin. Frame of a bodybuilder. Hung like a beast. But his frosty blue eyes steal every woman and man's breath. Even I am not immune to his presence. Christy only met him once, and we all kept our clothes on. If she saw the rest of him, I have no doubt my girl would want to sample the merchandise. Hell, the temptation to call her down here now weighs heavy in my groin.

Sitting on the stool next to me, his erection slowly taming, Chad orders a drink. After Tink delivers the shot of whiskey, he tosses it back and glances at me. "Got a name and number for you."

"Quicker than I expected," I say.

"In our industry, most of us know each other or can connect us. It was a matter of making the right calls. When I find my clothes, I'll get it to you." He laughs, staring across the room at the couple he walked away from. The woman up on all fours while the man takes her from behind.

After a few circuits of the club and several conversations, I take my break. I go into the back storage area where the music from the club is quietest. More than likely, night life is just ramping up in California. Taking the slip of paper with Chad's scribble out of my pocket, I dial the number and fidget as the phone rings in my ear.

"This is Rocco," a man with a throaty voice says.

"Rocco, hello. My name is Rick. Chad Wexler gave me your number in reference to a job opportunity."

The line is silent for a beat and I pull the phone away from my ear to be sure the call didn't drop. "Ah, yes. Chad near Savannah."

"Yes, sir."

"Good guy. Well Rick, I will have an opening in the near future. A current bar and night club I own is prospering, so I thought it was time to expand." Rocco proceeds to tell me about his current business. An upscale bar on the main floor called The Sophisticate. Beneath the bar, though, is P.I., an exotic night club. He opened the businesses seven years ago and they are thriving much quicker than he'd expected, hence he's decided to open a new establishment.

"Will the new place mimic your current?" I ask for

more than one reason. One—I don't care to manage a strip club. Not really my thing. Too much drama. Two—I was under the impression the California offer would be for a job exactly like the one I hold.

"Yes and no," Rocco states. "Yes, because it will structurally appear the same. The main floor, where patrons enter, will be a fine dining restaurant with hints of sensuality. Nothing obvious to those not in the life. No, because instead of an exotic dancer's club, there will be a club similar to what you work in now. I'm not going to call it a sex club, but, in essence, that's what it will be. The restaurant, Opulence, will cater to a set crowd just as my bar does. It's imperative we filter out the undesirables. There is a strict dress code and a contract to be a member of the club. The same will apply at Boundless, the new lifestyle club. From time to time, myself or people I deem suitable will "interview" patrons in the restaurant. If we find them compatible to possibly joining the club, we offer them a one-time invitation. Several of the members from P.I. plan to join Boundless, so there will be a base when we open."

Wow. Opulence/Boundless is a dream job. In a haze from everything he shared with me, I remain speechless when Rocco pauses. When I manage to form words, I ask, "When will the new business open?"

"Doors open in December." Elation kicks in. December is less than six months from now. "Next year," he adds. Now I'm flat on my back. A year-and-a-half. For this job, I would be more than willing to wait. But will Christy be open to waiting so long? Fuck, I hope so.

"Say you hired me. When would I start working? I imagine you'll need me prior to the doors opening." *Speak as if you already have the job*—the best advice I received from my first boss. It tells owners and interviewers how serious you are about the position.

"Right you are. If all goes to plan, I would need you to start—if hired—three months prior. If you're open to it, I'd love you to fly out, show you around The Sophisticate and P.I., and we can do a formal interview."

Holy fuck. One phone call and I have an interview. Not just any interview, but an interview for one of the best possible jobs. Am I in the *Twilight Zone*? How the hell does this even happen?

"Definitely. Tell me when works best for you and I'll coordinate with Chad."

"The number you called from, is it your cell?"

"It is," I answer, maybe a little too quickly.

"I'll text you dates that work for me once I'm back in my office and we'll go from there. Good with you?"

Hell yeah it is. "Perfect."

"It was a pleasure speaking with you, Rick. Look forward to meeting you soon."

"Likewise, Rocco. Thank you for your time."

The call disconnects and I stare at the phone in my hand for a moment. Holy shit. I landed the opportunity of a lifetime. Managing a club from the startup. With a man who sounds more like a mentor than a boss. Christy will flip her shit when I share the good news.

SEVEN

CHRISTY

Rinsing the last of the soap off me, I shut off the water and step out of the shower. The moment my phone pings with an incoming text, I perk up. After drying off somewhat and wrapping the towel snug around my torso, I amble over to the bed, snag my phone, and unlock it.

Rick: Exciting news. Will you be up when I get home?
Christy: No, but wake me.
Rick: Get some sleep, gorgeous. See you soon.

I start typing out what a tease he is for leaving me hanging, but know it's not intentional. Obviously, whatever he wants to share is better in person than via text messages. So, I delete the unsent message and toss my phone back on the bed.

Back in the bathroom, I brush the tangles from my hair, finish drying my body, and toss the towel in the hamper. Rick and I own nightwear for when we have guests stay over or when it gets really cold—which is almost never, if I'm honest. Otherwise, we sleep how nature made us. Bare.

After brushing my teeth, I shut off the lights, snuggle under the plush comforter, and read my current paperback. A rom-com by one of my favorite authors. Suddenly, I startle awake with the book flat on my chest. *At least I didn't lose my page.*

Sliding the bookmark into place, I set the paperback on the bedside table and shut off the light. Before long, Rick slips into bed beside me. Face to face. Inching closer to him, I weave my legs between his as he wraps his arms around me and inhales deeply.

"You can sleep," he whispers into the darkness.

I skim my fingertips along the front of his throat, down his sternum, over the ridges of his abs, and clutch his cock. He thrusts forward and moans in my ear. In a heartbeat, I straddle him and rub my clit over his fast growing erection. Teasing him with strokes up and down his length, I finally cave when he bruises my hips and tattoos my flesh with his grip. Slowly, I push him inside me, dig my nails into his biceps, and ride him until we both come undone.

Once our breathing settles, he bundles me in his arms and holds me close to his chest, chuckling. I sit up enough to see his face in the illumination of the alarm clock. "What's so funny?"

"You were passed out cold when I got in bed. Now, we're both wide awake."

"Worth it," I mumble as I fall back against his chest. "What did you want to tell me?"

He rolls us over, so he hovers above me. Tugging on a strand of my hair, he smiles. "I have a job interview next week. In California."

It takes a moment for all my synapses to fire, but once they do, I squeal. A little too loud for the late hour. "Really? When? Where? I need details."

Rick laughs above me, fingers still toying with my hair. He goes over all the details from the call he had earlier and what job he is interviewing for. The only kicker, if hired, the job wouldn't begin for a little more than a year. As far away as that is, it's a timeline. Rick stares down at me with trepidation, uncertain if the prospect makes me happy. Which it does. Another year will pass between now and then—because he *will* get the job—but I can handle it.

But he needs my reassurance. "This is great news. So excited for you. For us. How awesome to be at the startup of a lifestyle club. You get to help create something new."

"Most of the night, I was so worried the time between now and then would bother you," he admits. "A year is a long time. Especially if you're unhappy."

"Only part of me is unhappy." I brush my fingers over his jawline and relish in the prickliness of his stubble. "A small part. But having a possible timeline, it gives that small ounce of hope." Closing the space between us, I press a soft kiss to his lips and say, "You own the biggest part of me. Not just my heart. Many people can own slivers of that. No, you have my soul. The piece of me no one else will ever own."

Rick slams his mouth to mine and steals my breath. Renders me speechless with his kiss. Takes control of my body with his capable hands. And with every kiss and touch and inkling of intimacy, he possesses every ounce of my soul. As I possess his.

Over the next week, life is back to normal again. Our version of normal, anyway. We go to work, spend as much time together as possible, and get lost in each other at Apex. Rick mentally preps for his trip. He will only be in California two days, but he says his schedule should be packed the entire time.

The night before his flight, I walk into Apex wearing his favorite dress. All black with a corset top and a leather skirt that hugs my hips. Attached to my collar is a thin chain. Rick has never outright told me, but I know he wants to dominate me more than he actually does. Honestly, I think he holds back because he isn't sure if I would enjoy it.

But I want to give him what he truly desires.

Weaving through the crowd, I perch on a barstool and order a drink. After Tink delivers my martini, I sip on it and scan the sea of bodies. Tonight appears busier than usual, and there are several unfamiliar faces.

After a few minutes of people watching, I spot Rick across the club. He sits slouched in a chair by himself and watches two men as they whip and fuck a petite blonde. Typically, seeing Rick like this wouldn't bother me. Considering our lifestyle, it takes a lot for jealousy to surge in my veins. But something sharp jabs my chest, stabbing me as I sit on the opposite side of the club and watch him stroke himself through his pants. The stiffness of his erection is quite evident. His expression screams how desperately he wishes to join them.

The sole reason my heart thrashes like a wild beast is because he has no idea I stepped foot in the club tonight. I never want to question his loyalty to me, but seeing him like this... sweat highlights my skin as jitters shake my limbs.

A few minutes pass as the scene becomes more intense. More assaulting. More heated. And I can no longer sit on the sidelines and be a silent observer. I slip off my stool and step up to a pair of men a booth away. "Care to escort a lady?" I ask, popping my elbows out.

Each of them rises and takes an arm. Slowly, I guide them through the club. When we are twenty feet away, Rick's eyes leave the ménage and land on me. His hand flies to his side and he sits taller. If expressions were written in words across someone's face, Rick's would say *how long has she been here? What did she see?*

When we reach Rick, I thank each of the men with a

peck on the cheek and a groping of their balls. Rick doesn't utter a word. Not until the two men walk away.

"When did you get here?" he asks before kissing me.

For a moment, I stare at him, make him sweat a little, and remain utterly silent. It takes a lot for Rick to crack, but if there is one thing he hates, it's silence. When I have dragged out the torture long enough, I give in. "Maybe fifteen minutes ago. Looks like you've been enjoying yourself." I glance down at his groin, where his erection stands proud and tall behind his zipper.

"It's nothing, gorgeous. These guys asked me to watch. Nothing else."

I believe him. Really, I do. But there's a small piece of the whole scenario that eats away at me. His hunger to join. To get off with others. Without me. Dilated pupils and insatiable strokes up and down his fly told me as much.

Rick and I don't have your typical, "normal" relationship. We fuck and make love like every other couple. We also fuck other people. And get off while watching other people fuck. But we always do it together. *Always*. There has never been an occasion when we spent time alone with another person or couple for sex. Ever. Hence why my blood simmers as I stand in front of him a bit peeved.

"I don't doubt they asked. But for me to sit at the bar and watch you stroke your cock in your pants for more than five minutes…"

Pivoting, I walk away from him. I have no intention of leaving the club, but I need to breathe something other than him for a minute. Walking into VIP, I pass a couple sprawled out on a large ottoman. The woman is nude, clamps on her nipples and clit, chained together, and gripped by the man fucking her ruthlessly.

I sit in a chair beside them and get lost in the visual. The longer I sit here and absorb their energy, the more my clit throbs. The heavier my breasts grow in my corset. Spotting Rick out of the corner of my eye, I rub my hands over my thighs. His stare burns through me, but I ignore it.

When the man tugs the chain and the woman cries out, I slide my skirt up and expose my bare wanton flesh. When she begs him for more, I circle my clit then coat my fingers with my juices. And when she cries out in release, I dip my fingers inside myself.

"Enjoying yourself, kitten?" Rick hisses from behind me.

"As much as you were, *daddy*."

In a flash, Rick yanks me upright and steers me toward the large X on the wall. Anger vibrates off him with the pulse of the music. *Why does he get to be angry?* I only did what he was doing when I walked in. Tit for tat.

He rips my clothes away and straps me to the Saint Andrew's cross. Before I get to ask how this is remotely my fault, he walks off and toward a wall of implements. After selecting two, he returns and steps up to me.

Grabbing the chain connected to my collar, he yanks my neck forward. "For that" —he points to the chair I sat in a moment ago with a leather whip in his clutches—"you will be punished."

He takes three steps back and rears his arm, then brings it forward and whips me. Sharp stings prick over my lower abdomen and mound where he struck me. Only comparable to a thousand shards of glass piercing my skin. Not enough to bleed, but enough to feel their presence. When he does it again, the bite to my skin is more brutal and I scream.

"So, it's okay for you to get off watching others alone? But not me?" I bite out after I catch my breath.

The whip cracks my skin again and I hiss. He doesn't hold back and it hurts worse than expected. "I never got off, kitten."

His words infuriate more than the physical punishment he doles out. "Neither did I, asshole."

He freezes and just stares at me. His expression shifts. Eyes dilated. Posture taller, prouder. Gaze icy. I shiver under his scrutiny. Stepping toe to toe with me—if my feet actually touched the floor—he barks out, "What did you just call me?" His tone is as frigid as the arctic.

Un-fucking-believable. "Ass. Hole." When he just stands there, I continue. "How dare you. How dare you get pissed at me for doing exactly what you did. At least I had the decency to keep you in my line of sight the entire time. You... you were so enthralled with the blonde and her two brutes, you had no idea what was happening around you." I huff and slam my head back. "Is that what you want? Someone completely unlike me? A pretty little toy?"

I drop my head and let my hair shield my face as tears spill down my cheeks. Seconds pass and neither of us says a word. I'm still restrained to the cross as every emotion drains out of me. My body is exhausted and quivering from the onslaught of sobs that I couldn't hold back. Dozens of eyes are fixated on us and this whole show-down. Although we aren't yelling, we are most definitely fighting. And we both swore to never fight again. How did we get here again so quickly? Oh right, his earlier groping session.

A tug at one ankle gets my attention, then the other, followed by my wrists. I let gravity take me as I fall into Rick. He cradles me in his arms and walks away from the crowd. After he passes the chatty crowd, we step through a door and the music is muffled. When I peek up, I spy a cluster of black metal lockers, a small dining table with four chairs, a fridge and some cabinets, and an oversized couch. The employee's lounge. Rick places me on the soft cushions and drapes a blanket over me before he paces the length of the couch.

After a beat of silence, Rick walks over to the small table and leans his backside against it. "Is that what you think?"

I wrap the blanket tighter around me and peek up at him. "You'll need to be a little more specific."

He pushes off of the small table, walks across the small

space, and squats down in front of me. "That the blonde woman is what I want?"

"Yes. No. I don't know." I shake my head, confused by it all.

Rick reaches up and plays with a strand of my hair, tugging the end when he reaches it. "Hey," he says when I break eye contact. "Her." He points toward the door. "She is *not* who I want. You are the only one I want. But I'm not going to lie and say I wasn't enjoying watching the two men with her."

I nod and sit silent, pondering over his admission. He doesn't want *her*. But he wants someone *like* her. Someone willing to do things we have not. Things I wish he would ask to do with me, but has yet to. And I refuse to always be the one to reveal all the cards in my hand. He needs to be equally willing to do the same.

"Am I enough for you?" I whisper-ask.

The room remains silent for far too long. And with each passing second, a new pain mars my heart. A knife stabbing me again and again. Each thrust adding a new scar to the slow-beating organ. *Will I ever be enough?*

His knuckles stroke my jawline and I close my eyes. I count to myself—*one… two… three…*—before he tips my chin up and waits for me to open my eyes. When I do, his golden gaze sears my soul.

"I love you," he says. *Not a confirmation I am enough.* "And I love who I am because of you." *Still avoiding the answer.* "But do I wish we could be more? Sometimes, yes."

Hot branding iron to the chest. God, this fucking hurt.

Not that I expected him to answer differently. But hearing it aloud is a vicious slap to my confidence.

The door swings open and Tink steps in with my clothes. "Someone brought these to the bar," she says, holding them up.

"Just set them there, please," Ricks says, pointing to the table. She sets them down, stares at us a beat, then steps out.

I rise from the couch and drop the blanket on the floor. Ambling over to the table, I redress then head back to the couch, fidgeting and avoiding eye contact with Rick. It's silent for several minutes beyond comfortable and I am more than done with the night's events. Done being in this place. Just done.

Walking toward the door, I stop and glance over my shoulder. "Have a safe flight," I mumble, all energy drained from my body. "See you whenever you're back." And before he responds, I turn the handle and exit.

EIGHT

RICK

WHEN I GET HOME from work, I head for the bedroom and twist the handle to open the door. But it doesn't budge. I try it again. And again. It takes me a minute, but it eventually dawns on me Christy has locked me out of our bedroom. She shut me out after what happened tonight.

What the actual fuck is happening with us?

I love this woman fiercely. Like no other. Would give up everything for her. Hell, I'm flying to California for a job interview for her. Yet she infuriates me at times. Her fire is one of the traits I love most about her. But as of late, it seems we are constantly fighting. And I hate it. Hate the expanding hollowness beneath my sternum.

Her question tonight… *"Am I enough for you?"* threw me for a loop. How the hell could she doubt her worth to me? Christy is a vital, essential piece of me. My life would be absolute shit without her. Questioning my devotion to her was a slap to the face. And a knife to the heart.

After she left the club, I was tempted to run after her. Tempted to drag her back into the lounge and hash things out, right then and there. But I stopped myself. She needed time to sort out her emotions, and I needed time to reevaluate what happened.

When I sat down and really mulled it over, it dawned on me how badly I fucked up. I violated one of our rules. A rule I was adamant over when we started seeing each other. *Never be a part of an act without the other present.* Although I wasn't physically participating in the act in the club tonight, I was on the cusp of coming as I stroked myself. And honestly, that is equally as bad as participating.

Once I realized how at fault I was, I typed out a text to her, but didn't have the balls to send it. I fucked up and didn't want us in this questionable place before I left for California for days.

I walk into the guest bedroom and flip on the light. My suitcase and clothes for the morning, which were originally on our bed before I left for work, now lay sprawled out on the guest bed.

"Fuck," I whisper-hiss.

Taking my keys, phone, and wallet out of my pockets, I set them on the dresser and see a folded piece of paper with my name on it in Christy's swirly penmanship.

R,

Travel safe. Have a good interview.
C

The note cold and lifeless, but exactly what I deserve. Flipping off the light, I set the alarm on my phone then lay back on the bed. The wall isn't the only thing dividing me and Christy, but I attempt to sleep over the next five hours as my thoughts whirl in a never-ending cyclone of sadness and confusion.

The wheels hit the tarmac at LAX and I jolt in my seat. Flying never bothered me, but today felt different. Edgier. Unsettling. Not just because I have an interview for a dream job. But also because I didn't get to kiss Christy goodbye before I left. Our disconnect a constant dull pain in my solar plexus. Once I disengage airplane mode, I type out a quick text to her.

Rick: Just landed. Love you.

Notification after notification populates my phone screen, but not a single one of them is a response to my earlier text letting Christy know the plane was in cue for takeoff. The hollowness in my chest swells. She has every right to still be mad, and I understand her reasoning, but I just wish she would acknowledge she received my texts. From what I see, she either hasn't read them, or she turned the read receipt function off.

I wind my way through the maze that is LAX and locate the pickup area. Rocco told me he would send an employee out to pick me up. He also offered a room at his home while I stayed here—which I gratefully accepted.

I step through the sliding doors and the first thing that hits me is the smell of the city. Savannah is no small city. But it is far from being a metropolis. The Los Angeles air is drier. I inhale and capture a blend of salty ocean air, a soft floral perfume, marijuana, and a hint of burning wood. It's a strange mix, but not unappealing.

A man in black dress slacks and a black button-down stands beside a car at the curb and holds a small sign with "Matheson" in black marker. I head in his direction and offer my hand when I reach him. "Hi. Rick Matheson."

The man shakes my hand. "Ben." After he wheels my carryon to the back and stuffs it in the trunk, we get in the car and drive away from the airport. One of the first things I notice as we drive through Los Angeles is how busy and alive this city is. Savannah compared to Los Angeles is minuscule. The sea of people and commuters isn't as intimidating as I thought it might be. In fact, the bustle invigorates me.

Wrapped up in all the sights, time flies by and soon we park in front of an opulent building. Stone and pillars and perfectly manicured foliage. Ben gets out and retrieves my luggage. We walk up to the entrance of the building and another man greets us. A man twice the size and a hell of a lot more intimidating than Ben. He nods at us and we step past him.

Ben leads me through a bar/lounge, up a set of stairs, and down a small corridor before he points to a large, wooden door. "Rocco is in there." Other than offering his name, that is the most Ben has said to me since picking me up. Either he is not much of a conversationalist or his job requires him to be a man of few words. I nod and head for the door as Ben leaves.

Staring at the door, I close my eyes and take a deep breath. *You got this*, I repeat in my head. After a few inhalations, I knock and wait a millisecond before I'm invited in. I turn the handle, step inside, and Rocco rises from behind his large mahogany desk and smiles wide. "You must be Rick," he says, walking around the desk and shaking my hand. "Pleasure to meet you."

"No, the pleasure is all mine. Thank you for having me."

We exchange pleasantries for a moment, then get down to the formal part of the interview. Questions for a job of this nature are not quite like those in a typical job interview. Sure, he asks some of the familiar questions. Job history. Why the big move. What my boss and employees would say about me. But when we surpass those, we broach the ones some people may cringe hearing.

What sex acts have you witnessed? Are you straight, gay,

bisexual, pansexual, non-defined, other? Elaborate. Have you witnessed a sexual act that made you cower? If so, what was it? Tell me the most hedonistic scene you've been witness to. How did it make you feel?

The questions go on for more than an hour. Once he has asked me a mile-long list of questions, Rocco walks me around the bar and introduces me to several of the staff. We sit at a table in the lounge, eat lunch, and have a drink while discussing his and my lifestyle.

Hours pass and the crowd inside The Sophisticate multiplies. We chat and mingle with patrons. Rocco points to a couple—woman and man. "I'm going to talk with them in a minute, and I want you to listen. See how I filter out people I'm willing to allow into P.I. The only people who know about P.I. are those who have been invited in. They are told not to discuss the club outside these walls. If members want to bring friends, we allow them a one-time opportunity to bring a guest into the club. Names are taken and we track every person who sets foot in P.I."

I nod. "Got it."

We reach the couple and Rocco asks them how they are enjoying themselves. He introduces me as one of his managers, then continues speaking with them. Basically, Rocco asks them questions to check their integrity and determines if they would act civilized in the exclusive area of P.I. Some of his questions also ascertain if P.I. would be something they would be interested in. It is somewhat similar to what we do at Apex, only this is more personal.

Rocco invites them to join us in an elite area of the bar.

He doesn't divulge specific details, but tells them it is a club. When the couple agrees, we head toward a guarded staircase. Rocco tells the bouncers the couple will be guests for the evening. After the bouncers check their IDs, they are let in and we follow.

After descending a lengthy stairwell, we land in a dark corridor. Music vibrates the walls and light slowly seeps in. When we reach the open space, another bouncer lets us pass. The moment I scan the room, I remain rooted in place, awestruck.

If a strip club could receive star ratings, P.I. would get them all.

We walk over to the bar and take a seat. A nude woman pours Rocco a drink and offers me one as well. Once we both have drinks in hand, Rocco asks my opinion on the place.

"First of all, this place is stellar. I've never seen a business of this nature appear so *classy*. Now I'm eager to see your plans for Boundless. Is there only dancing here?"

Rocco points to a space to the right of the stage. Sheer curtains cascade and form a sense of privacy, but every person can see everything in the open area. "Most lap dances happen there, but the girls will stay at the tables if the patron accepts." Next, he points to a long wall with several doors. "Those rooms are for private dances. Only the dancers can take someone in them. And they are in control of what happens. No one except them and the patron are privy to what happens inside."

He tells me more regarding the club and the girls who

dance here. Just as Rocco is very selective with the clientele, he is even more so with the staff and dancers. Everyone receives a full background check and is given a probationary period. If anything undesirable happens in the first ninety days, the person is let go without notice.

After a couple hours in P.I., Rocco and I leave and drive to his home. Less than thirty minutes later, I strip my clothes away and take a quick shower. Once I hit the sheets, I send Christy another text. It's just after midnight in California, which translates to after three in the morning at home.

Rick: I miss you, gorgeous. Had a great interview. I love you. Sleep tight.

I plug my phone in and lay it on the bedside table. Just after I turn the light off, my phone vibrates and lights up the room.

Christy: Miss and love you, too.

Thank fuck. If we didn't exchange any form of communication during my entire trip, I was ready to throw in the towel on this offer. Why put in all the effort to move out of state if we're not in an amiable place?

The next day, Rocco takes me to where Opulence/Boundless is being constructed. Similar in nature to The Sophisticate, it has a few differences. Where The Sophisticate has touches of creams and browns in the bar/lounge area. Opulence is bold with black and silver on the exterior. On the interior, the base a slate gray with pops of purples, blues, reds, and occasional touches of silver. Describing it sounds like a disco ball, but visually it screams fine dining with a hint of sex.

We walk the floor plan and I see the restaurant slowly coming to life. Rocco points to a long wall on the left. "We'll have a bar along most of that wall." Then he points toward the back right corner. "An open kitchen there, with a doorway that leads to a closed off prep area and refrigeration." As we reach a stairwell similar to the entrance to P.I., Rocco stops. "And this will be the patron entrance to Boundless. The only traffic to enter and exit through other means is strictly staff or emergency personnel."

I nod, and we head down the stairwell. The entry mimics P.I., which I prefer. This way, there are no surprises or questions regarding the safety of everyone inside.

When we step into the massive open space, Rocco asks, "How do you envision Boundless?"

Whoa. Completely unexpected and humbling. I gaze around the vast interior and try to picture a club the way I would love it. Currently, there is absolutely nothing here. Just concrete, dust, and the beginning stages of drywall being hung. Spinning around, I point toward the farthest wall. "A bar spanning the majority of the wall. Slate or concrete to match the color scheme in the restaurant." Rocco nods and waves me to continue. "Along majority of this wall" —I point to the longest wall that butts against what could be the bar— "couches, chaises, and chairs with low tables. Same material as the bar top. With tables, couches, and chairs sporadically placed throughout as well. At Apex, we have a VIP section. Perhaps we could create a similar set up here. A secluded area where higher paying clientele or more frequent members can lounge more comfortably and be doted on more."

"I like the idea of having a VIP. We also intend on adding closed off rooms here, like in P.I., where people can explore new things without watching eyes. Not everyone is as adventurous their first time. At least two of the rooms, though, will be specifically for spectators."

This has my interest piqued. "Wouldn't everyone here be privy to the happenings of everyone else?"

"Yes," Rocco confirms. "But the voyeur rooms will be equipped with specialty items from different lifestyles. Bondage, D/s, fetish items, stimulation devices, and so on. Depending on what it is, we will also allow clientele to bring in their own items for play. But they must be approved by myself or club management. The voyeur rooms are intended to be more intense in nature than what happens on the club floor."

Boundless truly is a dream job. This place is everything I've ever wanted out of working in this industry. Freedom to express who I am without criticism. To be in a like-minded environment and not be shamed or made to feel guilty for being who I am. Other than Christy, nothing has ever felt so right.

"Rocco, I don't know what to say, except I hope you'll consider me for the job. I understand if you need time to—"

Rocco cuts me off. "Rick, after talking with you on the phone last week, I made a few calls. Several conversations later, and it was just a matter of meeting you. If your vibe fit what I was seeking, you were my man. And, I'd like to extend you an offer. Would love to have you join the family."

Floored. Absolutely floored. I met this man a day ago, shared nervous conversations with him, and just like that he is ready to bring me on. Speechless and stunned, I shake off my incredulity. "Yes. Let's discuss going forward."

That evening, I sit at the bar inside P.I. A young woman with long dark hair dances across the stage. If I had to guess, I'd say she is Native American. Her beauty rare and subtle. I sip on a glass of whiskey and bask in the day's events. The whole offer still blows me away.

Pulling my phone out of my pocket, I type out a text to Christy.

Rick: Best news, gorgeous. He offered me the job.

The little bubble pops up and the three little dots dance in the gray box, and it thrills me she is awake and responding.

Christy: I'm so excited. You'll have to tell me all about it when you get home. What time is your flight tomorrow?
Rick: 2:30 p.m. CA time. Think I land close to midnight.
Christy: I'll be waiting.
Rick: Fuck, I miss you. Love you, gorgeous.
Christy: Love and miss you more.

I glance at the time on my phone. Just after eleven. Which means it is after two back home. Honestly, I'm somewhat surprised Christy is still awake. But happy I got to chat with her a moment. It was one thing to have her in the room next to me after we had our fight. If I wanted to bad enough, I could have jimmied the lock, walked in, and laid with her. Being thousands of miles apart in a foreign city, though… there is no such possibility.

Honestly, I just want to wake up next to her, study the lines of her face, get lost in her expressions as she dreams, smell that distinct floral scent of hers, trace my fingers over her curves, and bask in her stormy blue eyes and supple body when she wakes.

Sometimes, it takes distance and not having someone completely accessible to grasp how much they truly mean to you. I have loved Christy for years. But I think time has made us comfortable and complacent with each other. Not having her curled up next to me at night—not even in the same living space—is lonely and cold and unsettling.

After I finish my drink, I exit the club and head back to Rocco's home. Never have I been so eager to jump on a plane and fly back home. Home is wherever Christy is. And if my girl wants to move to the opposite side of the world, I will go with her in a heartbeat. Because wherever Christy is is where I need to be.

THE BED DIPS beside me and a draft sends shivers across my skin. I groan into the darkness and yank the comforter higher on the bed.

Just as I drift off again, warm lips graze my temple, my neck, my collarbone. I moan and roll onto my back. Best dream ever. Wet lips kiss down my sternum, across my breast, and wrap around my nipple. When his teeth grind together, I bow my back off the bed.

"I missed you, gorgeous," Rick mumbles around my nipple, his fingers dancing down to my navel and dipping lower.

I open my eyes and see a head of dark hair sweeping over my ribcage. Still believing it's just a dream, I comb my fingers through his hair, make a fist, and tug. Hard. His teeth and lips part, freeing my nipple as he hisses.

A second later, he inches up my body as his lips crash onto mine and it is a battle to the death. When our lips break apart, he slips under the comforter and licks his way down between my legs. His tongue circles and laps my clit, over and over, like a savage beast. But the moment he inserts two fingers and pumps inside me, I let go.

"So sweet," he says, muffled by the blanket. "Fuck, how I have missed the sweet taste of your pussy, kitten."

He crawls his way up my body and hovers above me for a second before kissing me senseless again. The sweet and salty tang of my release hot on his tongue. As he breaks the kiss, he slowly pushes inside me.

It isn't often Rick makes love to me. Yes, our sex is intimate and passionate, but I wouldn't classify most of it as making love. We fuck. A lot. It's intense and hot and euphoric. And the majority of the time, it is straight up fucking.

But what's happening between us right now. How he rocks his hips with slow precision. The way his lips brush softly over my skin and ignite an inferno in my soul. This is so far from fucking, and tips the scale much closer to lovemaking. The pace at which he slides in and out of me. The passion whirling in his eyes. Yes, lust is present. But his longing to touch and see me is a million times stronger. Taking precedence. As does the tender kisses he presses to my lips, my forehead, and my chin.

More intimate than any other time we have been together. Our bodies in sync, this dance we're doing nothing short of hypnotic. I can't get enough of him.

We make love for hours. Kissing. Touching. Reacquainting ourselves with each other after days apart.

Not quite sure what happened while Rick was in California, but he seems different. More appreciative and affectionate. Saying I missed this intimacy would be just the tip of the iceberg. Over the last few months, things between us have been off. Maybe us moving across the country isn't such a bad idea after all. Maybe it is exactly what we need.

In the morning, we stumble out of bed after making love again. After a late breakfast, we dress, hop in the car, and then Rick says he has a surprise for me. We chat throughout the entire drive—Rick telling me every last detail of his time in California. Before I realize it, he drives up to and parks at a small airport, and we board a helicopter.

"Where are we going?" I ask as I buckle myself in and tug the belt as tight as it will go.

Rick winks at me. "You'll see. Figured it'd be fun to have a change of scenery."

After the pilot finishes the preflight checks, the helicopter lifts off the ground and we are high above the streets of Savannah. Beside me, Rick chuckles as I attach myself to the window and watch the city and trees change. In the sky, the world is an entirely different place. Quiet. Peaceful. Sure, all the chaos still happens below us, but it looks like ants marching in the forest. In the clouds, perspectives change. People change.

After we leave Savannah airspace, I sit back in my seat and wrap Rick's hand with mine. With no idea of what he has planned, a fresh wave of excitement ripples in my chest. Rick kisses my knuckles before drawing me closer and pressing his lips to mine. When he strokes my tongue with his, the world vanishes.

No helicopter. No pilot. Just him, and me, and the connection that magnetizes us and always will.

Less than an hour passes and we descend toward Atlanta. The city bustles with life, its energy a massive bubble luring me in. Before the helicopter hits the ground, I assault Rick with kisses. A couple years shy of thirty and I have never traveled very far outside of the city limits of Savannah. Most of my life I was sheltered, and in the years since meeting Rick, we've stayed close to home. Not because neither of us wanted to travel, but we just never had anywhere we dreamed of going.

A car sits idle near the airstrip, and I glance over my shoulder at Rick. His larger than life smile plucks the strings of my heart. "When did you do all this?" I ask.

He shrugs as we slip into the backseat. "I had some free time on my trip. Thought it'd be nice to take you somewhere new. Have a change of scenery. Things have been difficult the last month, and I missed seeing your smile."

I hop on his lap and kiss the hell out of him. After we are both breathless, I inch back into my seat and buckle my seatbelt. "Thank you," I whisper. "You don't know how much I love this."

Dropping a chaste kiss on my nose, he says, "Anything for my girl."

After we grab lunch at a chic cafe, we wander hand in hand through the streets of Atlanta. Rick steers us into a couple stores. The first stop, a jewelry store named Compulsion. Not your typical diamonds and gold bands jewelry store. But I love it the moment we step inside.

Rick drops my hand and lets me walk ahead of him. My eyes light up at all the pieces on display. Silver, platinum, titanium. Collars, cuffs, clamps. The small store is packed with a plethora of jewelry that would be appealing to people from all walks of life. Bands and gemstones and chains glint under the lights in each case.

When I stop in front of a case, a set of silver cuffs sparkle in the display. Simple and beautiful, yet so much more. The bracelets a half inch wide and a quarter inch thick. A small chain links them together, but is removable for normal daytime, public wear. Almost a perfect match to my collar.

Rick leans forward and presses his chest to my back. "Something catch your eye, gorgeous?" I nod and he laughs. "Haven't quite mastered reading your mind yet, so you'll have to tell me."

I swallow and clear my throat. "The cuffs," I mutter.

He leans in closer, his groin thick on my lower back. "Mmm... those would match this" —he brushes a finger along the edge of my collar— "quite nicely. Would you like them?"

I twist to get a better look at him. His honey eyes simmer, lips kicked up in a slight smile. "Really?" I ask. After a beat, his smile widens and reaches his eyes. "Yes, I would love them."

Rick signals for the clerk and, ten minutes later, we walk out of the store. Me with matching bracelets on my wrists. Rick holding a small bag with a chain and a few clamps tucked inside.

While I stare awestruck at my new accessories, Rick guides us into a second store. As soon as we step inside, the distinct scent of leather and latex grabs my attention and I snap my head up. Rick and I have experienced so much together, sexually. We also play a lot in the fetish department. At least I think we do.

For the most part, we enjoy sex together and with other couples. Yes, we have done things deemed not "normal" by the average person or couple. But we haven't introduced an arsenal of accessories. Honestly, that is why I lost it when he strapped me to the Saint Andrew's cross at Apex.

Was I turned on? No doubt about it. But the humiliation rang much louder and stole all the pleasure from my body.

We have never been shy, but our lifestyle wasn't centered around exhibitionism. So, when he caused a scene and everyone stopped to watch him —us—a piece of me shattered. A piece I pray is mendable.

I peek up at Rick, his eyes alight as he scans the store. "Why are we here?" I ask.

Kissing my forehead, he answers, "We have plans tonight. Thought you might enjoy a new club, for a change."

Staring at bodysuits, corsets, and crotchless panties, I zone out a second. When I come back to, I ask, "What kind of club?" Because we don't make a point to wear leather or latex in Savannah.

"Rocco told me about it." When I stare at him confused, he clarifies. "He wanted me to check out other clubs. More ideas for Boundless."

Ah… so this isn't just time away with your girlfriend for fun. This trip to Atlanta is also a work assignment. Don't I feel fucking special.

"Do we need to wear some of this?" I ask, waving my arm at the miles of fetish attire. A few pieces catch my eye and I wouldn't be opposed to wearing them. But there are several things I don't know if I'm quite ready to experience yet.

"No. But I thought it might add some flair." He bends down and kisses me on the lips. Slow and sweet. "And I didn't think you'd be opposed to trying something new."

Am I against it? Yes and no. Should I have to put on skintight, unbreathable material to turn Rick on? I hope not. But slipping into the second skin also adds a new layer of desirability. The chance to be someone new. Someone different. In a sense, wearing leather and latex is a form of role play. For us anyway, being new territory and whatnot.

"Okay," I acquiesce.

After what feels like hours of searching the aisles and racks, I chose a black leather cage bodysuit. Thick black straps span over my neck, breasts, abdomen, and between my thighs. And they are all that will mask my nipples, clit, and ass crack. When I pick it up and survey the design, Rick practically drools beside me.

I drape it over my arm and smile up at him. "What are you wearing?"

We walk to the men's attire and he lifts a pair of leather pants from the rack, hanging them over his forearm. We head to the dressing rooms and try on our selections. Needless to say, the cage bodysuit is a winner in my book. Can't wait for Rick to see me in it later. Before we head for the checkout, Rick walks us down a few more aisles and snags more toys for our collection.

Once we pay and leave, a gleam I have never witnessed lights up Rick's face. And it makes me wonder, once again, if I am enough for him.

TEN

WE STEP inside Entrapment and a rush explodes in my bloodstream.

Entrapment isn't a sex club like Apex. It is notches above.

The floor plan is twice the size of Apex, but smaller than the space for Boundless. A small bar sits off to the left of the entrance, dim red lights glowing along the liquor shelves. Black, studded leather couches, chaises, and ottomans spread throughout the open floor. The back third of the space lined with cages, suspension equipment, and varied restraints.

A buzz hums across my skin as I soak in every square foot.

I inhale deep as my eyes close and wrap my arms around Christy's waist. This is what I need. The energy. The lechery. Countless people with insatiable desires, dying to fulfill their utmost fantasies. This is what I want for Boundless.

Walking slowly toward the bar with Christy on my arm, I absorb every heady inch of Entrapment. A seductive beat echoes throughout the large floor plan. It vibrates beneath my feet as heat and lust ripple through my limbs and up my spine. The dim lighting adds another layer of allure to the club. The air is thick with leather and sex and sweat. Pure fucking bliss.

When we reach the bar, Christy orders us both drinks and sits on a stool. Sexy as fuck in the caged leather piece, I can't wait to peel it off her body. But as I wait for my drink and study her body language, I register her discomfort. Legs tightly crossed. Arms banded over her breasts as she fiercely grips her biceps. Head tipped down, eyes on the bar top.

This isn't my girl. Not one bit.

I tip her chin up and force her stormy eyes to meet mine. "You okay, gorgeous?"

The bartender sets our drinks down and her eyes dart toward them. Sliding her glass closer, she locks eyes with me again. "Yeah. I guess. It just feels..." She trails off and scans the men and women in the club. For a split-second, her eyes widen. "Everything is so different here."

Bending down, I kiss her gently. "Yes, it is different here. Things will be different at the new club in California, too." I paint a finger over her cheekbone and down the side of her neck. "Sometimes, different can be good, gorgeous."

Christy stares at me with questions in her eyes. Questions she refuses to ask. A huge part of me wants to introduce her to more than the tamer shit we have done. More than sex with other couples. Because the animal that has always lived inside me, the one I cage up and bury deep, yearns for more.

Not corporal punishment or open wounds. I understand the desire others have for that, but it doesn't resonate with me.

What I thirst for is more kink. More delayed gratification and foreplay. The ability to let go and release the beast clawing inside me. I want to be savage and rough and watch Christy's skin redden under a whip or paddle. I want to clamp her nipples and her folds, chain them together and yank them while I pound into her.

And I want Christy to want this with me.

"I suppose. But I feel so out of my element here. People here are more—"

"Intense," I finish for her.

"Good choice." She nods then sips her drink.

Was bringing her here not such a great idea? *Fuck*. I hope she is open to this. To being in a place similar to this. To experimenting with new things. Boundless will mimic the vibe here and I want her to accept the concept before I work there day in, day out. Christy means the world to me, and I want her to be comfortable with more beyond sex with other couples.

"Are you okay with the intensity here?" I pose the question and pray she says yes.

Taking another sip of her drink, she scans the crowd. Her eyes zero in on a group, and then another, before coming back to me. "I'm not narrow-minded. This is just a lot to take in without warning, I guess."

I mentally slap myself for being so vague with her today. But I wanted to surprise her. Show her the world wasn't just black, white, and gray. Splashes of color existed and it is okay to let droplets dye your skin.

After taking a sip of my drink, I kiss the crown of her head and leave my lips there a moment. Her amber-floral scent pricks my nose, and I close my eyes. "Sorry I didn't tell you, gorgeous," I mumble into her hair. "Just wanted you to be open to new possibilities. Boundless will be more like Entrapment than Apex. I'd rather you be shocked now."

Christy's arms snake around my bare torso and she tugs me closer. Cheek pressed against my pec, she says, "Okay, I'll try to enjoy the evening." She sighs, and a layer of goosebumps pop up on my skin. "Just please don't be upset if I don't want to try certain things."

I inch back from her, take her chin between my thumb and forefinger, and lock eyes with her. "I will never make you do anything you're uncomfortable with. Ever. And it won't upset me. All I want is for you to enjoy yourself. Okay?"

She nods. "Yes."

We finish our drinks and I wrap my hand around hers, guiding us around the club. Tucked close to my side, Christy gazes at couples and groups as they explore one another. When we get closer to the back of the club, where the cages, harnesses, and other contraptions reside, Christy pauses.

For a few minutes, we stand rooted in place and just watch. If I'm not mistaken, Christy seems a little more than curious. Her gaze is locked on the couple in front of us. A good sign.

A tall, lanky man stalks circles around a young woman. If I ventured to guess, I would say he is in his mid- to late-forties, and she appears barely legal. Age is easier to define when you aren't wearing clothing. Both their ages evident in the lines and curvature of their flesh. But in a place like this, as long as consent is provided, no one judges your tastes.

The young woman's ankles and wrists are cuffed and latched to a square, metal frame mounted to the floor. Her body is stretched completely and fully upright. A ball gag is buckled at the back of her head. Her breasts are small and the nipples pert, her thighs are glistening with arousal. As the man circles, he cracks a leather paddle over her body. With each thwack, the young woman jolts in the cuffs and my dick throbs behind my zipper.

I peek down at Christy. Her widened eyes haven't strayed away. From my current angle, it is difficult to tell how all this registers with her. As badly as I want to know, I don't wish to come off as pushy. More than anything, I ache to explore new things with Christy. Incomparable to any other woman I've ever had, it's imperative I know she is happy with our life and open to new possibilities.

When I can no longer bear standing here unaware, I ask, "How does this make you feel, gorgeous?"

She fidgets beside me a minute, her eyes still fixed on the man and young woman. Twirling a lock of hair around her finger, she answers, "Not sure. Guess it depends on what he does next. Right now, though, I don't want to look away."

This is a good sign. In the realm of possibility. Hopeful.

"Do you want to keep watching?" I ask.

"Yes," she whispers. "Please."

I release her elbow and step behind her, wrapping my arms around her waist. With my lips at her neck, just below her ear, I start kissing a trail down and across her shoulder. Her body trembles beneath my lips, and I trace my fingers along the cage straps on her belly. Soon, she audibly pants and starts grinding her ass over my groin.

Fuck yes.

The man switches out the paddle for a riding crop. As he circles, he stings her nipples, clit, and each butt cheek. After a few passes, the young woman's skin blossoms a glorious shade of red. A red I wish to paint Christy's skin.

"Does this turn you on, kitten?" I murmur.

Christy gyrates her hips and rubs her ass over my erection. "Yes, daddy."

Thank fuck. "Do you want to play, kitten?" I trail my fingers down her belly and between her legs.

"Please. But be gentle."

We step away from the suspension exhibition and

wander. After a few minutes, we spot a couple on a couch. They're still mostly dressed, with the woman bound to the couch while the man flogs her. For a moment, we observe before introducing ourselves.

When the man glances over at us, I nod and he stops. Extending a hand, I introduce us. "Name's Rick. This is my girl, Christy."

The man shakes my hand. "Jason. And this fine speci-men" —he points the flogger at the woman on the couch— "is my wife, Rachel."

Christy speaks up. "Nice to meet you both." Her smile illuminates the darkest night and the shadowed parts of my heart. Fuck, I love her.

"We wondered if you'd care for company," I state.

Jason walks over to his wife, leans down, and whispers in her ear. She glances our way, nods then kisses her husband. When Jason returns, we discuss our conditions for play. Once everything is laid out, I saunter toward Rachel on the couch.

Near her knees, that are bent over the seat edge of the couch, is a bamboo cane. Christy and I have never played with whips, canes, or similar items. The harshest implement we have introduced was a paddle or crop. I have wanted to try something *stronger*, something with a little more *bite*, but am worried Christy won't enjoy it. Hopefully tonight will change that.

I pick up the bamboo cane and scrape the end over Rachel's body—up her thigh, along her torso, tracing her collar bones. When I stand on the opposite side of her, I lift it up six inches and whip it back down over her breasts. Rachel bows off the couch and moans in pleasure.

Immediately, my cock stiffens and groans for relief behind my zipper. It isn't so much that Rachel turns me on, it's the pleasure she receives from the pain.

Stepping between her widespread knees, I lift the cane again and whack it against her clit.

"Fuck yes," she mewls. Between her thighs, moisture pools at her folds. Not yet, but I need to fuck the hell out of this woman.

I glance over at Christy and Jason. For a beat, my pulse roars in my veins. Jason has her spread wide on an ottoman, hands and ankles bound at the furniture legs. Clamps attached to her nipples, a chain linking them together as he holds the center in his clenched fist. He sweeps the leather tassels of a black flogger over her still caged body. Christy wiggles when the leather grazes between her thighs, and he tugs the chain.

When she gasps, eyes rolling back in her head as her mouth hangs open in pleasure, I freeze. *Have I been too scared to push harder with her? Maybe she wants more, and I have been resistant for the wrong reasons.*

An unfamiliar anger builds inside me. Not anger at Christy. Anger at myself for what has been lacking in our relationship due to my concern. A concern I plan to voice when we are alone.

I refocus on Rachel and take out my aggression on her with the cane. The fact she enjoys it only makes me angrier and my cock harder. Once I have licked her skin with the cane several times, I grab the paddle at her feet, undo my pants, and roll on a condom.

Jacking Rachel's hips up, I slip my knees beneath her ass and line myself up with her folds. She watches me with unadulterated lust in her eyes, and it makes me wild. Sneaking a side glance at Christy and Jason, I stare a beat as he rubs his thumb over her clit and slides in and out of her ass.

Motherfucker.

I whack Rachel's breasts with the paddle and she bucks beneath me, forcing me inside her. So fucking tight. After a moment, I find a rhythm of fucking and beating. The harder I hit Rachel, the louder she cries. Beside us, Christy appears to be enjoying herself more than past exchanges.

In a heartbeat, I see red.

In a heartbeat, I fuck Rachel like a rag doll. Except her limbs are frozen in place. I bang the fuck out of her. Punish a woman I only just met for circumstances beyond her involvement. Beat her with the paddle and mentally scream at the top of my lungs in rage.

Why is this eating me up?

The answer is simple. Christy is mine. She is mine and I have limited our relationship due to fear. Fear of rejection. Fear she will detest me. But most of all, fear she will leave me. Because a life without her isn't a life worth living.

And with all this building up inside me, I explode inside a woman who means nothing to me. A woman who

I hope got off, because I lost focus and am not sure she did.

But the worst part of this whole debacle... Not five feet away, my girl is screaming out the most intense sound I have heard leave her lungs. And I suddenly hate myself.

PART

two

ELEVEN

CHRISTY

August — One year later

RICK AND I, along with a dozen other people, sit in a dark private room at Bella and Daisy's Bistro. In a matter of minutes, Jackson and Sarah will walk into the pitch black room as Jackson pretends that just the two of them are having a private birthday dinner for her. Sarah has no idea we traveled here for her birthday. The other night when Liz and I talked on the phone with her, we played off our loud night out in the city and told her we were partying. A half truth. We were out at a bar drinking and dancing, but unbeknownst to her we were only a few miles from her house.

The moment she walks through those doors, her reaction will be picture worthy when she sees us all here. God, I have missed her face. Missed her carefree demeanor and smile. Talking with your best friend on the phone regularly is one thing. Being able to hug the hell out of them is so much more.

The door cracks open, and Jackson and Sarah step inside before the room goes dark again. Sarah is ten feet away and it takes all my willpower to not jump forward and plow into her. A few seconds tick by before the light flicks on. After a quick adjustment to the brightness, we all holler "Surprise!"

Sarah remains stock still with wide eyes. After realization dawns, she smiles so big the room glows brighter. I snap a few quick photos. The moment is one-hundred percent priceless.

After we all line up and give hugs to the birthday girl, we settle at our tables and spark conversations. Everyone made a special trip here just to see Sarah on her birthday. Sarah's parents, Jackson's dad, Liz, Tiffany, me, Rick, Eric, and some new friends they have made since their move to California.

Smiles light up every face in the room. Laughter ricochets off the walls. Family, friends, and the best of times. In my heart, nothing gets better than this. Well… I glance toward Jackson. Just as I suspected, pale as a ghost. I wriggle in my seat and lean toward Rick. "It's almost time," I whisper in his ear.

Rick pauses his chat with Jackson's father and glances at me with confusion etched in the crease of his brow. "Time for what?"

Sworn to secrecy, I haven't shared with Rick that Liz and I have been helping Jackson coordinate tonight. The pièce de résistance coming in five... four... three... two... one.

Jackson rises from his chair and Sarah peeks up at him. Concern mars her forehead as she studies his sweat slickened pallor. She asks if he feels okay and he brushes it off, kissing her cheek. When she returns her attention to her mom, Jackson clears his throat. "Hey, everyone. Can I have your attention for a moment or two?"

The room quiets and every pair of eyes hones in on Jackson. Poor guy. Sweat glistens along his forehead. His breathing is jagged and heavy. His fingers tap the outside of his leg as if he's playing a drum solo.

"Thank you, again, for being here tonight. I know it means the world to Sarah." Jackson gazes down at Sarah as if she is the sun, stars, and moon wrapped into one. "It means everything to me, too. It took a lot of man hours, and woman hours—" Jackson pauses and tips his head to me and Liz "—to get tonight put together. Countless hours, that turned into weeks, of planning. I couldn't have done it without help. So, thank you. You are the best friends either of us could ever have."

When I raise my wine glass, Rick leans into me. "You've been helping Jackson plan this?" Rick almost hisses, and I just ignore his pissy demeanor and nod. Rick and I have been *off* as of late. Not sure if our upcoming move to Los Angeles is to blame. Or if work has been a stressor for him. Either way, our relationship teeters on a slippery slope. A slope I wish would flatten out and right itself.

"Sarah's birthday isn't the only reason I wanted everyone here tonight." Jackson's lips curve up and display his bright smile. Gah! I have been waiting months for this exact moment. "I brought you all here tonight for another reason as well. I wanted all of you here, the people who hold the highest level of importance to both of us—individually or together—on this memorable evening."

Jackson pivots, shoves his chair back, and drops to one knee. I slap my hand over my mouth and gasp. Although privy to the planning for this very moment, I still shake my head in disbelief that it is actually happening. Tears threaten to rain down my cheeks any second. I'm so happy to be here to witness one of the happiest moments of my best friend's life.

"Sarah, since the day I met you, a little over a year and a half ago, you have turned my life into this astonishing place. You made me see things a little brighter, your aura like a glowing ray of sunlight. Before you, my skies were gray and life was monotonous. Now, everything is brilliant and bold and screaming with life. You make me feel whole. You make life worth living."

Jackson fishes a ring from his pocket and presents it to Sarah. After a shared, teary glance with his father, Jackson continues. "This ring belonged to my mother, MaryAnne. I wish you could have met her. She would have loved you immensely." Sarah wipes a tear from Jackson's cheek. I swipe at my own, not able to fight the urge to let them run free.

Jackson explains why he flew so many of us out here for tonight. Not just for her birthday, which he holds in high regard. "I could have held the door open for anyone that day. I was in such a rush to meet up with a client, I didn't have time to pause at the gym doors or say anything to anyone. I thought in that moment, I'd missed the opportunity of a lifetime. I thought I'd missed my one chance to talk to the most stunning woman I had ever laid eyes on. But I didn't know luck was on my side. I didn't know we were meant to see each other again."

Jackson explains how he whined to his friends for days about the beautiful woman he spotted at the gym. How he practically begged clients in her complex for another appointment, all in the hopes he would see her again. The story plucks at my heart as he shares his point of view.

"Eric was having way too much fun giving me shit for acting like a girl." Jackson glances over at Eric and they laugh a moment before everyone joins in.

As Jackson carries on, he shares how he ended up going to Liz's birthday party. Where the two of them met and spoke for the first time. "I watched you, waiting for the right moment to approach you and start a conversation. When I did… it was all downhill from there. I was hooked. I've been hooked every moment since. Sarah, I couldn't even imagine my life without you in it. I never want to."

I zone out for a moment and ponder over Jackson's confession to Sarah. How his life is incomplete without her. And part of me saddens at the reality of where Rick and I are right now. In some strange limbo. Do I love him? Without a shadow of doubt. Am I completely happy? In this very moment? I want to answer yes, but my hesitancy is answer enough. Whatever has shifted us off kilter, I want to force it back into place. Realign us. Piece us back together and make us whole again.

When I snap out of my introspection, Jackson says the one line most women swoon over. "…will you marry me? Will you be mine forever?"

The room goes silent. Utterly engrossed with Sarah and Jackson, I startle when Rick rests his hand on my thigh. Sometime after Jackson started his speech, maybe while I sat here deep in thought, Rick inched closer to me. For the first time in weeks, Rick displays a level of affection that's been missing from our relationship. Affection I crave on an unhealthy level. And in public, no less. Taken slightly aback, I peer at him out of the corner of my eye. I stare for a moment, wondering what circulates through his head as he watches our best friends get engaged.

Has Rick ever given thought to us getting married?

It crosses my mind for the millionth time. Sarah and Jackson have been together less than two years and he is proposing to her. Rick and I have been together five and a half years, and I wonder if he has ever thought of me beyond the term *girlfriend* or *kitten*.

At times, it feels like we're strangers. Passing each other in the thin timeline between our work schedules. Honestly, I can't remember the last time we had sex. A wild guess, at least three weeks to a month ago. Ever since that night at Entrapment last year, Rick has slowly distanced himself from me. I don't have it in my heart to assume he would cheat on me, but oftentimes my thoughts wander down that path. With his distance, how could they not?

When your partner prefers the company of everyone except you, it isn't difficult to believe you are the issue. Truth or falsehood.

The room booms with congratulations. I wilt in my seat, pissed, because I was so wrapped up in my own head, I missed the key part. Where my best friend accepted the marriage proposal. Not a second passes before a lone tear rolls down my cheek. Not from joy for my friends, but from the notion I may never have this. A happily ever after like Sarah and Jackson.

Rick reaches up and wipes the tear from my cheek. "Happy tear?" he asks as his eyes search mine.

A huge part of me wants to lie and tell him yes. But we swore to always be honest. Always. Although our relationship may not be in the best place, I never go against my word.

"No," I whisper. *Please don't let me ugly cry. Not here.*

He tugs on my chair and spins it so I face him. "What's wrong, gorgeous?" Gone is his pissy attitude from ten minutes ago. Now, a layer of charming and sweet sits out in the open. The sudden shift is like whiplash to my heart.

Damnit. I don't want to lie to him, but I don't want

him to do a one-eighty when I spill my honesty. Whatever. "Being here… are we okay?" I ask.

My question broken and vague, but he knows exactly what question I'm asking. There is no way he doesn't see or feel the distance growing between us. A gradual barrier erecting and widening with each passing day. If he doesn't recognize it, then we need to have a more serious talk.

His thumb draws small circles on my bare thigh beneath my dress. The motion soothing and equally disheartening. "We should talk later, but yes, gorgeous, we're okay."

I survey the lines of his face. Study his eyes with intensity. Drop down and stare at his lips. He gives nothing away. If there is one thing I have learned over the years, it is that if Rick doesn't want you to know something in a particular moment in time, you won't. He keeps secrets better than Area 51.

The rest of the party goes by uneventfully. Sarah flashes her engagement ring to me and Liz, and a boulder sinks deep in my gut. Flashes of being nothing more than Rick's *girlfriend* pop in and out of my head the rest of the evening. Nothing sets the tone better than a *"we should talk"* moment.

Bile rises in my throat and I excuse myself. Sarah and Liz offer to go with me, but I tell them I will be back in a minute, then walk away alone. Once in the locked bathroom stall, I sit on the seat, hang my head in my hands, and cry.

Cry for my relationship, which is going south faster

than a snowbird leaving Canada for Florida. Cry for my best friend, and the jealousy that runs in my veins like a drug every time I bear witness to her happiness. And I cry for myself, and the life I thought I would have but can't seem to grab hold of no matter what I do.

After I dry my eyes, I walk back to the party with my eyes downcast. If I keep them down long enough, maybe no one will notice their red and puffy state. The last thing I want is to ruin my best friend's birthday/engagement party.

An hour later, our Uber parks at the entrance of our hotel. We step out, walk to our room in silence, and head inside. The quiet irks me more than anything. Lack of communication is the devil taunting me. If I know Rick at all, he will bring everything up as soon as I hit the sheets.

I turn on the shower and start stripping out of my clothes. The continuous silence kills me as I watch Rick remove his clothes. Once undressed, I step under the hot spray, close my eyes, and sigh. A river of tears sits restrained by my internal dam. I refuse to cry. Not now. Not when it won't solve a damn thing.

As I run my hands through my hair, cool air licks my skin for a beat before Rick grabs both my hips. It has been too damn long since the last time he touched me intimately. I hate to admit it, but I have almost forgotten what it feels like to be caressed by Rick. After another pass through my hair, I swipe it to the side and Rick peppers soft kisses from the base of my skull to the edge of my shoulder. So sweet. So gentle.

At any given moment, that internal dam I built is going to shatter.

His strong arms wrap around my belly, tug me out of the spray, and spin me around. Then his lips graze mine. "I'm scared," he whispers.

My eyes pop open and lock on a swirl of golden fire. I reach up and frame his face. "Why?"

For the first time in weeks, the bond that brought us together flickers. "I'm scared to leave Georgia. It's where my life came together. What if us moving out here tarnishes that?"

I shake my head and press a chaste kiss on his lips. "It won't. We won't let that happen."

"How can you be so sure?" The way his voice cracks… it breaks my heart.

"Because you are the strongest man I know. And if you want something, you go after it."

His brow furrows as he stares into my eyes with uncertainty. "Not that I've purposely withheld from you, but there are skeletons in my past I don't wish to unearth. And moving might do that. My lifestyle—" I cock a brow at him. "Our lifestyle, sorry, is an outlet for me. And if we're being truthful, sometimes what we have isn't enough for me."

"Like what?" I challenge.

Rick starts playing with my hair. "After Jackson and Sarah's engagement today, and seeing the way your face lit up when he asked her, it was a knife to the heart." His eyes wander to where his fingers toy with the strands. "I love you, Christy. More than I love anyone else. But sometimes I wonder if we give each other what we need."

I inch back from him and his eyes refocus on mine. "What is that supposed to mean?" I bite out.

"Please don't be upset." He pauses, eyes bouncing back and forth between mine, and he takes a deep breath. "What I mean is, I'm not sure we're both satisfying the other physically."

My blood boils. *Is he serious right now?* "We have to have sex for that to count."

He flinches, then nods—my words a slap in the face—and returns to playing with my hair. "After that night in Atlanta, a light came on. I'd never seen you so euphoric during sex—with me or anyone else. At first, I disregarded it and blamed it on my imagination. But the next time we had sex, it replayed in my head. How much you got off with that other guy. Your cries. The way your body begged for more of *him*. For the first time ever, I felt inadequate."

I lean back, my hands still on either side of his face, and study his eyes. Rick's eyes hold the keys to all his secrets. "You feel inadequate? I don't understand how that's possible. Especially seeing as I never give you what you need."

He slowly shakes his head, eyes watching my lips a beat before they come back to mine. "Christy... you *are* everything I need."

Pressing my lips to his, I kiss him as if I never will again. "Are you sure?" I hold his gaze. "Because that club in Atlanta… The new club in LA… They're so different than what I'm used to. And you're not the Rick I've known in those places. White hot fire blazes in your eyes in that setting." Inhaling deep for three breaths, I continue. "Baby, I want you to be happy. If doing things I'm not quite comfortable with makes you happy, I'll do them."

He strokes his knuckles over one cheek while his other hand tinkers with my hair. "That's not what I want, gorgeous. I don't want you doing things, especially uncomfortable things, to make me happy. This isn't just about me. It's about us. What we enjoy individually, and together. You're in control, more than me."

His words seep into my consciousness and filter through every molecule. As much as I would love to believe I hold more control in our relationship, it isn't true. Yes, I love the thrill of having new sexual experiences and partners. But it isn't the end all, be all. If Rick told me today he no longer wanted to have another person in our bedroom—so to speak—I would stop for him. And I hope he would react the same. It isn't strictly the thrill of a different partner, but also what they do and how they behave.

Hard to explain, but it is a yearning deep inside that begs to be fulfilled. A hunger. An insatiable drive for more. Could Rick give me what I need? No doubt about it. And that is why I am willing to experience new things. Besides another shape or set of hands on my body. If I expose myself to more, maybe I can be enough for Rick. Be enough for him to not need another in our bed.

I shake my head. "No baby, we're both in control. And all I want is to love you."

For the first time in weeks, Rick makes love to me for hours. As if it were our first time. And I fall asleep with his arms wrapped tight around my waist. Sated and peaceful.

TWELVE

RICK

Walking through Boundless, I scan the floor as workers lay planks of graphite gray tiles. The walls coated with fresh paint two days ago. Once the floor is finished today, another set of hands will come in and construct the bar. Everything is coming together quickly, and it is hard to believe the doors will open in a month and a half.

After looking over the concept drawings for Boundless, Rocco and I added our opinions and notations. Within days, we had contractors and workers lined up. Everything kicked off faster than expected. Watching it all come to life is unreal. The pull I have in decision-making even more surreal. Rocco instills an unfathomable level of trust in me, and every day I work with him I am beyond thankful.

Christy doesn't start at the California Hammond Life office until Monday. So, over the next few days, she spends her time going through box after box and unpacking our home. Liz and Tiffany are scheduled to arrive week after next. At first, I considered it odd Liz also wanted to move. But then again, I never shared a bond with friends like the three of them do. The only person I have ever been somewhat close to—on that level—was Harriett.

"Mr. Matheson?" One of Opulence's bartenders calls across the room.

"What's up, Jake?"

He points a thumb over his shoulder toward the stair-well. "There's someone upstairs. Says they have an interview."

I nod. "Thanks, Jake. I'll be up in a minute. Get them a drink, please."

Jake spins on his heel and heads for the stairs. Taking my phone out of my pocket, I type out a quick text to Rocco.

Rick: Next interview is here.
Rocco: Be there in a minute.

I head for the stairs and up to the restaurant level. Opulence/Boundless has a third, upper level dedicated to office space for Rocco, myself, the restaurant manager, and shared space for our backup managers. I consider myself the club manager, but Rocco corrects me each time. "You're not strictly the club manager, Rick. You're also my number two. My right hand." When Rocco isn't here, employees come to me in his stead.

Today, we are interviewing for the open managerial roles. Tomorrow, we will see a long line of people applying for positions within Boundless. Bartenders, bouncers, drink servers, dancers, security, janitorial. The list goes on and on. We have seven managerial interviews today—an hour blocked for each. But the interviewees tomorrow will get fifteen to thirty minutes max, especially with the mile-long list.

When Rocco rounds the corner, I wait for him to join me. Together, we walk over to where a man sits. Before we sit, I quickly observe him. Bouncing knee. Palms wiping his thighs beneath the table. His eyes dart to me, then Rocco, then back to me. The glass of water on the table in front of him half full.

Why the fuck is he so nervous?

After talking to Mr. Scared Shitless for twenty minutes, I give a pointed look to Rocco. Something tells me this guy has never worked in a place like this before. Part of me questions whether he has ever seen a naked woman in person. Or if he's even been with someone else. Honestly, I pray we don't attract an obscene amount of pervs. I don't have it in me to deal with them.

We dismiss him and let him know we'll call him some-time next week. As soon as he walks out, I turn to Rocco. "We need some sort of signal. Something to tell the other we don't like the candidate."

Rocco laughs. A harsh, genuine roar. "Thought it was just me. How about this?" He brushes the side of his index finger knuckle against his nose. The gesture could pass as an itch. Vague enough only he and I would understand it means more.

"Perfect," I say. "If either of us feels we need to cut the interview short, we signal the other."

"Agreed."

The next three interviews come and go. Two of them potentials. One a dirty old man looking to get off. Wasn't hard to detect. If I have seen one, I have seen them all. Wrinkled button-down and slacks. Greasy hair slicked back. Cologne strong enough to smell a mile away. But that wasn't the worst of it. That belonged to the devious smile—sans a few teeth—and the glint in his eyes every time we mentioned anything sexually related. Within five minutes, Rocco and I both rubbed our nose.

Fucker.

Three more to go. Hopefully, they will be more professional. Rocco and I discuss the two potentials as we wait for our next candidate. We both agree we prefer Grayson over Charles, but both have potential. Once we finish discussing them, Rocco starts asking me personal questions.

"So, tell me about you and your girl. Christy, right?"

"Yeah. She's my light. Things have been a bit rocky since her friend moved to Santa Barbara a little over a year ago. But I hope we're on the upswing."

Rocco nods. "Me, too. I wouldn't imagine either of you moving thousands of miles with the other if things were bad. You love her?"

"With everything I am. But we both have our demons,

and every once in a while they make us doubt the other's happiness. Couldn't imagine life without her, though."

"So why isn't she more?"

I cock my head. Not wanting to assume, I ask, "How so?"

"If I remember correctly, you said you've been together almost six years. No ring?" Rocco gestures to my left hand.

Twisting the ring on my right thumb, I shake my head. "Not yet. Funny thing, I know she'd say yes if I asked. And it's not that I don't want her forever. But before I ask her to be my wife, I need to eradicate my demons first. Demons I haven't shared with her."

"Take it from me," Rocco says as he taps the table, "don't wait too long. You love her. She loves you. The longer you wait to share, the harder it will be. Plus, her trust in you may change."

"You speak from experience?"

"Yes and no," he tells me. "My wife and I have been married almost twenty years. She spends a lot of time with her family in New York—her mother isn't well. At times, it's hard on us, but we're completely open. Do I miss her? Every goddamn day. She misses me too. But for the longest time, I kept my tendencies to myself, and she didn't tell me about her mother's illness. It wasn't until we'd been married a few years—we dated four years—that I introduced my kinky side. Needless to say, she was shocked. Initially, I hid it from her because I didn't want her to leave me. Not that I thought she would, but you never know. She is sweet and gentle, and I feared losing her."

I sit beside him, running a finger over my upper lip. "Christy only knows half the kink I enjoy. I introduced her to more last year and she seemed open to some of it. My worry is she'll see me in a different light and leave me. Plus, we haven't talked much about my past. It's a touchy subject for me, and every time I think about telling her about it, I chicken out."

"Dive in head first. Get it over with. Thinking about the what if's will only have you questioning everything. If you're constantly in your head, she'll think the worst. And you'll never know her reaction unless you bring it up."

I nod. "True. Thanks for the advice, Rocco."

The last of the interviews pass and thank fuck there aren't any other assholes. Once we have spoken to every-one, Rocco and I go into his office and narrow down the candidates. Between the seven candidates—well, six because the perv was automatically eliminated—we narrow it down to four people. Through a second inter-view, those four will dwindle to three. A manager for the restaurant and each of our assistant managers.

Rocco hands me a few small slips of paper and I write their names and numbers down. Tomorrow, I plan to do call backs and schedule second interviews. All in all, the day went much smoother than expected and we are on par with our opening timeline.

After a long day, I park in the driveway at home. Christy and I found a small, two-bedroom home just outside the city. The cost of living in California is dramatically different than Georgia, but Rocco offered me a substantial salary and Hammond gave Christy a cost-of-living pay increase. It worked out perfect and we're financially more stable than before.

As opposed as I originally was to us moving across the country, everything has fallen in line. I have never been a firm believer in destiny. Not after what happened to Harriett. And with Sarah. But the concept grows on me more with each passing day.

When I walk in the house, Christy bangs pots and pans in the kitchen. From the sound of it, you might think she is cooking for a party. Tiptoeing from the front door to the kitchen, I stay out of her line of sight and watch her a moment. She must not have heard me walk in. Obviously slaving over the stove to make us dinner. Christy enjoys cooking, always has, but cooking doesn't like her.

I lean against the pillar that breaks up the open floor plan. The kitchen sits opposite the front door, foyer, and small breakfast nook. Off to the other side of the front door is the living room. Our black leather couch with a chaise on one end dominates one corner of the room. The television is mounted so it swings out from the wall and points toward the couch, but otherwise it is flush. Across from the living area, but next to the kitchen, is the formal dining room. Not a huge space, but our table expands to seat ten comfortably.

We have yet to set up the bookshelves or hang photos

and art. But that will come with time. And we have plenty of that ahead of us.

A frustrated huff puffs up a tuft of hair over Christy's glasses. On both of her denim-covered butt cheeks is a flour handprint. Only a small island separates the kitchen from the open space. On the island lies the evidence of where her flour prints came from. She stirs a large pot on the stove before lifting the spoon out and tasting the contents.

"Shit," she yells, tossing the spoon in the pot and slapping her fingers to her lips.

I push off the post and walk toward her. "Did you burn yourself?"

Christy jumps with a shriek before spinning to face me. "Holy shit! You scared the bejesus out of me." She play slaps my chest and leaves a flour handprint over my left pec. But I give two shits about the handprint. Whether or not she burned herself is far more important.

"Are you okay?" I drag her closer to me and inspect her lips. Before she answers, I kiss her. She tastes like herbs and chicken with a hint of her sweet honey flavor.

When the kiss breaks, she inhales deeply. "Yeah," she says, breathily. "Just hotter than I expected."

"Mmm. Whatever it is, it tastes good." I kiss her again, dragging her body closer and erasing all space between us.

After I devour the taste of dinner off her tongue, I break the kiss and head to the bedroom to change out of my work clothes. Christy walks in a minute later and slips on a cute, skimpy pajama set. Whether dressed to the nines or in her frumpiest outfit, Christy is drop dead gorgeous. A glowing burst of love and energy. She owns every room she steps in. Most of all, she owns my heart.

I twist the band on my right thumb and admire her. Christy is the reason my heart beats. Why I have purpose. The years before we met, I filled the void in my life with countless sexual partners. To be honest, I don't remember a single one of their faces, let alone their names. That probably makes me a cold prick, but the truth is what it is.

Without Christy, days trickled by and felt lackluster. Hell, I probably fucked half or more of the patrons from Apex before meeting Christy. From the second I laid eyes on her, life transitioned from a cold, cloudy existence to a sun-laden paradise. For years, my heart was this hunk of frigid stone in my chest. Unmoving. Never warming. Until the night she walked into Apex. Even at the lowest points in our relationship, she jumpstarted my heart with just her presence.

There is no way to explain the way she lifts me up. All I know is, my life would be shit without her.

We sit on the couch with large bowls of chicken and dumplings and watch *Meet Joe Black*. Christy loves this movie on an unhealthy level. A few years ago, I bought her the digital copy after the DVD got scratched and she ugly cried for an hour straight. Just couldn't bear to see my girl in such agony. She enjoys the love story most of all, but I find the rest of the storyline intriguing. So, we both get sucked in every time.

Curled into my side with a blanket over her legs, her

body sinks deeper into mine and her breathing evens out. The movie has another hour to go, but I shut it off. I scoop her up from the couch, cradle her to my chest, and walk down the hall to our bedroom.

Once in the bed, she lies on her side and gravitates toward me. I sweep fallen hairs off her cheek after I set her glasses on the bedside table. She sighs in her sleep and leans closer to me. It is moments like this that I treasure. The ones only I get to keep locked tight in my heart. The ones where I am most tender with her.

I kiss her softly on the lips and whisper, "Love you, gorgeous. Sweet dreams." She stirs beside me and drapes her body over mine. This is all I need in life. Christy in my arms.

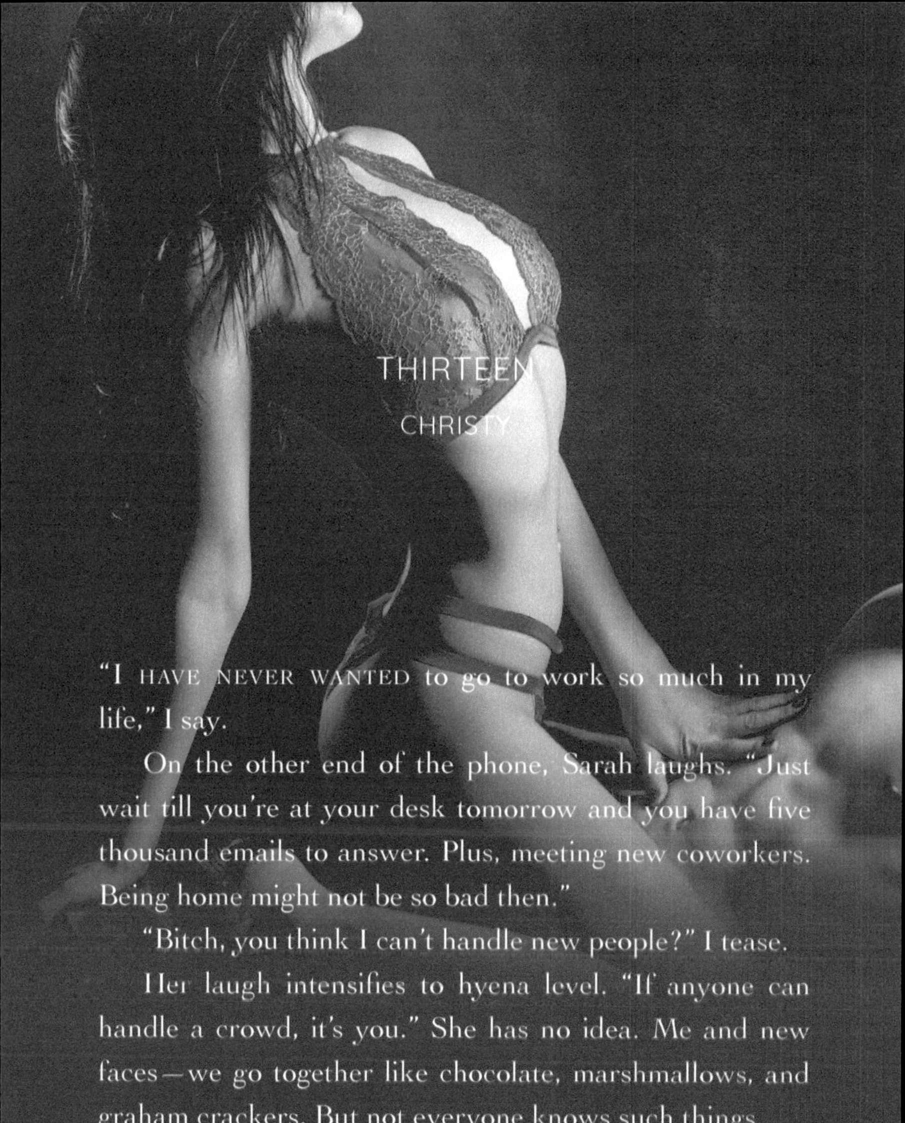

"I HAVE NEVER WANTED to go to work so much in my life," I say.

On the other end of the phone, Sarah laughs. "Just wait till you're at your desk tomorrow and you have five thousand emails to answer. Plus, meeting new coworkers. Being home might not be so bad then."

"Bitch, you think I can't handle new people?" I tease.

Her laugh intensifies to hyena level. "If anyone can handle a crowd, it's you." She has no idea. Me and new faces—we go together like chocolate, marshmallows, and graham crackers. But not everyone knows such things.

Rick and I arrived in California a little more than a week ago. Hammond was more than generous and gave me ten days off to transition from Georgia to California. The drive stole a couple of those days and exhausted the hell out of us, but we made it.

Marco, my manager in Georgia, gave me a company

laptop before I left. Although I wasn't required to work during the transition, I had the option to do so. So, when I needed the occasional break from unpacking, I cleared out emails and responded to clients. That little bit of work would make my first day at the new office less stressful.

"What's that supposed to mean, bitch?" I ask.

Since moving closer to Sarah, my favorite word has resurfaced. Honestly, I only threw *bitch* out with Sarah and Liz. After Sarah moved, and Liz stayed home with Tiffany more often, I stopped saying it. Throwing my favorite word out felt wrong. They were my *bitches*. No one earned it like them. Saying it with one of them gone was a betrayal.

"Nothing bad. Just that you have the ability to make a crowd fall in love with you," she confesses.

"Thanks," I mumble. God, why can't I find the nerve to tell her more about who I am. About my and Rick's lifestyle. Sarah rejecting me for who I am isn't something I picture. At least a big part of me believes this. But until I know for certain she will accept the other side of me, the side I shelter from half of my life, I plan to keep it to myself.

With the phone pinned between my ear and shoulder, I toss towels into the laundry basket and walk it to the washing machine. Sarah continues talking to me about her new job at a magazine as I add clothes to the washing machine.

I pick up a pair of Rick's work pants and something crinkles in the pocket. Fishing out a piece of paper, I unfold it and freeze. Is this real? I pinch my eyes tight, take a couple deep breaths, then open them again. Sarah still talks in my ear, but the last thirty seconds are a blur.

"What the fuck," I blurt out.

"Christy? You okay?" Sarah asks.

I stare at the small slip of paper, dumbfounded. "Yeah, I'm… I'm good. Uh, I got to go. Talk to you later?"

"Sure," Sarah says, a hint of confusion lacing her voice. "Call whenever. Love you."

"Love you, too." I disconnect the call and throw the phone down on the dryer.

What the actual fuck? Why the hell does Rick have this?

Scorching my hands is a small slip of paper with the name *Elizabeth* and a phone number written on it. In Rick's handwriting. Beneath the number, he has written *Monday 1:30.* Is he meeting up with this woman tomorrow? And who the hell is she?

My eyes refuse to look away while my thoughts scream *Rick wouldn't cheat on you.* I pinch my eyes shut as a vise tightens around my ribcage. I work to control my breathing, but it refuses to calm down. This cannot be happening. We are better. Things between us are better. Not as great as they once were, but on the upswing.

I snatch my phone off the dryer and vigorously type out a text to Rick.

Christy: Hey, for my first day back tomorrow, want to have lunch together?

Generic and innocent enough. Every once in a while, Rick would have lunch with me on his off days when he worked at Apex. So my asking wouldn't be out of the ordinary. Especially after our move.

Rick: Sorry, gorgeous. I have a meeting tomorrow. Tuesday?
Christy: Okay. Tuesday.

I shove my phone in my pocket and finish loading the laundry. Once done, I walk to the kitchen, grab a bottle of wine and a glass, and plop down on the couch. My head drowns in thousands of crazy thoughts and I have no idea which one I should believe. My heart tells me Rick would never mess around. But the paper scalds me like a branding iron.

Two bottles of wine and hours later, Rick walks in the front door. His body silhouetted by the outside lights. Since opting to drink my feelings, I haven't flipped on any inside lights. So, the second Rick flips on the light switch in the foyer, I squint and shield my eyes as if the sudden contrast burns my retinas.

"What are you doing?" Rick asks as he walks in my direction.

I bring the bottle of wine to my lips, tip my head back, and drink straight from the bottle. When I finished the first bottle, I left the glass in the kitchen sink. Honestly, using a glass just made extra work.

Rick sits on the couch beside me and studies my face.

Etched in the lines around his eyes as he half-squints is worry and confusion. As far as he knows, everything is on the up-and-up. I stare at him a beat before glancing at the paper on the coffee table. When I don't look back at him, he follows my line of sight. His body deflates next to me.

"Who is she?" I ask.

He picks up the weathered paper. I crumpled and straightened the small slip several times over the last few hours. At one point, I was half tempted to call the number, but stopped myself. What would I say? *Who the hell are you and why does my boyfriend have your phone number?* I'm not some lovestruck teenager. No, I'm a grown ass woman, and we don't make petty phone calls. We get even.

"Really?" Rick stares back at me, a fire roaring in his eyes. "Are you sitting in the dark because of this?"

"Not an answer." I take another swig from the bottle. "Who is she?" I ask again.

"Is this why you asked me to have lunch with you tomorrow? Because you found this." His face reddens and he is on the verge of yelling, but I give no fucks. Because he still hasn't answered my question. His evasion like poison in my veins, slowly eating me alive.

"Lunch would've been nice on my first day back, but yes," I hiss.

Rick rises from the couch, stares down at me, and shakes his head. "No words." He turns his back on me and walks to the bedroom as if his non-answer is acceptable.

Are you fucking kidding me? Not answering me adds fuel to the fire blazing beneath my sternum. I bolt up from the couch, slam the bottle on the table, and hold my hands out in front of me to stabilize myself. Whoa, I definitely drank too much. But it was the only thing to do that made time not drag by.

Once the room stops spinning, I storm toward the bedroom. I step past the threshold and see Rick stripping, then heading for the shower. Following in his wake, I stare at him through the fogged stall glass. He still looks pissed. But I don't fucking care.

"Why won't you answer me?" I ask, loud enough to be heard over the shower.

He stands under the spray, unmoving. The water pounds his face and torso. His eyes pinched shut as he grinds his jaw. Fists clenched at his side. After a minute, he turns his head in my direction. Eyes sad and red. Deflated and small.

"Do you think so little of me?" He mumbles so soft I almost don't hear his question.

Is he crying? Fuck. What have I done? Did I take something and spin it completely out of context?

He hangs his head, chin an inch above the hollow of his throat, and lets the water rain over him. I strip out of my clothes and hop into the shower behind him. Running my palms down his back, I wrap my arms around his waist. He doesn't move. Not an inch. And I simply hold him.

"I'm sorry for assuming. But why won't you answer me?" I whisper against his skin.

After a minute, his arms band over mine and he tugs

me closer to his backside. "The fact that you thought I'd cheat on you shatters me. The name on the paper" —he slowly spins around and looks me in the eye— "she was someone Rocco and I interviewed. I had her number so I could call her back in for a second interview."

Stupid, stupid, stupid. How could I be such an idiot? And why the hell did I automatically jump on the cheating train? Yes, our relationship has been a bit wishy-washy recently, but I never doubted Rick's loyalty to me. Ever. So, why now? Maybe because we are in a new place. A new life. And our whole world is a hot mess.

I close my eyes and mentally berate myself. "I'm a jerk. A goddamn idiot. Sometimes I wonder why you're still with me," I admit. "Recently, all I seem to do is cause problems between us."

"Hey." He tugs my chin up and waits until I open my eyes. The usual fire in his golden irises is a dull amber. I hold his bloodshot, somber honey eyes. For a moment, the world fades away as we get lost in each other. "You still don't get it, do you?"

No, I don't. I don't get why this beautiful, intelligent, and highly desirable man chooses to stay with me. Not after so many others rejected me. Rejection is a strange creature. Has the ability to twist your mind and make you believe you're not worthy. Worthy of trust or love or happiness. How could you be worthy when every person who mattered left?

The only person who repeatedly sticks by my side is Rick. And when I found that paper in his pocket, I automatically assumed the worst. Assumed he was sick of me. Of all the shit I have dished out in the last year. Of my lack of willingness to do more physically. And he was ready to move on with someone less drama-laden.

"No," I mutter. "What's so great about me? When you can have so many others who will give you more than me, how do I believe I'm it for you?" Especially after spending so many years together, and our relationship not evolving. Then again, we have never sat down and discussed our relationship being anything more than it is.

"Christy, I don't want anyone but you."

I shake my head. "That's not true. If it were, we wouldn't live the life we do." We wouldn't have sex with other people is what I really want to say. As exciting as it is, sometimes I just want it to be him and me.

"Fucking other people… I'd quit if it meant that much to you." He leans down and kisses me. "When we're with other couples, the only reason I get off is because you're with me. Before you, fucking was fucking. With you, it's so much more. I won't deny the pleasure I get from us fucking other people. But if you weren't in the same room, if I couldn't watch your face, imagine my cock inside you, it wouldn't matter."

His confession has me awestruck. "Why?" It's all my mind can conjure.

He shakes his head in disbelief. As if I should be aware of the answer. "Christy, you make my blood sing. Before you, sex was an outlet. With you… you breathe life into me."

"Will you tell me?" Rick hasn't told me much about his past. And I haven't pried. But this is the second time he has alluded to it. Almost as if he wants to tell me, but hasn't found the nerve.

"Let's finish showering."

He drags me under the spray and kisses me fiercely. When he releases me, we take our time washing each other. Hands and fingers touching and caressing as we lather and rinse. After we finish, he dries off before wrapping the soft cotton around me and toweling me dry. Rick walks into the bedroom, goes to our dresser, and fishes out nightwear for both of us. Once we dress, he curls me to his chest on the bed and holds me impossibly close.

After a sweet press of his lips to my forehead, he speaks up. "During my senior year of high school, I started using sex as an escape. Not that it was the first time I had the desire to be more *brutal* in the bedroom. Honestly, I think the urge has always been there. But most high school girls weren't into being strapped to the bed and hit before getting fucked. So, I found older women who were interested."

"What changed that year?" I ask as he dances around telling me.

"My sister," he whispers.

I lean away and peer up at him. "You have a sister?"

He nods. "I *had* a sister." Tears pool in his eyes. "Just before senior year started, sophomore year for her, she was hanging out with a new group of friends she'd made during freshman year. My parents and I never questioned anyone she was friends with. Harriett was a good kid. Made good grades. Was ambitious. Dreamed of traveling the globe and photographing all different walks of life. She wanted her photos in *National Geographic*. So, when my mom got a call from the police department telling us to come to the hospital, we were shocked."

I wipe away the tears rolling down his cheeks. He trembles beneath me, and I realize I have never seen him like this. So vulnerable and scared and disarmed. So different from the strong, always-in-control man I always see.

"Twenty minutes later, when we got to the hospital, it was too late. How can someone die so quickly?" he mumbles to himself, and I don't answer. I'm not meant to. "The *friends* she'd been hanging with were into drugs. If Harriett smoked weed, I wouldn't care. There was no harm in it. But obviously it wasn't weed. After we could walk again, the doctor brought us to her in the ER bay. They'd draped the sheet over her entire body, but my parents wanted to see her. They refused to believe she was dead until they saw it with their own eyes. I'll never forget how blue her skin was. Ash blue. After the toxicology report came back, we learned she took a mix of pills with alcohol. The cops spoke with the other kids' parents and learned they regularly had pharm parties. And a boy Harriett had a crush on dared her to take the pills. Told her how amazing it felt. We'll never know what actually happened, but I assume she wanted him to really like her and caved. Five pills. That, and a few ounces of vodka, is all it took to take Harriett's life."

Rick tips his head back and smacks the headboard. Eyes glued to the ceiling, he silently cries for Harriett. For the sister he lost and will never hug again. Will never tease or give advice to again. For the life she would never have because of a boy she crushed on. I squeeze him tighter, whispering how sorry I am over his heart. Words will never replace the loss he has suffered. Nothing can make up for the pain he has endured. And I understand why he needed an outlet. How else can someone get through such a tragedy?

"Sex was the only healthy way to release my anger. After the way Harriett died, there was no way I'd resort to pills or alcohol for reprieve. A few weeks after Harriett's funeral, I met a woman at my job. I worked part time at an auto body shop. Basically, I was a bitch boy while I learned about auto mechanics. A woman brought her car in for routine maintenance, and something inside me sparked. She was several years my senior, and looked at me like she wanted to eat me alive. After her car was finished, she slipped me a note with her number. When I met up with her, I fucked her in the backseat of that car. It turned her on when I wrapped my hand around her throat and clamped down. We fucked several times over a three month period. That's when I wondered if other women like her existed. Women I could take my aggression out on and get off on it. Turns out, there're tons."

He chuckles beneath me and I wring my arms tighter. "Do I give you the outlet you need?"

Tipping my chin up, he presses a sweet kiss to my lips and nose. "I don't really need the outlet now like I did then. Do I enjoy rough kink? Yes. No lie, the rougher it is, the harder I get. But, do I need it? No. As long as I have you, I don't need it." He slides down the bed and lays eye-to-eye with me. "Christy, you fill in all the gaps. You make my life remarkable. Worth every beat and breath and minute. As long as you're by my side, life is complete."

I comb my fingers through his hair and he melts into my touch. "Well, just so you know, I like the kink. And I'm willing to try new things. Okay? I see how turned on you get with some of it."

He kisses me as one hand comes around the back of my neck and the other traces down the curves of my body. Slipping a leg between mine, he grinds his hips against my pubic bone. The second he breaks the kiss, he stares into my eyes and strokes a thumb over my lower lip. "How did I get so lucky?"

"Is it you who's lucky? Or is it me?" I propose.

"Gorgeous, I don't know how, but you're making me believe in fate," he says, twirling a lock of my hair around his finger.

For the next several hours, we exhaust each other between the sheets. Just him, me, and the bond we have shared from the start.

FOURTEEN

RICK

EVERYONE SCURRIES around the restaurant and club frantically.

Upstairs, bottles are dusted and lined up on the glass bar shelves. Candles, salt and pepper shakers, and a single red rose in a small glass vase sits at the center of each table. Black cloth napkins are intricately folded and sitting on silver-rimmed white plates. Warm, ambient lighting brightens the restaurant with an array of wall sconces, while fairy lights drip from the ceiling. Opulence screams its namesake.

Downstairs, the bartenders and barmaids stock glassware and check that all the liquor is accounted for at the club. Janitorial staff does a last once over, wiping down all the furniture and cleaning the floors. In the club, there is less to straighten out and manage. The bar and the basic janitorial cleaning will be the biggest things to prep each shift.

Tonight, we will have a soft opening. Family, friends, and members of P.I. invited to enjoy Opulence and Boundless before heavier crowds occupy both. P.I. members will be offered special pricing if they opt to have a membership at both clubs. Rocco and I sat down, crunched numbers, and came up with what we thought was a hell of a deal. Hopefully, they will think the same.

Hours pass faster than seconds, and it's not long before Christy strides in. Glancing at her from head to toe, I openly check her out, swallow and adjust my cock. With the soft opening for both the restaurant and club, I asked her to dress accordingly. As always, my girl never disappoints.

Clad in a sultry yet classy dress, she smirks knowingly when I bite the inside of my cheek. The base layer of her dress is a nude fabric that hugs her body in all the right places. Over the top is a layer of black lace. From a distance, the nude material is unnoticeable. Sleeveless, the neckline plunges and displays just enough cleavage to keep it semi-appropriate. The material stops mid-thigh and accentuates every curve, dip, and groove like a second skin. Her toned legs are bare and glistening under the amber lighting. But it's her black heels that pull it all together—long leather straps wind up her calves to her knees.

When she reaches me, I exhale and pull her to me. "Fuck, gorgeous. How am I supposed to work?"

Christy laughs and I bask in the sound. Over the last year, she hasn't laughed as much. Part of which was my fault. But she was also sad with Sarah gone. Now, it feels like my girl has returned. Her smile, her laughter. You never realize how amazing those small tidbits are until you don't get them on a regular basis.

She brings her lips to my ear and whispers, "Wait until you see what's underneath." Kissing the angle of my jaw, she inches back and flaunts a wicked smile. "I want to play tonight."

One line is all it takes. One line and my dick strains against my zipper. I grip her tighter and hold her hostage. Lips at her ear, I whisper-hiss, "You can't walk in here dressed like a goddess and say things like that. Now you have to stay put until my cock calms down."

She clucks her fucking tongue and it does nothing to settle my erection. "Patience. I brought a couple things with me." Lifting her oversized purse, she raises her brows. "Where can I set this down?"

I walk her downstairs and introduce her to the club staff. Since it's our soft opening, everyone works tonight. After introductions are made, I show her the staff only lounge/breakroom. It's a complete kitchen, bathroom, a small wall of lockers, and two couches. In the center, a table where employees can sit and eat. A work version of a tiny home. Rocco wanted to be sure the staff had a place to relax and get away.

Unlocking my personal locker for her, I give her the combo, and Christy tucks her bag inside. We walk out together, and I direct her to my office on the upper level. Inside, I get her an access bracelet. For tonight and the first few visits, members will have these bracelets. Once officially signed up, we will issue member ID cards. Rocco has already ordered cards for employees and their significant others, but they didn't arrive in time for tonight's event.

When we reach the restaurant floor, I hook Christy's arm on mine and walk her to a table. I pull her chair out and she glides onto the leather. "Stay here, gorgeous. I need to make rounds and shake hands. Order dinner for both of us. I'll be over soon." I bend down and kiss her. As much as I don't want to, I break the kiss and hold her gaze a beat. "Be back shortly."

The next thirty minutes involve a lot of schmoozing. Several members of P.I. arrive and they chat with myself and Rocco. I wouldn't go so far as to say we are brown nosing, but it is pretty damn close. A key foundation for Boundless is dependent on current P.I. members and their word of mouth. Although our lifestyles aren't exposed for everyone to see, we know people in the life. And people in our circles talk.

After speaking with a couple who has been with Rocco since the start, I head over to where I left Christy and join her for dinner. Before taking a seat across from her, I kiss the crown of her head. "Thank you for waiting, gorgeous. What'd you order?"

As she relays our dinner order, I bend over the plate and inhale. "Garlic and caper grilled salmon served with dill creme fraiche and a side of roasted herb root vegetables."

I peek up at her. "You could've started eating without me."

She waves me off. "It's been here maybe five minutes. Besides, I had salad and bread to tide me over until you got here."

We eat our meal and I pass on who some of the guests are. Christy asks me questions about P.I. and I explain how it is basically an upper-class strip club... with benefits. When it comes to the benefits, the dancers run the show and dictate what they are willing to allow.

Soon, dinner ends and Rocco says a few words of thanks to everyone who came out tonight. He announces anyone present is allowed to stay and join us downstairs in Boundless. Tonight is a one-time glimpse for everyone here. Their one chance to see Boundless without membership. He continues to explain membership, how it works, cost and the rules while downstairs in Boundless. At any point in time, anyone can be removed from the club, if their behavior is deemed inappropriate.

Rocco reiterates, several times, that Boundless is a safe space and environment. If anyone does not feel this way while inside, they are to seek out management or an employee immediately. Rocco and I pride ourselves in keeping Boundless a place where people don't cringe when they express their sexuality. Instead, they feast on it and share it with others.

After his speech ends, everyone rises and ambles down the stairwell at the back of the restaurant. As we hit the final steps, I clutch Christy closer to my side. Adrenaline hits my bloodstream like an avalanche. Beside me, Christy bounces on her toes. Music thumps and vibrates the walls. Low lights illuminate the corridor. A mysterious and alluring vibe oozes from the walls.

When we reach the end of the corridor, I breathe in the visual masterpiece laid out before us. Seeing Boundless with all the overhead lights on is one thing. Seeing it how we want everyone else to see it is a wholly new perspective.

Industrial Edison sconces glow around the room while large Edison bulbs hang from the open ceiling, dimly lighting the charcoal walls with an amber radiance. The entrance sits off to one side with the club management office in the small crook beside it. Fifteen feet into the club, a concrete bar top starts and spans for thirty feet, connecting with the wall to form a large rectangle. Just past the bar is a sectioned off area for VIP members. All in all, VIP is about three hundred square feet and is for selected clientele. The small nook has minimal furniture but has a suspension grid and wall restraints. Along the back wall, and slightly onto the wall opposite the bar, is a variety of furnishings—poles, long, padded tables, cages, more suspension options, as well as an array of tools and implements. The second half of that wall and part of the entryway wall has a handful of private rooms, which can be utilized for up to thirty minutes. The rooms are generally utilized by people who haven't gotten up the courage to be so open and/or explicit. Two of the rooms are completely private. The others have a small adjoining room with a two-way mirror for voyeurs. In the center of it all, leather couches, chairs, chaises, ottomans, and concrete topped tables. Small clusters of candles illuminate each table, which can be decorative or for play.

Boundless is beyond what I expected and I hope Christy loves it.

Once inside, we head to the bar and order drinks. Slowly, everyone wanders in and breathes in the piney leather polish and amber scented candles lining the bar and tables. A few minutes pass and Christy tells me she is going to change and will be back in a moment.

While I wait for her, I prop a foot on the stool behind me and sit. People watching in the clubs always fascinates me. Always a fifty-fifty with the crowd. Half are eager and ready to rip their clothes off. The other half wander in circles and watch the people ready to rip their clothes off. Eventually, though, most people open up and free their mind. In no time, there will be more bare skin than clothed skin.

Out of the corner of my eye, I see a pair of toned, delicious legs. Legs I have memorized and would know in the darkest of nights. They don't just belong to any woman. They belong to my woman. But when I scan my eyes up her body, my mouth goes dry and I swallow hard.

Fuck.

Christy struts toward me. No longer in the dress I saw her in less than ten minutes ago. The closer she gets, the more my cock swells. Fuck, she is gorgeous.

Thin leather straps cage her thighs and calves, hooked

to a garter belt at her waist. Black, strappy panties shield a small patch of her flesh. Nipples marked with an "X" in black tape, she wears a sheer black top. Another set of leather straps cages her breasts and torso and hooks onto the belt around her waist. Her long, russet curls hang loose and drape the front of her body.

But the thing that shocks me the most. The single thing I can't rip my eyes away from is her eyes. Stormy blues stare back at me, but not through her glasses as usual. *Is she wearing contacts?* What incinerates my blood in this very moment is the mask covering half her face. Black. Leather. *Kitten.*

Christy is sex fucking personified. Every set of eyes in the room is on her, watching as she slowly saunters across the club and in my direction. My heart swells as much as my cock and only one thought runs through my head. *This woman belongs to me.*

An inch away, she stops and I can't avert my eyes from her cherry red lips. I don't move. Not a breath. My limbs forgetting how to operate. As she leans into me, I gasp and beg for her to touch me. Kiss me. *Fuck me.*

"Hey, daddy," she purrs. "Kitten wants to play."

When she inches back, I lock eyes with her. A hurricane spins around her pupils and makes landfall on a path headed straight to my groin. I adjust myself and tug her back into me, whispering in her ear. "Good girl, kitten. Come," I extend the crook of my elbow to her, "let's go play."

As if we're the power couple in the room, patrons step

aside and allow us to pass. We walk in leisure, reaching the wall of toys. After I slip a few items from their holsters, I walk us to one of several couches nearby.

"Do you know what seeing you like this does to me, kitten?"

"Tell me, daddy," she cajoles.

Lifting a hand, I pinch her chin between my thumb and forefinger and tip it up. When her stormy blues land on my lust-laden honeys, I keep her stock still a moment. There is something to be said about a non-verbal exchange between lovers. Bonded couples, such as ourselves, exchange a million sentiments without uttering a single word.

We don't have to.

Eyes connected, I take her hand in mine and drag it over my erection. Fingers contracting around my length cause me to swell even more, I watch her lips part and her eyes that dare to close. But they won't. She yearns for our connection as much as I do.

"This is what you do to daddy, kitten." I rub her hand up and down my length. "Are you ready to play? Do you want to play new games tonight?"

Her breathing spikes. "Yes, daddy. Teach me some new games."

With her invitation and permission, my chest heaves and cock pulses. I'm not quite sure what shifted with Christy, but this is new. It hardens my cock to steel. Has me ready to come in my pants. Maybe it's the mask. Maybe it's her unprovoked exhibitionism. If I am honest, perhaps it's a combination of the two and the fact that she has never been so eager to please me.

Before I sit on the couch, she reaches around her backside and retrieves something. Once in her hand, she extends it to me and I take her offering. The cool metal is a light weight in my hand, and I glance down to see the leash. *Her leash.*

I can count on one hand the number of times we have used this. The tally wouldn't tick off all digits either. For Christy to dress like this, to hand this to me… A rush of blood whooshes behind my ears like white noise. The gush all I hear. But beneath my sternum, a war wages between my heart and lungs on which organ can pump fastest. Currently, my heart takes the lead.

Stepping into her, I brush my lips against hers, then clip the leash onto her collar. She sighs as her eyes close for a blink. Her satisfaction shoots adrenaline throughout my body. How long has my girl needed this? Craved this? And I neglected to give it to her. All because I didn't know if it was something she desired. In essence, I disregarded us both under the assumption she didn't want this in our relationship.

Obviously, I was wrong.

Over the next several hours, I tease and torture and do questionable things to Christy. With each lick of the paddle, she begs for more. While suspended by her wrists, I whip her flesh and revel in the pinking and sting marring her alabaster skin. Her whimpers and cries all in the name of pleasure. A pleasure only I fulfill.

Several people crowd around and ogle us. Voyeurs fucking and petting as they watch our interaction. It sets me off, and I am certain it urges Christy on too. The evidence is in her dilated pupils. As she bows her body and silently pleas for more. In her slack jaw and parted lips. And the dampness soaking the flesh at the apex of her thighs.

Never have I seen my girl aroused to this degree. As I stare at her now exposed skin, sans the black tape over her nipples, I relish in all we have done together. All we have done here, tonight. She never ceases to amaze me.

I unclip her and slide her body down the front of mine. Walking her over to the nearest couch, I bend her over the back of it, and whisper in her ear. "Fuck, gorgeous. You have no idea what it does to me knowing you're mine."

Christy peers over her shoulder, mask still in place, and grins wickedly. Her hand dips between my thighs, clutches my balls and massages. "And you're mine. Always." She faces away from me and grinds her ass against my erection. "Now fuck me."

In seconds, my pants hit the floor and I wrap my hand around her throat as I ram into her from behind. The world disappears as euphoria clouds around us. Just me and my girl. Savagely fucking like beasts. Her cries of pleasure the only sound in my ears.

It will always be her. Only her.

"WHERE DO you want the sweet potatoes?" I yell from the dining room.

I spin around in search for an open space. Any open space. So far, there is zero to be found. "On the side table, next to where Tiffany's sitting," Liz hollers back from the kitchen.

Scanning the side table, I shake my head. The side table is already stacked with a mountain of mashed potatoes and cranberry-orange relish. If I scoot things around, the sweet potatoes still wouldn't fit. How on earth did Liz think we would have enough space for all this food? So, I glance back at the four-person, square dining table and ponder what I can shift to create more space. We still need space for the rolls, butter, and green beans.

"We need another table," I say, walking back into the kitchen after countless attempts to shift plates and glasses and serving bowls. Liz bustles around like a maniac, washing dishes and wiping down countertops. She pauses and stares at me with tightly pinched eyes and deep creases in her brow like I requested her left lung.

She shakes her head and breezes past me. If Liz has a better solution to the table setup, I would love to see it. You can only fit so many platters and casserole dishes on the space provided. If the table had space for another two people, we would have more than enough room today. But it doesn't. So we don't.

I follow her back to the dining room and watch as she shifts cups, plates, and dish after dish. Exactly what I did before coming in and telling her it wasn't possible. Minutes later, she steps back and points to the tiny open spot she created. "There. Put it there."

"Okay, bitch. But where the hell are we putting the rest?" A fair question. One that any normal person would ask. But a second after I ask, I wish I could retract my question.

Liz huffs, rolls her eyes, and throws her hands in the air. She looks like a bomb ready to detonate any second. "Why am I the only one figuring all this out? Where the hell is Rick and Tiffany?"

I shrug and bite the inside of my cheek. No chance in hell I would tell Liz she frightened them with her *perfect Thanksgiving* demands. Last I saw, Rick and Tiffany were on the back patio. They stepped out an hour ago, just after Liz's first "this is how you baste the turkey" moment. It came with a full tutorial of how much of the drippings to suck into the baster and where the best place was to disperse it.

Liz isn't a perfectionist. Just… particular. And when it comes to holidays, events, and parties, it kicks up a notch. Sarah and I always ignored her neurotic tendencies. It is the only way party planning ever gets accomplished. I love Liz, but her demands can be over the top at times. Rick never joined in during the planning phase, and Tiffany is still somewhat new to it all. She and Liz have only been together a little more than a year.

"Um." I squint as my lips tighten into a straight line, exposing my teeth. "On the patio," I say hesitantly.

She rolls her eyes again, groans, and storms back off to the kitchen. "Maybe *they* should help you figure out the table situation."

Not mad, but definitely peeved. As soon as we all sit down to eat, she will relax and enjoy the day. Until that moment strikes, though, Liz will be a twisted ball of yarn, wound tight and ready to fall apart any second.

I head for the sliding glass doors and step out onto the patio. A shiver rolls up my spine as the cool air whips my hair across my glasses. The smell of wood-burning fire-places trickles through the air. Nothing like cozying up near a fire on a cool fall day.

Rick and Tiffany stop their conversation and glance up at me. Apologies written in their eyes and the lines crinkling their faces. For a moment, I sit beside Rick and take a deep breath.

"Would you guys mind helping me in a minute?" I ask.

Tiffany's shoulders cave forward. "Sorry," she says. "Didn't know Liz got like this. Last year, we went to friends and family during the holidays. She gets so flustered, and I just feel like I'm in the way."

I nod. "Yeah. She just wants everyone to have a good time. Which equals everything being perfect." Peering over my shoulder, through the glass doors, Liz is a madwoman cleaning the kitchen. "Help me?"

Rising from the loungers on the patio, we walk on eggshells once inside. I tell Rick and Tiffany a few more dishes need to be brought out and we need to shift things around to make room. After a minute of our best Tetris skills, Tiffany pauses and her eyes light up.

Without a word, she turns on her heel and walks away. A minute later, her feet pad across the floor and she walks in with a small side table. Thank God. If we had to spend another second squeezing and semi-stacking dishes, I would pull my hair out.

Tiffany sets the table off to the side. The second the legs hit the ground, I set the mashed potatoes, balsamic roasted Brussels sprouts, and brown sugar candied carrots on top. With all the food made, we had enough to feed a dozen people. Leftovers inevitable. But leftovers were one of my favorite parts of holiday meals. Some foods just tasted better the next day.

"Thank you, Tiffany. You saved the day." I pull her into a full body hug. "If Liz is ready, I say we eat."

When I release Tiffany, she ambles to the kitchen, hesitant. So cute how gentle she is with Liz. Not wanting to agitate the lioness. "Baby, whenever you're ready," Tiffany coos.

Once we all sit around the table, laughter and smiles and chatter consume us. Plates piled high with tons of delicious food. Wine glasses full to the brim. Banter all around. This is the perfect gathering.

Tiffany updates Rick and me with her job. After finishing her master's degree in Georgia, she scoured for open positions. For months, she had zero luck. When the topic of moving west came up, she and Liz were open to the idea. Low and behold, Tiffany was equally lucky as Rick in acquiring a job before the move.

Her job at Lewis House is more rewarding than imaginable. The facility, armed with several psychologists and psychiatrists, is an organization which helps teens and young adults up to age twenty-five who deal with or have dealt with depression and/or suicide. An admirable practice. The organization was founded a few years after a fifteen-year-old boy, Taylor Lewis, ended his own life. Tiffany astounds me. The fact she works with individuals who feel no one cares, and then guides them down a path of hope. Not just anyone can do what she does. I applaud her and the others working at Lewis House.

After our bellies are full and we clear the table, we all slump on the couches with heavy eyes. Eventually, Rick flips on the television and engrosses himself with the football game while Liz, Tiffany, and I chat.

Liz and Tiffany banter constantly. The way they are with each other is adorable. "If you don't behave, I'll tie you to the bed later," Tiffany teases. My eyes widen and I stare between the two of them. They smile like idiots.

Kinky? Let's find out.

"I love being tied to the bed." The bait set.

Liz stares at me like she doesn't know who I am and I squirm. Beside me, Rick sets a hand on my thigh and strokes his thumb against my skin in a slow, measured motion. Although his eyes haven't left the game, he listens to everything. Always. The weight of his hand meant to comfort me. Since Rick and I don't discuss our lifestyle with friends not in that circle, this is a big step. One I second guess.

Other than the game commentator screaming from the television, the air around us remains eerily silent. My lungs burn as I patiently wait for someone to say something. Anything. My stomach shrivels and sinks like a lead weight. The silence and not knowing how she feels about what I just said is a dull knife to the torso, again and again.

All I ever wanted was acceptance. Especially by people close to my heart. For them to know me. The real me. And not just a fragment. But every aspect of who I am. And love me just the same. Ever since my family disowned me for being myself, the desire for acceptance and love has been the biggest reason I shelter my life. Rejection, especially from someone close to me, would shatter me.

Time ticks by as if days have passed and not seconds. The room spins and I remind myself to breathe. Just as I inhale, Liz tips her head back and laughs at the ceiling. A rich, hearty, everyone-within-a-mile-will-hear-her laugh. Is this good? God, I am so fucking confused.

"Don't tell me how, but somehow I knew you were a kinky bitch," Liz states. She belts out another torrent of laughter. "Call it intuition. Maybe it's your extroversion. Who the hell knows. Maybe it's because you never talk about sex. *Ever.*" Liz glances at Tiffany. "What is it they say… it's the quiet ones who are the kinkiest."

I throw a pillow at Liz's head and hit her smack dab in the forehead. "Have I ever been quiet?" A stupid question. But I threw it out more teasing than anything. Her laughter was exactly what I needed. The perfect antidote to settle my anxious heart.

"Not in general, no. But you never talked about sex with me and Sarah. Most girlfriends do. Sarah and I did. A lot. But you… you just sat there and listened and never said a single word about your sex life."

"That's different and you know it." I give her a pointed stare. Before Sarah and Jackson got together, Liz and Sarah hooked up all the time. They never brought it up around me, but after I caught them making out one day, it was rather obvious.

"Guess you're right. But it still holds true."

Not that I need his permission, but I peer over my shoulder at Rick. A smile spans his cheeks while his eyes follow the football game on the screen. Before I turn back to Liz and Tiffany, he squeezes my thigh. His way of telling me it is okay to talk about who we are as long as *I* am comfortable.

And I am. This is Liz. One of my best friends. Someone I trust my life with.

"Whatever, bitch. You want to hear me talk sex? Better grab some more wine. You have no idea what you asked for," I tease.

For the next few hours, I divulge just how kinky my and Rick's life is. Liz and Tiffany sit completely silent and captivated. They ask questions, truly interested in the answers. Rick inches closer to me and adds more pressure to my side. His way of supporting without hovering.

By the time we leave, I feel twenty pounds lighter. An unknown burden lifts off my shoulders and floats away. But that is by far the best part. Which happens to be the fact my friends still accept me. Us. And this year, I am thankful for this life. A life of love and acceptance and happiness.

SIXTEEN

RICK

Servers bustle around the dining floor, fold napkins, set them on the plates on tables, and add silverware. Bartenders with pen and paper scan inventory, fill ice, and wipe water spots off glassware. In the kitchen, chefs in tall white hats chop, dice, and julienne vegetables. Roasts and whole birds cook in the oven for hours, the back of the restaurant smells of lemon and garlic and rosemary. Another group of chefs off to the side are putting the final touches on dessert plates.

I slap a hand to my stomach as it growls, begging for a morsel. *Later.*

After surveying the dining area one last time, I head downstairs.

Inside the walls of Boundless, loud music pours from the hidden speakers in the walls. A low, sultry beat throbs at the pace of my heartbeat. For the next nine hours, Boundless will stir to life. After the soft opening two-and-a-half weeks ago, we added over two dozen members. Some of them members of P.I., others referred by those members.

If all went as projected, Boundless would have close to a hundred members by end of year. We set a maximum membership number to one thousand. For now. As it stands, Boundless can comfortably hold a thousand people at one time. With room to breathe. After we determine the pattern of our regulars, we plan to gauge whether or not to increase membership capacity.

But being exclusive has its perks. Not just anyone can walk inside Boundless. The membership a pretty penny, but worth every cent. Worth having a safe space to express yourself amongst similar individuals. What we offer is not comparable to any other establishment within a three-hundred-mile radius. Rocco and I did our fair share of research.

A few hours after Opulence and Boundless open, Christy waltzes in. She goes to the end of the bar nearest the entrance and club office. After a glass of merlot is set in front of her, she sips it and scans the club. Catty-corner to where she sits, she spots me after a minute. She blows me a kiss and I wink at her.

Once I make another circuit around the club, talking with several patrons and thanking them, I head over to where Christy sits at the bar.

"Hey, gorgeous." I kiss the crown of her head. "Did you eat yet?"

She shakes her head. "Figured I'd eat with you when you have a break."

The club is somewhat quiet, so I tell the bartender, Cheyenne, I am heading to the kitchen to grab dinner, but will bring it back down here to eat. After I hook Christy's arm with mine, we head upstairs and make a bee-line straight for the kitchen. Christy and I wander past the swinging double doors and I order us chicken, risotto, and whatever vegetable is on the menu tonight.

In no time, we walk back downstairs to the club's office and eat our meal. The office set up with a two-way mirror of sorts. Inside the confines of the office, I see everything happening in the club. But from outside the office, no one sees in. Instead of a mirror on the club side, the glass is made to look like the wall. Don't ask me about the fancy tech behind it all, but I love it. Able to monitor all activity in the club while doing other managerial tasks.

Once we finish eating, I lock the office door, bend Christy over the large mahogany desk, twist her hair around my wrist, and fuck her senseless. Sure, I could have fucked her on the club floor. Had every pair of eyes in the club on us. But tonight, I wanted Christy all to myself. What can I say... I am a greedy bastard sometimes.

"How long you staying?" I ask as I zip up my pants.

Christy straightens her dress and combs her fingers through her hair. "Thought I'd stay until midnight or so. Want to people watch in a new place."

At times, Christy enjoys being the voyeur more than the exhibitionist. She teeters back and forth, giving equal love to each. Another astonishing quality I love about her. An equal opportunist.

"Staying at the bar? Or you want to sit in VIP?"

"The bar for a little longer. Then I'll hang out in VIP."

She continues to mess with her hair, doing her best to settle the wayward strands. I grab her hands, lower them, and kiss her forehead. "You're perfect, gorgeous." Her body melts into my touch and, for a beat, I don't want to leave this room. For a minute longer, I want to hold her in my arms and kiss the hell out of her.

I love her warm skin against me. The way she leans into me as if I am the only solace she needs. And I love the way my heart jackhammers when she is in proximity. No one has kickstarted my heart the way Christy does.

We leave the office. I mingle on the club floor while Christy sits at the bar with another glass of wine. By the time I make it to the VIP lounge, Christy has already made her way over. In a tall-backed, leather throne chair, she sits like a queen. *My queen.*

I join her and another couple she has been chatting with for a bit. Ella and Thomas. Like us, they enjoy the company of other couples. The four of us talk about Boundless. All the walks of life inside these walls. I mention Apex, and how different that club is compared to Boundless. Christy jokes about her boring day job and how tiring it is to sell life insurance to people. Although, she does admit to hearing some of the oddest stories. Ella tells us she owns an indie bookstore just outside the city. The traffic was slow going at first, but sales have picked up drastically in the last quarter. Thomas works at a law firm in the city. Jokingly, he says he won't bore us with the details.

Thomas and Ella are easy to talk with. Comfortable. No strange vibes. Almost as if we have known them years. I ask my standard list of questions in casual conversation. And I take note Thomas does the same. Obviously, we are both interested in each other, and our exchange easily goes from minutes to hours in no time.

On occasion, I excuse myself and meander the club. Each time I glance at Christy with Ella and Thomas, all I see is smiles or laughter or in-depth conversation. Since moving to California, things hadn't been what they once were. But seeing Christy so at ease in her own skin, hope surges in my veins. Before Ella and Thomas leave tonight, if Christy hasn't already asked, I plan to extend an offer to meet up outside of the club.

As I make one last circuit on the way back to VIP, a woman steps in front of me and halts my path. "Hey, sugar." The bleach-blonde places her hand on my chest and pets me. Immediately, anger simmers in my blood and I step back.

"First things first," I say, giving her a pointed stare. "Without permission, you do not touch people here. Understood?" It is a fundamental rule in Boundless. Although everyone in these walls enjoys sex, not everyone wants other people touching them. And everyone needs to respect that. We aren't all into the same lifestyle.

A gleam lights her smile. "Okay, sugar."

I cringe and bite my cheek a second before I say something unprofessional. "Second of all, I'm not your *sugar*. Do not address me as such."

She steps closer to me and pops her breasts closer in the tacky, tight one-piece she wears. "Bossy one, aren't you?" Not a question. Her tone is intended to be sexy and appealing. Honestly, it makes bile rise in my throat. "I like them bossy."

I clench my jaw and take two steps back. "If you'll excuse me."

But before I turn to walk off, she reaches out and touches my bicep. I glance down at her hand, curl my top lip, and look back up at her. The acid in my stare tells her I'm not fucking around and she yanks her hand away. Thank fuck. "Sorry. Just looking for a good time."

Obviously, this woman can't take a hint. Stepping farther away, I point at the crowd around us. "There are plenty of options here. But I'm not one of them. And just a reminder, if you cannot abide by the rules of the club, you will be asked to leave and not allowed to return."

Her wicked gleam makes its return. Tongue jetting out to lick her lips. A single lick of the lips usually sparks interest for me, but with this woman, there is not an ounce of attraction. If anything, the more she tries, the more turned off I become.

"I'll do my best." She winks then walks off. Finally.

When I rejoin Christy, Ella, and Thomas, my girl is talking about previous partners we have had in our bed. I sit on her left, hand wrapped around hers, and we chat. Another hour passes, the conversation flowing smoothly, and all I want is my shift to be over.

By the time Ella and Thomas stand to leave, Ella and Christy have exchanged phone numbers. An unspoken agreement that we'll meet up in the not too distant future. With certain people, we find it more comfortable if the women meet up alone in a public setting, and the men too. This way, we get our own vibes without disruption.

Not long after Thomas and Ella leave, Christy decides to head home. It's well after midnight when I kiss her goodbye, and I promise to be home in a couple hours.

Minutes after Christy leaves, my hackles rise. A pang twitches in my gut. Sharp and nauseating. I scan the club and spot the bleach-blonde staring at me. Strapped to a wooden table. A man yanks a chain attached to her nipples while he fucks the hell out of her. But she stares at me, licking her lips. Disgust swims in my gut. *What the hell is with this woman?*

I shake my head and go to the bar. "Cheyenne, keep an eye on the blonde on the restraint table. I'm getting a bad vibe from that one. I'm going to the office for a bit."

She pours a beer from the tap, nods and doesn't look up. "You got it, boss."

With that, I head into the office and shut the door, bolting the lock. I stare out at the club floor, my eyes landing on the blonde. Although she can't see me in here, she stares where I stand. It sends a chill down my spine—and not the ball-clenching, explosive type I enjoy either. *Who the hell is this woman? And why is she so fixated on me?*

Hopefully she's not a member. More than anything, I also hope to not see her inside these walls again.

SEVENTEEN

CHRISTY

Over the last two weeks, Ella and I have texted daily.

It is wonderful to have a friend to talk about everything with. Although Rick and I haven't met up with her and Thomas outside the club yet, we have chatted in VIP a few times now. Mostly, when Ella and I text, we discuss normal life stuff. Work, best places to eat, annoying habits our significant others have. Plain Jane normal. Getting to know one another. And it makes me so happy.

Two nights ago, at Boundless, I finally learned where Ella's bookstore is. Actually, not too far from our house. Now that we have developed a level of trust, I want to see Ella outside the club walls. See her in her element. Her love for books and how she interacts with others. Which brings me to here and now.

I park under a shady tree and stare at the hand-painted oak sign over the bookstore. Cozy Corner Books. The storefront has large glass windows and white painted brick with a pillar supported overhang. At either end of the store, an iron post sticks out from the wall with a matching store sign hanging from two rings. On the front door is the store name in a font that matches the signs. An appealing blend of modern and antique/vintage. Quaint. Unique. I love the vibe.

Cutting the engine, I loop my purse over my shoulder and step out. The bookstore is freestanding but has a coffee shop next door as well as a bakery and delicatessen. The area is busy yet quiet. A perfect place to grab a coffee, pastry, and read a good book. Ella has it made here.

I tug the wood and glass door open and am hit with a smell I haven't inhaled since grade school. Fresh paper and ink. Binding glue and worn leather. I inhale deeply and close my eyes. Bookstores and libraries are high on my list of favorite places. The paper grain against my fingertips. The weight of the words in my palms. Nothing replaces a good paperback novel.

Aisles and aisles of six-foot oak shelves fill the space. Along the walls, the shelves go to the ceiling. I spy a rolling ladder on each packed wall. At the front of the store, several distressed tables sit stacked with new releases or sale priced books. Off to the far right is a small reading nook with a few couches, chairs, and a large window that looks out on a small patch of greenery, trees, flowers, and a fountain.

Is it possible to fall in love with a store? Yes. Because I just did. I don't know how Ella leaves here every day. But I can definitely see why she loves it.

As I wander past some of the tables in the front, Ella walks up from farther back in the store. "Welcome to Cozy—" she pauses a second "—hey, Christy!" Ella steps up to me, wraps her arms around my shoulders, and hugs me like we have known one another years instead of weeks. "What are you doing here?" Her excitement to see me warms me like a mug of hot cocoa on a winter day.

"I had some free time and wanted to check out your store. Think I'm in love." I swoon at the shelves and she laughs.

"It's pretty great. Have you seen much of it yet?"

"Nope. Walked in a minute ago."

Ella grabs my hand and yanks me. "Let me show you around." Her jubilance is palpable. I practically stumble behind her as she drags me through the store and points to this and that. Her two favorite parts are the reading area —inside and out—and the indie author section. The way her eyes light up as she gives me a tour, you would think this was the first time I'd been in a bookstore.

She tells me to wander and check things out but invites me to have lunch with her in thirty minutes. After I scan hundreds of book spines, not even a quarter of the way through the store, she finds me down the indie romance aisle. After I store the books in my hands behind the clerk counter, we head to the delicatessen for lunch.

Once we pay for sandwiches and drinks, we take them to the outdoor garden by the bookstore and sit at a picnic table. The air whips my hair and sends a chill throughout my body. Although it's winter, it has been unseasonably warm. Noticing my shiver, Ella cranks on a small outdoor heater next to us. Within minutes, the air warms as we start eating.

"So," I start, "I stopped by to ask if you and Thomas would like to join Rick and me for dinner."

Ella finishes her bite of roast beef and wipes her mouth with a paper napkin. "I'll check with Thomas, but I'd love to. When were you thinking?"

"Rick has tomorrow off. If that's not too soon for you."

She nods and takes a sip of her water. "Should work for us. After I check with Thomas, I'll text you."

"Cool," I answer.

We eat the rest of our lunch, and I reiterate how much I love Ella's store. When we finish, Ella gets back to work. I purchase the books I stashed behind the checkout then head home. Energy zaps and funnels through my veins on my drive home. The same sensation I get every time when we plan to meet up with a couple. The natural chemical high is addictive and intoxicating. And with Ella and Thomas, it feels ten times more powerful.

Chopping a plethora of veggies, I add them to a large wooden bowl filled with lettuce. Lemon and garlic wafts throughout the kitchen before Rick adds shrimp to the scampi sauce. After he tosses the shrimp a moment, he drains the cavatappi pasta and adds it to the shrimp and sauce. Just as he pulls garlic bread and roasted carrots from the oven, the doorbell jingles.

Tossing the final slices of red onion in the salad bowl, I rinse and dry my hands, then go to greet our guests. Before opening the door, I face the mirror in the foyer and fix my hair. After a quick swipe down the sides of my dress, I open the door with a warm smile.

"Ella. Thomas. Please, come in." As each of them steps in, we exchange hugs. Of all the couples Rick and I have been with, none have resonated with us like Ella and Thomas. With them, life clicks into place a little more.

Giving Rick a moment to finish in the kitchen, I play tour guide and show Ella and Thomas around. The tour doesn't last long and when we reach the dining room, Rick is placing dinner on the table.

"Hey, man," Thomas says as he and Rick shake hands and do a one-arm bro hug. Slap on the back included. "How've things been?"

"Good. You?"

"Good. Feels like you and I have been missing out. Our girls chatting all the time." Thomas laughs and Rick joins him. Ella and I shrug, not caring that we have been talking day in-day out, and join the laughter.

We all sit, eat dinner, and chat. In such a short period of time, Ella and I have developed a wonderful friendship. Our daily texts just typical girl chatter. I love how easily we have come together. Other than Sarah, I have never had a friendship form so quick and simplistically.

After we finish our meal, we make our way into the living room with wine. The guys talk sports for a bit, while Ella and I discuss a book we have both read. The conversations flow and the time breezes by.

When the wine is gone and the conversations simmer down, Rick sets his palm on my knee and gives it a light squeeze before sliding it up my thigh, slow and steady. Midway up my thigh, he turns in his seat to face me head-on.

While his hand continues toward my center, the other cups my jaw and he kisses me. Twisting to face him better, I spread my legs and give him better access. Rick savors me with his tongue as his fingertips dance over my wet folds. Completely absorbed in his touch, I startle when soft lips graze the top of my shoulder. Ella.

Opening my eyes, I peer to my shoulder as Rick kisses me. Ella slides the thin dress straps off my shoulder and kisses from where the material vanished and further up my neck. Thomas stands behind Ella, sweeping her curly red locks off her neck. Kissing her neck, his hand cups her breast, squeezes, then glides down her abdomen.

I can't see, but I know Thomas's hand dove between Ella's legs. Behind me, her hips circle. Begging for more. Her eagerness shoots a bolt of lightning to my core. I want my fingers between her thighs. To taste her on my tongue.

"Oh, god," I moan.

Rick circles my clit. Once, twice, thrice. I gasp, breaking our kiss, and rock my hips forward. In an instant, two digits slip inside me. Reaching down, I hike the skirt of my dress up my hips and gaze between my thighs. Watching as my hips rock back and forth, Rick's fingers sliding in and out of my folds.

Shifting my weight, I press my back against the couch and gain a better view of everyone. Beside me, Ella moves onto her haunches as she kisses along my collarbone and Thomas plays with her clit, occasionally dipping his fingers inside. I run one hand up Rick's thigh, gripping his cotton-covered erection, then run my other hand up Ella's thigh. Her knees slowly part the closer I get to the junction of her thighs.

When I reach her slick core, Thomas removes his hand and lets me take over playing with her. A zipper unlatches in the room, and I assume it's Thomas undoing Ella's dress. My assumption answered a second later when the top and bottom of her dress bunches at her waist. Thomas kisses his way along Ella's collarbone before he dips down and wraps his mouth around her nipple, sucking and teasing the pert bud.

Under my touch, Ella thrusts forward and I pump my fingers in and out of her. Rick continues to finger fuck my pussy as he slowly peels my dress away. Once my dress drops and exposes my breasts, Rick slips off the couch and sucks each in turn. My breasts grow heavy with need. My nipples taut and begging for more after Rick releases his grip on each. Rick kisses his way down my abdomen, biting the sensitive skin below my navel. I pause my fingers inside Ella long enough for Rick to rip my dress away.

Beneath the soft cotton, I'm bare. No panties. No bra. Not a lick of hair on my body.

As I resume pumping my fingers inside Ella, Rick spreads my knees wide and bites his way up the inside of my thighs. With each nip, I jerk forward and hiss. By the time Rick reaches the apex of my thighs, I have scooted to the edge of the couch.

His mouth clamps down. Tongue swirls. Heat pulses through my limbs and soars where he continues to taste me. "So fucking sweet," he growls.

Thomas stops teasing Ella's tits and replaces my fingers at her folds. I paint her juices over her lips before sucking them off my fingers. Damn, she is divine. Like honey and cinnamon.

Rick laps at my pussy while Thomas does the same to Ella. Beside me, Ella mewls. Whimpering as Thomas licks and sucks her clit. Watching the two of them spikes my high. I grip Rick's hair and grind against his face. Hard.

Leaning toward Ella, I pinch her nipple and roll it between my fingers. Soon, she tips over the edge. Not long after, I follow suit.

The rest of the night progresses much the same, except we transfer to the bedroom. Hours later, when we are all spent and it seems impossible to stay awake another minute, Rick and I offer the spare bedroom to Ella and Thomas. They thank us for the offer but decline. Their departure is far from awkward. If anything, there is more of a level of comfort with them than any previous partners we have been with.

After Rick closes the door behind Ella and Thomas, he faces me and walks us back to the bedroom. "We got lucky and found great new friends," Rick says, kissing the top of my head.

"Agreed." Hope soars as my heart flutters. California went from originally being a questionable idea to being one of the best decisions we have made. Fate. Because I feel like Rick and I are finally home. In the place we belong. Together.

EIGHTEEN

RICK

THE CLIENTELE at Boundless has been gradually growing. Just as Rocco and I predicted. As business booms downstairs in the club, it also booms on the floor above. Rocco is a smart businessman and has mastered the art of prospering.

Oftentimes, Boundless patrons dine upstairs and flaunt their wealth in well-tailored attire and flashy jewels. Once they have enjoyed dinner, they descend the "members only" stairwell and step into the club for dessert.

Since having Ella and Thomas at our place three weeks ago, things have flourished between the four of us. Christy smiles more often. As do I. Our relationship, and happiness, has never felt more alive and electric.

Thomas and Ella stop by Boundless once or twice a week. Most nights they're here, so is Christy. When I'm able to join them, we sip on drinks and chat inside VIP. On my last night off, the four of us went out on a normal date—dinner and a movie. After we stepped out of the theater, Thomas invited us back to their house for a nightcap.

Best damn nightcap I ever had.

We also spent time together over the holidays. It was so… normal. The most normal our lives have been in a really long time.

I love how easily our ladies mesh together. Christy and Ella are two peas in a pod. They text or talk on the phone all day, every day. Thomas and I exchanged numbers after the first night we had them over at our place. We occasionally catch up, talk about football and the girls. Occasionally, we bring up our past, but nothing too heavy. After our times together and the conversations Thomas and I have had, one thing holds true. I trust Thomas. As a man. As a person. And with my girl. There is no doubt in my mind that he would admit the same.

Trust is challenging in our lifestyle. We have to test the water with so many people. Some just don't click, while others only pretend to be into the life just to get in your bed. But it soothes my insecurities that Christy and I have found the level of trust we crave with Thomas and Ella.

"How you two doing back here?" I ask Cheyenne. Currently, Cheyenne is training our newest bartender, Xander. Between the two of them, they have served thousands of drinks over the last week. They keep up and never complain. We are lucky to have them at the club, and I try my damnedest to let them know how much I appreciate their hard work every chance I get.

"Good, boss man." Cheyenne pours a shot of Patrón and slides it in front of a middle-aged man with salt-and-pepper hair. "But looking forward to my day off."

"Both of you" —Xander glances over at me— "keep up the great work. Never seen a bar tended this perfect."

A heap of flattery, but I meant every bit of it. Over the years at Apex, Tink poured drinks faster than my eyes could keep up with. But Cheyenne and Xander… I never see their hands. Drinks just magically appear in front of people. I have mad respect for them both and their abilities.

I sit at the end of the bar, near the office, and survey the crowd. As per usual, hundreds of bodies tempt and tease and dance. Bass shakes the walls. The scent of salt and sex whirl in the air. Skin slaps skin as lungs gasp for breath. Whiskey lingers on the tip of my tongue after I down a shot Cheyenne places in front of me.

Turning the glass over and setting it on the bar top, I signal to Cheyenne and let her know I'm going in the office for a bit. Unfortunately, a stack of invoices with my name on them call out for my attention.

As I close and lock the office door behind me, the music fades away. Not completely, but enough for me to focus on the pile of paperwork on my desk. This room, as well as the break room, had special insulation added to semi-soundproof them from the club. A bit more professional to have phone calls that don't involve loud music, screaming, or moaning pleas for more.

The invoices slowly shuffle from *to-do* to *done*. Just as I finish inputting figures from the invoice in my hand, I glance up from the computer and out onto the club floor. A man in tight-fitting leather stands at the bar, waiting for a drink. On his elbow… the bleach-blonde.

Fuck.

I don't have time to deal with pests tonight. Especially those who don't respect others or rules. And I refuse to be holed up in my office because some woman is incapable of controlling herself. I take a deep breath, promise not to let this annoying woman rain on my parade, and continue working on the task at hand.

An hour later and I finish the last of the invoices. Surveying the club through the two-way window before I exit, I see no sign of the blonde woman. Perhaps I got lucky and she left. One can only hope.

I straighten my shirt and slacks, step out of the office, and start my rounds of the club. Halfway through my first circuit, and a handful of conversations, I spot the blonde near the wall. I shift my trek and walk closer to the center of the room. Twenty feet later, a small hand grips my elbow and I spin around to see who it is.

Goddamnit.

Why won't this woman leave me the hell alone? What the fuck is her deal?

"Last warning," I tell her, glancing at her hand on my elbow. "You touch me again without permission, and you'll be banned from the premises."

She removes her lanky fingers from my elbow and coos, "No need to spit out threats."

I grind my jaw and hold back what I really wish to tell her. That threats are undelivered promises. I deliver on my promises. "What is it that you need?" I have lost my patience with this woman. She is a thorn in my side.

Leaning far too close to me, yet not touching me, she says, "Someone to fuck me hard."

I step back from her, annoyed at her presence. Five seconds away from booting her out, the man from the bar latches on to her side. Completely oblivious to what is happening. Another step back, I create a wider gap between us. "If you'll excuse me."

Before I take another step, she steps into my personal space. Again. Her hand running down my side and pissing me the hell off. "Think about it," she purrs.

"Actually," I pause and lock eyes with one of the bouncers. I signal him over. When he reaches us, I stare coldly into her eyes and speak to her as if she were a child —slow and exaggerated. "There is nothing to think about. You are banned from Boundless and Opulence. If you are caught on the premises again, we will call law enforcement and have you arrested. Jake will escort you out."

I turn and walk back to the bar. First person to be kicked out and banned from the club. Joy and happy day. Open for two months and the aggravations are already popping up. Hopefully we don't see any more for a while. I never enjoy dealing with these situations.

The rest of the night goes smoothly. I shoot Rocco a text and let him know I had to ban someone. His response —*won't be the last*. Too true.

The club shuts down for the evening and we all go about our closing routines. After the tills are locked in the safe, and everything is ready for the janitorial crew, I walk Cheyenne and Xander to their cars. Xander told me he was more than capable of walking to his car alone, but it's a habit from over the years. Just because he's a man, doesn't mean I can't extend him the same courtesy as the female staff. Once their cars start up, I head out of the lot and home to Christy.

Since starting at Boundless, my schedule has been a bit wonky. But since things are starting to level out, the management team decided it was time to set regular shifts/days off. Day after tomorrow, I officially have weekends off. Which means more time with my girl. Which also means a sense of normalcy in our lives.

Finally, everything is falling into place for us.

The next morning, I wake to Christy sucking my cock under the sheet.

Her hot, wet tongue glides up and down my shaft as she fondles my balls with her fingers. I growl when she takes me to the hilt, and she fists my balls tighter.

"Fuck, gorgeous." I comb my fingers through her hair and fist a cluster of locks, holding her head in place as I plunge down her throat.

"Mmm," she muffle-moans.

The faster I pump my hips, the more she moans. As my cock swells in her mouth, she rakes her teeth over my shaft and I explode down her throat.

"Goddamn. Son of a bitch. Motherfucker." I prattle off the curses as she takes everything I give then licks me clean.

When she pops out from under the sheet—hair a disheveled cute mess and eyes bright and wide—she licks her lips like the goddess she is and singsongs, "Breakfast. Best meal of the day."

I yank her down to my chest and wrestle with her a minute. Her giggle floats around the room and my heart bursts with joy. Best goddamn sound in the world. One of them, anyway. The second being her whimpers as she comes on my cock.

"Shouldn't you be getting ready for work?" I ask, tickling her sides.

"Yeah. Just couldn't resist going in the tent on our bed. Only time I really enjoy camping." She laughs and I join her.

Can't help I'm hard half the night. Happens when you sleep next to a woman like Christy.

Pushing up onto my elbows, I suck her bare nipple a second, slap her ass, and shoo her away. "Go shower, gorgeous."

The most adorable pout jets out her lip and creases her forehead. "Fine," she huffs. "I'll get ready for work." She takes her sweet time slipping off the bed, purposely strad-dling my cock and grinding for a beat.

Before the shower starts, I fall back asleep. When I wake, there is a note on the bedside table.

Looking forward to the weekend. Should we see Ella and Thomas?

I am one lucky son of a bitch. To find someone as amazing as Christy and live a life we both enjoy. Grabbing my phone from the charger, I shoot Christy a quick text.

Rick: Yes. Want me to set it up?
Christy: Nope. I'll take care of it.
Rick: Love you, gorgeous.
Christy: Love you, too.

TOSSING dirty laundry into the washer, something crinkles in Rick's pocket. Déjà vu strikes as I reach inside and pull out a slip of paper. This paper is different than the previous, though.

Folded on a Boundless receipt is a phone number, smeared lipstick, and a message.

You want a real woman? Call me.

I stand frozen, staring at the wrinkled slip of paper. Who the fuck is *this* bitch? And why the hell is this in Rick's pocket? When we were in Georgia, this shit never happened. Ever. As great as California is, it seems the place comes with new challenges.

I drop the note and pants and go locate my phone. *Breathe, Christy. Assume nothing.* If Rick was actually trying to hide something from me, he wouldn't leave notes from other women in his pockets for me to find. Plus, the context of this note is somewhat juvenile. Similar to a note a girl would slip a guy in high school.

After I snag my phone from the charger in the bedroom, I shove it in my back pocket and sit a moment. Once my thoughts have simmered down, I walk back to the laundry room. With trembling hands, I slide my phone from my back pocket and lean against the washer. I pick up the paper and flatten it out on top of the machine and snap a photo. Opening up my and Rick's text history, I attach the photo and type out a brief message.

Christy: What is this?

While at work, Rick doesn't always feel his phone vibrate when I text. Sucking in a deep breath, I slip the phone back into my pocket and go back to my chore, doing my best to ignore the menacing slip of paper. He will text back as soon as he sees the message. No doubt.

An hour and a half later, almost every surface inside the house sparkles and glows. Clean cotton wafts in the air from a lit candle in the living room, mixing with the artificial lemon scent from the floor cleaner I used not long ago.

Sometimes, when I get a touch frantic, I clean. And not just a little cleaning here, a little cleaning there. More like shit-can't-possibly-get-any-cleaner OCD cleaning. The clothes are twenty minutes away from finishing in the dryer. Then I'll swap the bedding from the washer into the dryer while I fold and put away the items from the dryer. I swept, vacuumed, and mopped every room. Dusted every surface above ground level, especially those pesky floorboards. Cleared out any old leftovers in the fridge. Washed the dishes. Wiped down the shower, toilet, and bathroom sink. Swiped wood polish over the dresser, bookshelves, entertainment center, and tables. Changed the sheets on our bed as well as the spare bed. Reorganized the linen closet, then decided to reorganize our bedroom closet. Shredded all the mail I couldn't throw in the trashcan.

Now standing in the middle of the living room with my hands on my hips, I spin around and look for something else to do. Maybe reorganize the books on the shelves? Should I alphabetize them? Sort them by color or author or genre?

I still haven't gotten a response from Rick and I'm losing my freaking mind. Ugh! It never takes him this long to answer me. Of course, every second that ticks by right now feels like a week passing.

Part of me is half tempted to jump in the car and drive to the club. Business has picked up, from what Rick told me, but he still gets breaks and does office work.

Just as I slip on my shoes and throw my purse strap over my head, my phone pings with an incoming text.

Rick: Not sure. Could be from this crazy bitch I booted out the other night.
Christy: Crazy bitch?

Rick: Yeah. She got in my face one too many times. Propositioned me. I kicked her out.
Christy: So how did this get in your pocket?
Rick: Beats me. But she kept touching me. Maybe she slipped it in my pocket.

Deep, steady breaths, Christy. You know what they say about assuming. So, don't be an ass.

Rick: I swear, gorgeous. Didn't know she did that. She's actually made work a pain in the ass. Until I banned her.
Christy: Good. Glad you banned her. Otherwise, I might have to kick her ass.
Rick: There's my girl. Gotta go. See you in the morning.
Christy: Love you.
Rick: Love you, too.

Just breathe. Everything is fine. God, I need to quit jumping to conclusions. Especially when I don't have enough information. Nothing is going on. Nothing except crazy bitches in the club trying to steal my man. Another day in the life. But I definitely need to chill the hell out.

I crumple the paper and toss it in the trash bin. Once my heart settles, I fold and put away the laundry, make myself dinner, and head to bed. Soon, Rick will be home. Soon, we will share our first weekend off together since moving here. And it will be absolute perfection.

We meet Ella and Thomas at a bistro near the beach.

The chic decor grabs my attention as soon as we walk in the door. Oil and watercolor paintings hang sporadically on the walls. Most of the art naturalistic. Botany. Flowers. Pops of yellow and blue amongst the creams and greens. Chunky tables resemble smooth driftwood. Matching chairs draped in cream crocheted blankets and fluffy pillows. A cluster of tea lights glow in the center of each table beside a small fern filled vase.

Rick pulls out my chair for me. After he scoots me forward, he presses a kiss atop my head and sits in the chair beside me.

"This place is super cute," I comment. "Thanks for inviting us."

Ella waves off my gratitude. "Someone in the bookstore mentioned it after sitting in the reading nook. And you never need to thank us for an invite."

My heart swells. Rick and me being here with Ella and Thomas is so normal. A couple's date night out. Although the four of us have been intimate, tonight isn't about that. For the first time, we thought it would be a nice change to have dinner and enjoy the company of one another. As great as the sex is, it doesn't rule our lives.

Thomas discusses the crazy case he just landed. Says

he will be bombarded for months unless a miracle happens. His client suing a large corporation due to one of their employees driving under the influence and running them off the road. The client's spouse passed away less than twenty-four hours after the accident. Now they're suing for negligence, pain and suffering, and how the loss will affect the living spouse's future financially.

The more he shares—as vague as possible—the more I tremble. If anything ever happened to Rick, I would be absolutely devastated. He has been my rock. The only solid foundation I have known. Once upon a time, my parents were my foundation. But the moment they shamed me, the earth tilted on its axis and shattered beneath my feet. Lucky for me, Rick righted my world, slowly sealed those cracks, and gave me a solid place to set my feet.

As if he senses my wayward thoughts, he clutches my hand and strokes his thumb softly over my palm. His assurance through touch that nothing like this will ever happen to us. And I want to believe it, so I let all my anxieties fall away.

We order dinner. Chat about life before we met. Enjoy each other's company and share laughter.

Before Ella owned the bookstore, she worked several retail jobs. In her words— "nothing of significance."

"So, how did the bookstore come to life?" I ask out of curiosity. Rick and Thomas carry on a separate conversation beside us.

"Sheer luck. An older woman lived next door to us. Grace. Such a sweet and kind-hearted woman. Unfortunately, her children only visited during the holiday season. She wouldn't confess it, but I think they only showed for the check she put in their card." Ella shakes her head and purses her lips, obviously upset over the matter. "Every day, Thomas or I would go check on her. Visit with her for an hour. Sometimes, we'd make enough dinner for the three of us. It saddened me that her family basically sat on the sidelines and waited for her to die."

I slap my hand over my mouth and shake my head. Working at a life insurance company, I know just how often this happens. It always shocks me when people call in and ask to cash in the policy. Their loved one barely gone, and their only concern is the check they will receive. Unfathomable.

"What happened?" I ask.

"Grace passed in her sleep a few years ago. I went to check on her in the morning. When she didn't answer the door after a couple minutes, I let myself in with the key she gave us. She laid so peaceful in her bed. Afghan tugged up to her chin. Not an ounce of suffering on her face. I kissed her forehead, said my goodbyes, and called the non-emergency number for the police."

Ella swipes a tear off her cheek. And it isn't until she does this that I realize I started crying at some point. She sucks in a jagged breath, then continues. "Anyway, a month later, Grace's attorney called. Asked us to come down to their office. A few days later, we learned Grace altered her will months prior and left Thomas and me her savings. She'd left the house to her children and instructed them to sell it and divide the proceeds. In the end, her four children sold her house for a quarter of what she left us. They were bitter, but we ignored them."

"Wow," I say. "Sorry you had to deal with the drama, but after all you did for her… what a wonderful gift she left you."

"Yeah. Grace loved books. Always had one nearby. The man who previously owned the bookstore had been in the red for some time and put the store up for sale. After weeks of negotiating, Thomas and I became the proud owners of Cozy Corner Books. With some of the remaining money, we gave the store a facelift and made it more inviting. Soon, the coffee shop and delicatessen moved in and business has boomed since."

I love this story. Although the part about Grace was sad, it tells me what kind of people Ella and Thomas truly are. Considerate. Loving. Generous. Rick and I are more than lucky to call them friends.

After we finish dinner, the four of us bundle up and walk down the street to Confectionate. One of my coworkers bragged for ten minutes straight about the sweet shop's pie selection. The second I mentioned it to Ella, she told me it wasn't far from the restaurant and we should go.

Once we have our fill of sugar, chocolate, and fruit, we call it a night. For the first time, we don't take the evening any further. A flutter erupts in my solar plexus. Ella and Thomas are so perfect for me and Rick. Not only do we pair well as sexual partners, we also bond perfectly as friends.

There isn't a single couple Rick and I have ever had a relationship with that was similar to this. Fate is a strange creature, but I believe everything happens for a reason. Ella and Thomas fit into our world so simply. Like the missing pieces to our puzzle.

With each passing day, life here gets better and better.

TWENTY

ALEX

A BLOCK AWAY, he opens the passenger door for her. Kisses her. A little too long for my liking. Then shuts the door and gets in on the driver's side.

The black Audi starts and pulls onto the street. Behind them, another black vehicle. A BMW SUV with the other couple. They both drive away but turn opposite directions at the traffic light down the street.

As soon as they are out of sight, I crank the engine of my dying sedan and veer into traffic. Five minutes later, I drive three cars behind the Audi. My eyes lock onto it and watch its every movement. It turns left, and I follow suit. Then takes a right a few blocks later, and I continue behind them but keep my distance.

On the quiet neighborhood street, porch lights glow and highlight well-manicured lawns. Houses decorated with wreaths on the doors or accent lighting showing off their prized plants. It is all a little too prissy for my taste.

The Audi parks in a driveway, and the couple steps out and walks hand in hand to the door. Once they go inside, I drive slowly up to the house and stop in the street, staring at the large windows.

That should be my house.

A light flips on inside and their silhouettes come together and blend into one.

That should be me in there. Lips crashing and hips slapping. Me.

Soon… soon it will be.

Might not see me coming, but they will soon learn.

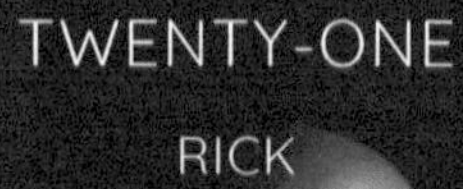

TWENTY-ONE

RICK

Tonight, we closed Boundless for a private event. A fucking bachelorette party to be more precise.

The squealing women and shit ton of glitter everywhere has me ready to puke. *If I ask Christy to marry me, would she behave like this at her bachelorette party?* An errant thought I shake off.

The bride paid a pretty penny—five thousand, to be exact—to make Boundless hers for the evening. Currently, she and twenty of her closest friends dance naked in the vacant space. Body glitter on every lick of their skin, shimmering like a disco ball under the lights. And spreading onto every surface they touch.

Honestly, I hate that the janitorial crew will be cleaning twice as long tonight to get all this shit off the furniture and floor. They will no doubt hate us by the time they clock out.

But Rocco told me the bride is a close friend to one of his dancers, and that is the *only* reason he allowed it.

Two men walk out of the entry corridor, half-dressed as law enforcement, and I roll my eyes. I really have no desire to stick around and watch what is about to unfold. Amateur hour with a couple of scrawny dweebs and women who obviously don't get pleasured often enough.

Walking up to the bar, I look at Cheyenne and she rolls her eyes. She loves tonight just as much as I do. "Cheyenne, I'll be in the office. Let me know if you need anything."

She harrumphs and nods. The last thing she wants to do is spend the next several hours watching these women as some ridiculous male dancers twirl their cocks in banana hammocks. At least Rocco agreed to pay her a normal night's salary. Which is the only reason she hasn't stormed out yet.

"Yeah, sure," she says, then goes back to slicing lemons and stocking the bar. At least tonight will give her a chance to prep more for tomorrow.

After I weed through a stack of invoices on my desk, I call Christy. Before leaving for work, I forgot to tell her we were closed for the party. If she walked in and saw the flock of sparkly women mobbing the male dancers, she would probably turn around, walk out, and call me with a million questions.

"Hey," she purrs, answering the call.

"Hey, gorgeous. Forgot to tell you tonight the club is closed for a private party. We'll be out early."

"Yay." Something shatters in the background and she curses.

"What was that? You okay?"

"Dropped a glass. I'm fine. Just need to clean it up," she huffs.

"Just a glass. It's replaceable. Don't cut yourself." A gust muffles her phone speaker and I imagine her blowing her hair off her face. So fucking adorable. "I should be home in a couple hours."

"'Kay. Love you."

"Love you, too."

I walk Cheyenne to her car before I slip into mine.

After five hours of squeals and hollers and enough glitter to wipe out the unicorn population, the bachelorette party ended. Thank fuck. Seriously, if Christy ever has a bachelorette party, I know it would never be packed with all that fake bullshit. Not even sure she would ever have a bachelorette party, to be honest.

I shake my head. There I go again. Imagining Christy as my wife. Not that I don't love her with every beat of my heart, or enough to want her as my wife, but her in such a traditionalist role seems odd to me. Matrimony doesn't quite fit our mold. But what really does?

Marriage has always set me off-kilter. Not in a bad

way. Never comprehended the point, I guess. Why do two people need a piece of paper and words uttered before other people to be committed? In my eyes, they don't. Christy and I have been committed to each other for the last seven years. We don't need a government certificate to validate our love. At least I don't.

But does she?

For the first time, I consider she might dream of such things. At Sarah's birthday party, she bawled as Jackson proposed to Sarah. Starry-eyed, she smiled at me in a way I had never seen before. She cried that night and I assumed it was happiness for her friend.

Maybe it was more than that? Maybe she wished for the same. To have a ring on her left hand. To flaunt it to the world and lay claim to me. Little does she know, she claimed my heart seven years ago.

"Am I blind?" I ask the steering wheel.

I twist the black band on my right thumb. Have I failed this part of our relationship?

Sure, we have had our ups and downs—like every couple. But I don't imagine a single day of our lives apart. Ever. From the second I laid eyes on her in Apex, Christy was mine. She would always belong to me. We may share ourselves with other people, but only our bodies. Never our hearts. Hence why we don't allow kissing. Far too much intimacy comes with kissing.

Christy has never given me any indication she isn't happy. With me. Or our relationship. But I can't help but wonder if I deprive her of what she truly wants.

Years ago, we discussed other important life topics. Mainly children. Thankfully, we were both on the same page. Neither of us wants children. When she eventually told me about her parents, it made more sense. She never wants to expose another life to the pain that comes with rejection. Especially from family. The people who claim to love you the most.

Me? The minute I lost Harriett, my perspective on life changed. Mom shut down. Dad finished a bottle of whiskey every other day. Neither of them gave two shits about me anymore. Their baby died and nothing else mattered. Not even their living, breathing son.

I never want to suffer a loss like Harriett's again. She may not have been my daughter, but she was my world then. We never bickered like most siblings. If anything, we spent more time with each other than our friends. Harriett wasn't just my sister, she was my best friend.

Losing her flipped a switch in my brain. A switch that turned off my emotions and erected a wall. A barrier to shield my heart. I never wanted to get close to anyone again. Never wanted to love someone again. Because love equals loss.

But Christy scaled that wall, wrapped her warm arms around my heart, and jump started the slow beating organ.

"Holy shit," I whisper into the darkness as I park in our driveway.

I sit in the car a minute and wrap my mind around this

revelation. True, I may never have imagined myself married. But with Christy, my imagination runs wild.

After clearing my thoughts, I go inside to greet my girl. Barely after eleven, and she is sexy as fuck on the couch. Curled up with a knitted, heather gray throw blanket, head propped on the arm of the couch, she snores softly as movie credits scroll up the television screen.

For a moment, I squat beside the couch and watch her chest rise and fall. Steady, even breaths. A lock of her russet hair drapes her left eye. Glasses cock-eyed on the bridge of her nose. Her eyes dart behind her lids and I wonder what she dreams about. Wishing it would project onto the screen and show me her inner desires.

She inhales and sighs in her sleep. "Always," she mumbles.

The corner of my mouth perks up. She's dreaming about us. Often, I dream of her. Of us. My heart inflates and jackhammers behind my ribcage as I stare at my girl. My gorgeous, amazing girl.

I click off the television and scoop her up in my arms. Automatically, she wraps her arms around my neck and curls into my chest. Even asleep, her body clings to me. As does mine to her. Like second nature.

After laying her in the bed, I undress and slip under the comforter. A second later, her arm and leg are draped over me. I tug her impossibly closer and kiss her forehead. "Night, gorgeous. Love you," I whisper into the dark.

Her body hugs me tighter. "Love you, too," she mumbles.

Am I really here?

Thomas stands next to me and pats my back. "Overwhelmed?" Overwhelmed is putting it lightly.

I stare around the small, independently-owned store. There isn't much to look at, but there is plenty. And everything fucking sparkles. Every. Goddamn. Thing.

"Uh, yeah."

After my revelation a few nights ago, I shot Thomas a text and asked for his help. Not that I am incapable of doing this type of thing on my own. Just thought it would be nice to have support since I'm swimming in uncharted territory.

"Any idea what she likes?" Thomas asks as he scans the blinding jewels in one of the cases.

Did I know? Christy never wore anything flashy. Most jewelry she owned was simple—not plain, but not a piece someone would shriek over either. "Classic. Silver. Nothing gaudy."

We survey a few of the cases before he points out a selection to me. "How about these?"

Walking over to him, I scan the rows and rows of sparkling stones. If there aren't spots in my vision when we leave, I will be shocked. All the twinkling and prisms is starting to make every one of them look the same. And it is a little much. Ready to give up after scanning a few more rows, I freeze.

Locked in my gaze is a platinum, antique filigree band. At the center, the two-carat, round cut black diamond sits high. On either side, woven into the band, is five vibrant, red rubies. Absolutely stunning.

You have heard of women seeing a wedding dress and instantly knowing it is "the one". Right now, staring at this small, delicate piece of jewelry, one truth is absolute. It was crafted for Christy.

After shelling out a small fortune, I leave the store with the black velvet box tucked in my pocket. My palms sweat and my throat dries. Nervousness has never struck me this hard. Like a closed fist to the sternum.

Am I *ready* for this? To propose to Christy? What if proposing fucks everything up between us? Will she say yes? God, I hope she does. More than that, I hope I don't make a fool of myself. But what if she says no? I love her more than anything, and it would shred me if I ask and she says she doesn't want to be my wife. Not sure how we would move forward after that.

Thomas and I grab a quick bite to eat before he heads back to the office. The entire time, he shares how nerve-wracked he was before proposing to Ella. He had the same fears that currently wrench my heart in a death grip. Before we go our separate ways, Thomas does his best to soothe my distress and tells me to call him if I need help.

After lunch, I head to Boundless and lock Christy's ring in the safe upstairs. Only Rocco and I have the vault combination, so I know it will be secure. Once I'm in my office, I sit at my desk, surf the web, and distract myself from the torrent of *what-if* questions.

An hour later, the perfect date is planned for proposing and I breathe a little easier. My nerves seem to have settled a fraction, thank fuck. Taking a deep breath, I mutter, "She'll say yes. Quit worrying."

I speak nothing but truth. No doubt Christy will say yes when I ask her to marry me. Our love is endless. Timeless. And we have proved it time and again with every obstacle that has hit us.

So then why is there still a boulder lodged in my gut?

Rick has been acting weird.

I let him sleep a little longer while I cook us breakfast. After tearing open the pack of maple bacon, I lay several strips on a drip pan and put them in the oven on low. While they start, I dice up potatoes, onion, garlic, bell pepper, and avocado.

Once the onions caramelize, I remove half and add the potatoes and garlic. As I start whipping the eggs for omelets, Rick wraps his arms around my waist. I freeze mid-whisk and close my eyes, basking in his warmth. He kisses the back of my head and I shudder as tingles run down my spine.

"Morning, gorgeous. Smells good."

I set the bowl down on the counter, twist in his arms, and kiss him. "Ten more minutes."

He nods, presses his lips to my shoulder, then walks off. "Gonna brush my teeth."

Over the last few days, Rick has lavished me with more kisses than normal. Soft, sweet kisses. Not that I don't love them, but they aren't the typical sort of kisses we share. Yes, he has been tender with me. And it is not as if I don't enjoy the softer side of his affections. But the ratio between gentle and harsh kisses is a ten-ninety split. Not the opposite. It's as if everything has suddenly flipped.

What the hell changed?

Before I delve too deep into my wayward thoughts, he walks back into the kitchen. "Need help?" Another shoulder kiss.

"Coffee?"

He nods and heads for the single brewer, popping a mug under the drip, loading a pod, and starting it up.

Once everything is plated and the coffee is ready, we sit at the small table in the breakfast nook. Silence stretches out the minutes like an overused elastic band. I want to scream. Ask him what the hell is going on. But, instead, I sit in silence and keep my thoughts to myself.

I shovel another forkful of omelet into my mouth, ready to lose my shit and fling the pronged metal at him. Just as I work up the nerve to blurt out and ask him what the hell is going on, he figures out how to speak again.

"Made us plans for Valentine's weekend."

I shake my head. *W-w-what?* "We never do anything on Valentine's. Always agreed it wasn't a real holiday."

"True. But indulge me. Please?"

I tilt my head to the side and study him for a beat. Is this why he has been acting weird? Because, for the first time in seven years, he planned a Valentine's Day surprise. Was he reluctant to tell me? Possibly.

"Sure," I say before eating another bite of omelet. "What did you have in mind?"

He taps his temple and smiles, the corner of his eyes crinkling. "It's a surprise. Can you get the day off? Would be nice to have a long weekend together."

Valentine's falls on a Friday. If Rick wants a long weekend together, I assume he already asked for the day off. Which means he has put in more effort than imaginable to make our first celebrated Valentine's Day one to remember. I study him as he eats another bite of potatoes and wonder what he is up to.

"I'll email Ingrid after breakfast," I tell Rick. "She should be good with it."

Ingrid is the new Marco. My direct supervisor. Her dedication to Hammond Life is admirable. She isn't just a boss, but also a leader. Honestly, I didn't understand the difference until I met her. When it comes to work-life balance, she advocates as if it was the most important part of the job. Lucky doesn't describe how fortunate I am to work for her. Someone who urges employees to take time off at least once per quarter — whether one day or five.

"Good." Rick winks then gobbles down his forkful of potatoes.

After we clean up the kitchen, we dress and head out

for the day. Once Rick mentioned he made plans for us on Valentine's, a weight lifted. Obviously, he was worried about how I would react. But I'm happy he finally spit it out and things feel like our version of normal again.

Rick steers us through traffic, his hand wrapped around mine as he draws circles with his thumb over my skin. A small smile perks up the corners of my mouth as warmth radiates from our joined hands. Before we left the house, Rick asked if there was anywhere I wanted to go today. I told him to choose. So, our first destination… the zoo.

Although nature is less than a couple miles from our home, the outdoors in California is vastly different than the outdoors in Georgia. The air thinner and lighter on my skin. The trees a more pungent pine and the earth damp and musky. When the sun beats down on me, I enjoy its warmth rather than melt into a puddle. Also, elevation is a legit thing here—not that it wasn't in Georgia, but the difference is noticeable. And the wildlife—no comparison to what we normally saw in our neck of the woods in Georgia. Life out here is just… different. And I love it.

After Rick parks the car, we follow the other zoo-goers and head for the entrance. Once we have our wristbands and step through the turnstile, I feel like a little kid for a moment. Twenty feet in and the scent of cinnamon and sugar and buttered popcorn wafts under my nose and has me searching for its source. A vendor sits off to the side with churros, popcorn, cotton candy, and a variety of drinks.

It doesn't take much to convince Rick we need junk sustenance. "Thank you," I say as I bite down on my churro.

He pays the young man behind the cart then laughs at my gluttony. "You're welcome, gorgeous." Before I can yank my churro back, Rick chomps a bite twice the size of mine.

"Hey. That's my churro. Get your own, mister," I tease as I tuck the confection behind me.

After I finish eating my morning snack, we stroll hand in hand along the paved paths and check out the lemurs, tigers, and hippos. At each animal enclosure, we stop and read the posted signs. All the animals here were rescued from horrendous circumstances. Injured or loss of habitat. Rejected by their herd. The zoo takes them in, rehabilitates them, and provides them with a better place to live.

Before we leave, I coerce Rick into a small photo booth to take pictures with me. We make goofy faces in the first two pictures. The other two are much more passionate as he kisses me deeply. Thank goodness for the booth curtain. Normally, kisses like the one we just shared don't bother me. But the zoo is packed with kids and our kiss was nowhere near a PG rating.

As we step out, I run my hands over my dress then do my best to fix my hair. I stand near the drop chute where the pictures print out. Don't need any curious children and pissed parents peeking at them. When the small sheet of images drops, I snatch it and smile at the photos.

I brush my finger over my lips. That kiss. The intensity. The way he cradled my face and held me prisoner while he expressed how deep his feelings for me run. Why have those been so far and few between recently? Does he think I want gentle and cute? On occasion, soft and tender fits a special moment. But for us, it isn't often. Maybe he needs a reminder how much I love it when he is rough and assertive. How I love it when he kisses me like he will never have another opportunity.

Shortly after leaving the zoo, Rick drives us to a café and we eat lunch. As we sit across from each other and eat paninis, I grant him a little more time. I plead with the universe for any sign his saccharine behavior has changed. No such luck. If anything, it has gotten softer. Wispy touches. Hushed tones. Delicate kisses on my shoulders, knuckles, forehead.

So tender.

So wholesome.

So not Rick.

When we get back in the car and drive toward home, he strokes the backside of his fingers up and down my bicep. Gah! I love it and hate it, all at the same time.

That is it! I can't deal with this anymore. "Are you okay?" I ask bluntly. Better to get right to the point. Really no sense in pussyfooting.

Rick takes his eyes off the road for a split-second and glances at me. When he looks forward again, he says, "Yeah. Fine. Why?"

I shift in the passenger seat to face him and tuck my

feet under my butt. "You've just been acting strange the last few days. Everything okay at work?"

His grip tightens around the steering wheel for a blink. So quick I almost miss it. But Rick and I learned to watch each other's body movements years ago. With our lifestyle, knowing when your significant other is unhappy is vital. His eyes pinch tightly as if he is upset with himself. Why would he be mad? What is he hiding? Rick and I have always been open and honest with each other. Not sure what has changed, but it is eating me alive not knowing.

In an instant, I'm a hawk and he is my prey. Eyes locked on target and tracking every move. If he shifts an inch to the left, I will know. His every move an instant blip on my radar.

"Work is fine. The bachelorette party was a waste of time and money, in my opinion. But Rocco is the ultimate decision maker in those instances. Nothing else has happened."

I narrow my eyes and study him as we drive through Los Angeles. After a beat, I retract my claws and let him drive without me being a distraction. The last thing we need is Rick to glance over at me and cause an accident because I stir the pot.

"Has something else happened with that person you kicked out?"

We exit off the highway and wind our way through the city. Rick waits to answer until after he navigates us to a street with less traffic. When we stop at a red light, he faces me. "Haven't seen her again. Hopefully we won't. We take copies of IDs and have marked her as "no entry permitted". She shouldn't be an issue."

I stare into his honey-swirled eyes, searching for clues. Any clue. Something to shed light on his recent change in behavior. Rick isn't someone who changes without just cause.

But he also has one of the best poker faces. When necessary, he is a master at masking the truth. He isn't lying to me. Just skirting around the truth.

"That's good," I mumble. "Still doesn't explain…" I let my words trail off as I spin to face forward. If this conversation isn't going anywhere, I am done talking. No sense in making us both upset.

His knuckles brush my forearm before he laces his fingers with mine. "Does it bother you? Me more tender."

I whip my eyes back to his just as the light turns green and he has to look away. "Yes and no," I confess.

"Tell me why, gorgeous."

Gazing down at our joined hands, I fumble over what to tell him. Will I come across as an idiot? Embarrass myself? Both equally possible. "It's just… not us. Yes, I adore the sweetness. But usually it comes in small bouts. When it's days, I wonder if something happened. If I did something wrong. Or if you did. So, I question it because we aren't a softhearted, mushy couple. Not ninety-five percent of the time, anyway."

He turns the car right, then left, and a few minutes

later, he pulls into the driveway. Throwing the car in park, he faces me full on. "It's true we aren't gentle lovers," he says, chuckling. "But every once in a while, it's nice to be like this. Don't you think?"

My brows furrow as my eyes narrow. "Yes. But what brought it on?" Because I truly want to know. As if a coin flipped and Rick went from heads to tails without warning.

"I had lunch with Thomas a few times recently. He said some things that resonated with me. Guess part of me is opening up. Trying things a little different. Should've brought it up with you, but thought *that* would be weird."

Trying new things? I suppose that is possible. But would we enjoy life the same if we did things different?

What if our relationship suffers? What if trying to be something we are not, knocks us down? God, I cannot imagine a life without Rick. Nor do I want to. I shake the horrible thought away and swear to not think it again. *See the bright side, Christy. Stay optimistic.*

Optimistic.

What if this change is exactly what we need? Will it make our love stronger? More powerful? Unbreakable? These are the questions and ideas I need floating in my head. Notions that scream positivity and love and strength.

"You're right. It would've been weird," I say, giggling. "Let's give this sweeter side a try. But we need to talk about it. Weird or not. So we're both on the same page."

Rick spins in his seat, opens the door, and exits the car. Before I grab the door handle, he opens my door for me and offers his hand. "Perfect plan, gorgeous," he coos. "Now let's go inside. I need to make love to you."

And with that, we bolt to the front door like two horny teenagers who can't keep their hands off each other.

TWENTY-THREE

ALEX

THIS IS FUCKING BULLSHIT!

Sitting in cold ass temperatures and watching them. As if I don't have better things to do. Complete. And utter. Bullshit. How the hell did I manage to get myself coerced into this?

If it was only me involved in this whole operation, things would already be next level. Strides would be made. Not this amateur stalking shit. Honestly, wouldn't shock me if they knew they were being followed.

People sense that shit. Intuition and whatnot. Not much of a believer in it myself, but sometimes you can't explain how you just know that shit. So saying you had a "gut feeling" fits the bill.

With these two, I can't be sure. Maybe they are oblivious. Maybe they are that fucking stupid. Answers will come with time.

Not much longer, though. Soon, shit will hit the fan.

Soon, I will get to twist rope around their wrists and ankles and throats. Tie them down on chairs and play my little games. That is when all the real fun begins.

My cell pings in my lap and startles the shit out of me. "Fuck!" Ever since this whole stalking game started, I have been a live wire. Been far too long since my last fix. And it can't come quick enough.

L: Anything to report?

"If there was anything to report, you'd know. Dumb ass," I say to the screen sarcastically.

Alex: Same shit. Different day.
L: Keep me posted.
Alex: Yep.

"Nah. Thought I'd sit here day after day for shiggles." I roll my eyes at the screen then toss the phone on the passenger seat.

The last thing I need is to be patronized. I volunteered for this gig because it would fulfill the urges living deep in my bones. Not to mention, I would do anything for L. The bond we share has proven it time and again. This isn't our first rodeo. Definitely won't be our last.

I suck down the last of my energy drink and toss the can onto the passenger floorboard. Leaning the driver's seat back, I undo my pants and stare at the house's far right window. The one I know is their bedroom.

Daydreaming of all the things soon to come, I fist my cock and tug hard. When I was a teenager, I got off on inflicting pain. After the first few people in my bed, word spread quickly and most steered clear of me. *The sicko with a torture fetish.*

Can't help what you love.

And soon, I will satiate the beast inside me.

TWENTY-FOUR

RICK

Nervous fucking wreck.

The only logical way to explain the thunderstorm of nerves brewing inside me right now. And I don't understand it at all.

Christy and I have been together seven years. Seven. Years.

The only other time I remember being remotely this nervous was in the beginning. When our relationship status was questionable and I had no clue as to what kind of person she was. A guessing game as to the level of her desires. Didn't take long to learn what my girl liked, though.

Hopefully, I guessed this right too. If not, I am royally fucked.

Beside me, Christy stares out the passenger window and bops to the music playing. Is she nervous too? Maybe keeping this so under wraps wasn't the smartest idea. Both of us on are on edge, and neither of us are speaking.

I reach across the console and twine our fingers together. Her eyes glance away from the passing scenery and stare at my jawline. She draws faint lines with her eyes along the angle of my jaw to my chin. Subtle and heated.

"Where are we going?" she asks.

Over the last forty-eight hours, she has asked me about this weekend again and again. I simply smiled at her and tapped my temple. From the glint in her eye, I know a part of her is excited. But another part of her wants to bite her nails off and spit them at me. Surprising Christy is not something I do often. Not like this.

"Not much longer and you'll see."

She sighs and it is the cutest thing. I tuck the sound away, hoping it's not the last time I hear it. "Don't know why you still need to be so secretive. We *are* on the way there."

I laugh, and she smacks my forearm. "Why ruin it now? After all the effort I put in, I'm not caving when we're minutes away from it all starting."

Her eyes snap up in attention. Like a child, she peers out the window and searches for invisible clues. As if a neon sign will flash in the distance and point out our destination. Once I pull onto the Pacific Coast Highway, I know the restaurant is roughly five minutes away. Watching her—giddy and excited—makes tonight, and this weekend, worth every second of anxiety I suffered.

When I drive up to the valet attendant, Christy ogles the restaurant. The valet opens her door and helps her out. Another attendant does the same for me before handing me a ticket. I walk around the car to Christy, offer her my elbow, and we stroll down a small path toward the restaurant.

I lean into her, my lips a breath from her skin, and whisper, "What do you think, gorgeous?"

She stares at the creamy stacked rock exterior. Along the roofline, planks of mahogany add a pop of warmth. We walk along a boardwalk path, winding through tall grass plants and perfectly manicured bonsai. Near the entrance to the restaurant is a small deck with muted gray outdoor couches, matching ottoman-style tables, and wide cream canvas umbrellas overhead.

From where we stand, you can see nothing but the Pacific Ocean for miles. The cirrus cloudy sky tinted cornflower blue with hints of peach, watermelon pink, and ruby as the sun starts to sink closer to the horizon. Absolutely perfect.

After a minute of getting lost in the scenery, I take out my phone. "Let me take a picture with the sky behind you," I tell Christy.

Just as I snap the photo, a man steps up beside me and offers to take a photo of the two of us. A few clicks later, I thank him and we head inside. At the podium near the entrance, I inform the hostess of our reservation. Probably not the first person to say this, but securing a reservation at a popular restaurant on Valentine's Day is a pain in the ass. But when the night ends, it will be worth every hassle.

The hostess seats us at a table near a large window with an ocean view. On the opposite side of the glass, outdoor heaters warm the patio seating. I considered us sitting outside when I made the reservation but wasn't sure how the weather would be. Our current table is perfect for the two of us. Neither Christy nor I have ever been the type to need fancy or over-the-top.

Once alone, Christy peeks over her menu at me. "Rick, this place is expensive." Her brows pinch together with concern. It only makes me love her more.

"If the cost was an issue, I wouldn't have brought us here. So, please, don't let it bother you, gorgeous. Find something you want to eat and ignore the price."

She chews on her bottom lip a moment and studies me. Once she sees my resolve, her shoulders drop and she sinks further into her seat. "Okay."

We order our meals and a bottle of wine. Christy slowly unwinds and enjoys the view and ambiance. Below the table, my hand swipes back and forth over the lump in my pocket. Each time my hand passes over the chunky band, my palm sweats a little more.

When dinner arrives, we dig in. After we both have a moment to savor our meals, we agree a walk by the surf after dinner would be the perfect way to end our night here. Originally, I hadn't planned for us to go down by the water. Now, it seems like an excellent opportunity. Before long, we finish our dinner, order dessert, and drink a little more. I drink only enough wine to settle my nerves, but not enough to inhibit my driving.

"Ready?" I ask as Christy drinks the last of her wine.

She nods. "Yeah."

Fifteen minutes later, I park at a beach access lot. The closer we get to the water, the more Christy's hair whips across her face and her dress threatens to fly up. The sun set over an hour ago, but the sky hasn't turned ink black yet.

Hand in hand, we stroll near the surf. A hundred yards away, a group of people sit in a circle around a bonfire. The flames lick the sky and light the beach where we stand.

I bring us to an abrupt halt, jerking Christy in the process. "Sorry," I mutter.

"Everything okay?"

This is it. Right here. Right now. In this exact spot with the waves crashing behind her and the bonfire brightening her skin. Her russet locks pelt her cheeks and mask her glasses as she faces me.

I nod. "Yeah, gorgeous." Pulling her to my chest, I brush her wild strands away and kiss her. Soft at first. My tongue painting delicate lines on her lips and tongue. Once the taste of her hits me, I frame her face in my hands and kiss her harder. Christy moans and fists my shirt, dragging me impossibly closer.

Fire and lust and my need for her drive me forward. But before things get out of hand, I break the kiss and press my forehead to hers. Her breasts rise and fall as she gasps for air.

"Why'd you stop?" she whispers against my lips.

Breathe Rick. You got this.

"Because there's something I need to say. And if we keep doing that, I'll never get it out." I laugh nervously, holding her face in my palms as I stare into her stormy blue eyes. "Valentine's has never been a day we've celebrated. But this year, I wanted to do something special."

"You didn't—" I press a finger to her lips and cut her off.

"Let me finish." She nods and I remove my finger. "We've been together seven years. Not a day goes by where you're not on my mind. Since you walked into my life, your happiness is what makes me whole. More recently, things have been challenging. But there is no other person I'd want beside me during those challenges. And just when I thought I had you figured out, you surprise me in all the best ways. You make me a better man. No one loves me the way you do. And that's why I wanted to do something special tonight. Because you deserve to be celebrated and adored and cherished."

A tear escapes her eye and I swipe it away. I close the space between us, kiss her sweet and tender, and reach inside my pocket. Then I drop to one knee and take her hand in mine. "Christy, no one has healed my heart the way you have. No one, but you makes me whole. And I would be honored for you to be my wife."

I pinch the ring between my thumb and first finger

and present it to her. She slaps her free hand over her mouth as tears flood her cheeks. "Oh my god!" She squeals.

Seconds tick by. Waves continue to crash along the surf. Chatter from the bonfire floats in the air. My heart expands and contracts at such a rapid pace, I wonder if a heart attack is imminent. Just when I am about to stand up—cause fuck if I didn't plant my knee on a rock or shell—she nods.

"Is that a yes?" *Please let her answer yes.*

She continues to nod. "Yes! A thousand times, yes!"

I rise from the sand and squeeze my arms tight around her waist, lifting her off the ground and swinging her in circles. She cups my cheeks, hooks her ankles at my back, and kisses me fiercely. The idea of fucking her on this beach—here and now—crosses my mind. But, after a moment, I plant her back on the sand and take her left hand. Sliding the ring on her ring finger, I smile so big my cheeks sting.

Fuck. Nothing compares to the symphony playing in my chest cavity right now. The zips and flutters and whirls as my pulse thumps, thumps, thumps. Never would I have thought I could feel so many emotions in a split-second.

Elation. Joy. Beholden.

Only one person gives me everything. And she just agreed to be mine for eternity.

The weekend ends far too soon.

After I asked Christy to marry me, I swept her off her feet—literally—and brought her back to the Airbnb I rented us for the weekend. The place is cozy and cute, but Christy didn't see a square-foot of it until Saturday morning after I woke her up with my head between her legs.

We stayed inside all weekend, minus one trip to a grocery store for food. After fucking on every surface of the small cottage, we watched movies, fed each other chocolate-covered strawberries, soaked in the tub, and laid around naked. Pure heaven.

The best part... Christy stared at her ring every chance she got. Better yet, her smile never faded. Nothing has ever made me this happy. Nothing.

With an hour left at the Airbnb, we relax on the couch and watch television. Christy manages to find a channel dedicated to weddings. And it has been on for the last three hours as we packed and ate breakfast. Her excitement palpable. Hopefully she picks up on mine too.

"Do you have ideas for our wedding?" Part of me is scared to hear her answer. But another part of me jumps internally at what her answer will be. The wedding getup doesn't matter to me, so long as I get to marry her. We could be as fancy or plain as she wants. As long as she says yes at the appropriate moment.

"I'd like to get one of those planning books to organize everything. But I was thinking we'd have a small ceremony. You, me, and a few close friends. Nothing fancy. Never been one of those girls who dreamed of the poufy white dress. A red dress to match my ring feels more appropriate."

Her response is exactly what I expected—and hoped—from her. "So why are you watching all these bride shows?"

She laughs. "Just for fun. Big weddings may not be our thing. Watching these reminds me why. Too much drama. No, thank you."

Less than an hour later, we are on the road and driving back home. Out of the corner of my eye, I spot Christy staring at and twirling her ring. The way her eyes light up when she stares at it… I picked the perfect one. If one thing holds true; I know my girl. Inside and out.

As we turn onto our street, I glance up and spot a tattered, champagne-colored sedan in the rearview mirror. The same sedan I have seen a dozen times over the last week and a half. Never close enough for me to see the person behind the wheel or clearly read the license plate. And I'd chalk it up to being a neighbor, except I see the car in various places around town in my commute. No way a neighbor drives *all* the same places I do.

The car turns left on the side street before our house, and I breathe easier. Maybe it's nothing. Or maybe that person travels a lot and it's a coincidence I see them as often as I do. Maybe.

AFTER I FINISH up at work, I decide to stop by the mall. Although neither Rick nor I desire a large, elaborate wedding, I also don't want our magical day to be a hot mess. Hence why I currently stand staring at a wall of wedding organizer books in the bridal boutique. The whole decision-making process of which planner to go with is a bit overwhelming, but I'm determined to find the one for me.

Three times, a sales associate has approached me and asked if I need help. And each time, I declined. Maybe I should have taken one of them up on their offer. As much as I would like to pick out the planner for me, I really have no idea what I'm searching for.

"Excuse me," I say, walking up to the first woman who offered to help me. "Can you help me find a planner book thingy?"

She smiles, and the way her lips curve up is endearing.

"Sure thing." We walk back toward the wall of a million magazines, books, and organizers. "Anything in particular you're looking for?"

"Just something simple. We plan to have a small wedding. So I need an organizer for the basics. A place to keep track of dates, phone numbers, appointments, and so on."

The woman taps a finger over her lips and scans over the plethora of options. Her eyes scan the wall a minute longer before she bends down and scoops up a small planner. "Take a look at this one and tell me what you think."

She hands me the planner and I open the cover. Soft paper grazes against the pads of my fingers as I flip each page. Inside, the planner is divided into several sections. Each is packed with pages and pages of things I might easily forget. Since we want a small ceremony and reception, these checklists are exactly what I need. After skimming through each section, I nod to the clerk. "This is perfect. Thank you. I would've been here another five hours without your help."

"That's what we're here for. Glad to help."

Back at the register, I pay for the planner and leave the shop with a little pep in my step. Something as simple as an organizer has made my day all that much better. After window shopping a few other stores, I exit the mall and head for my car.

As I weave through the rows of cars, I glance over my shoulder a few times. A shiver rolls down my spine and I can't help but feel like I'm not alone. Each time I look behind me, there is not a soul in sight. I tremble again. Somewhere in this lot, someone is watching me. No denying their eyes are on me, burning my skin.

Picking up the pace, I dash to my car and slip inside, quickly locking the doors. As soon as I start the engine and back out, I inhale deeply and shake off the layer of unease.

There was no one there. No one was following me. I'm fine. Just imagining things.

Driving away from the mall, I swing by the grocery store. Usually, we grab groceries on the weekend, but since Rick swept me off my feet, asked me to marry him, and held me captive all weekend, it never happened. But you will hear zero complaints from me.

In the store, I grab a cart, pull out my shopping list and a pen, and start my rounds. While waiting at the bakery counter for my loaf of sliced bread, I spot a woman out of the corner of my eye. Staring at me intently. I play cool and pretend to not notice her. But her eyes bore into me like a drill mining for oil and I keep an eye on her in my periphery. The level of intensity she exudes in my direction is unnerving.

The baker hands me the bread and I set it in my cart, happy to step away from this woman. I drift over to the deli area for lunch meats and cheese. After tugging a number from the deli ticket dispenser, I spy the same woman in my periphery again. Her eyes are locked on me like a hawk swooping in on her prey. Just as I suck up the courage to face her and ask why the hell she keeps staring at me, the deli clerk calls my ticket number.

"What can I get for you this evening?" the man asks.

I deposit my ticket in a small basket on top of the case. "One pound of applewood turkey and half a pound of Havarti, please."

He nods and walks off to slice my order. In the reflection of the case, the woman stares at me. Top lip curled in disgust. Eyes pinched tight. Hip cocked out with her hand resting on it. Studying her reflection in the glass, I try to place her, but come up with nothing. Nothing about her is familiar.

Perhaps she had a bad day and is one of those people who project their anger onto others. Who knows.

After I collect my order, I wander off and pick up the rest of the items on my list. During the rest of my time in the store, I never see the angry woman again. Thank god. I can't quite put my finger on it, but something about her just didn't sit right with me.

When I mark off the last item on my list, I make my way to the checkout lines. The grocery store on a Monday night is such a pleasant experience. Honestly, the lack of foot traffic and people bumping carts in the aisles is a delight. Perhaps I will change our grocery shopping day to Monday. Rick wouldn't care. He just tags along to be with me.

The bagger sets my bags in the cart and offers to help me to the car, but I decline his gesture. Parking the buggy in the corral, I heave the canvas totes on my shoulders and walk to the car.

Staring out at the vacant and dark parking lot, I change my mind about shopping on Mondays. It may be a quick and stress-free trip inside the store. Alone in the dark parking lot... I'm not really keen on that. If Rick were with me, I wouldn't care. But he isn't, and the feeling I had earlier—like someone is watching me—returns with a vengeance.

Fifty feet away, my brilliant red SUV gleams at me. I scurry across the lot and press the unlock button on my key fob. Almost there.

I open the hatch, unload the bags from my arms, and set them in the back. Just as I close the hatch, boots thud loudly behind me. Before I spin to see who walked up, the world around me goes black.

TWENTY-SIX

ALEX

"Load her in the backseat and drive her car to the meet," she demands.

What the fuck? "Since when do you make all the decisions? And since when do you tell me what the fuck to do?"

She rolls her eyes and cocks her head to the side. "Just shut the hell up, get in the car, and go. We need to get out of here. I'll meet you there after I make a quick stop."

I growl under my breath before shaking my head. "Whatever. Don't be long."

Sliding into the driver's seat, I start the car and back out. I tip the mirror down low enough to see Christy draped across the backseat. Her long hair hangs over her face, matted in clumps with blood. The gash on her temple is only a couple inches long but is enough to spill blood everywhere. Nothing bleeds worse than the face. From what I have noticed, anyway.

Twenty-three minutes later, I park near the warehouse entrance. I slip out of the front seat and open the back door. For a moment, I stare at her unconscious body. So pretty in her red and black swoop neck dress. The material hugs her curves and stops at her knees. Right now, with her completely out of it, I'm half tempted to push the dress up and see what is hidden underneath. If I ventured to guess, I would say nothing. Just her bare, pink flesh. Hot and wet and begging to be touched.

I rub my palm against my zipper and try to settle my eager cock. But the only way my hard-on will fade is after I finish this.

Grabbing her hand, I sit her upright before cradling her in my arms. Dead weight in my clutches, I carry her inside and set her in one of two wooden chairs. The chair with ropes secured at the legs and armrests. Quickly, I secure her limbs to the chair. Then I take a longer rope and wind it around her torso. Lastly, I tie a piece of rope to the top of the chairback and secure the end in a loop around her throat, creating a noose effect. That way, if she jerks forward in an attempt to free herself, she will instantly stop before choking.

Once she is fully bound, I step back, take out my cell, and snap a picture. I attach it in a text message and send it to L.

Alex: Let me know when you get the pic.

Less than a minute later, my phone dings.

L: Got it. Be there soon.

Lowering myself in the chair opposite her, I scan up and down her body. When I sat her down, I purposely hiked the skirt of her dress up to her waist. For my benefit and to up the ante with the photo. Beneath the tight fabric, her panty status is just as I suspected. Absent.

So while I wait for L to arrive and for the real party to start, I jack off to the delicious view of her pussy staring back at me.

TWENTY-SEVEN

RICK

THE LAST PERSON leaves the club and I itch to get the hell out of here. If I had it my way, the club would have closed hours ago.

After the most amazing weekend of my life, I'm dying to leave and get home to Christy. Our life has never been so stellar. Head over heels in love. Unbelievable sex—just the two of us or with Thomas and Ella. And as much as I never considered marriage, I am more than ready to run down the aisle and call Christy my wife.

Mrs. Christy Matheson.

Once everything is wrapped up, I hop in the car and push the gas pedal a little harder than normal. The traffic is minimal at this hour and I arrive home in no time. Just before I pull into the driveway, I notice Christy's car isn't parked in its usual spot. *Maybe she parked in the garage.* I hop out, open the garage, and bug out when the space is empty. I shake my head, confused as to why her car isn't home.

Where is she?

After closing the garage, I step inside and stop abruptly while my eyes adjust. Not a single light inside is on, which is normal when I get home this late. Although, after this weekend, I expected Christy to be up. I tiptoe through the house and go straight for the bedroom. When I open the door, my heart drops to the floor.

The bed is perfectly made and there is no sign of Christy. My pulse thrums loud behind my ears as I leave our bedroom and check the guest room. Nothing. Sweat pricks every inch of my skin and my hands start to shake. Next, I reach the living room and scan the couch. Not there.

As I go room to room through the house, I flip on every light and check every possible nook and cranny. "Christy," I shout. I wait but get no response. Nothing except the echo of my own voice. "Where are you, gorgeous?"

Yanking my phone out of my pocket, I call her cell. It goes straight to voicemail. What the *hell* is happening? She didn't leave me, did she? After everything this weekend, did she freak out and bolt? Not possible. She was just as giddy about my asking to marry her as I was.

Rick: Gorgeous, where are you? I'm worried.

I wait a few minutes, but she doesn't text or call back. Where is she?

After a few minutes pass without response, I call Liz. Maybe she went over there after work and they drank too much. Wouldn't be the first time. But when Liz answers, her voice thick with sleep, I immediately apologize. "Hey Liz, sorry to call so late. Early. Or whatever. Is Christy there?"

"No," she groans. "Why would she be here?"

"Don't know. But she isn't home and I'm worried. Tried to call her, but it went straight to voicemail. Then I texted, but she hasn't answered."

In the background, I hear Tiffany ask who called. Liz puts her hand over the speaker, but not completely, and tells her it's me.

"Haven't seen her since lunch today. Where she flashed her ring at me. Congrats, man."

If Christy flaunted her ring to Liz, that means she is over the moon about us getting married. There is no way she would show her best friend her engagement ring if she wasn't serious about us getting married. Which worries me more now. *Where is she?*

"Thanks. Hey, if you see her first, tell her to call or text. Please?"

"Of course. Sorry I'm of no help."

"'Night, Liz."

"'Night, Rick."

I disconnect the call and ponder over calling Sarah or Jackson. She could have gone there, but that would have been a heck of a commute after work. So, I hold off on waking them.

Instead, I wander around the house and look for something. Anything. A note. Her phone. Any clue. Once I scour each room for the third time and come up with nothing, I hang my head in frustration.

I'm sick of asking myself the same question over and over, but *where the hell is she?*

My head pops up with an idea. Not sure why, but my gut tells me to check the front porch, seeing as I came in through the garage. Maybe I missed something out front. I walk through the foyer, unlock the door, and flip on the porch light. After I swing the door open, I step out and am greeted with a bunch of nothing. Not really sure what I expected, but I hoped to find something.

Hanging my head again, I stand at the threshold and stare at the ground. A solicitation near the bush catches my eye and I bend down to retrieve it. It's a request for canned goods for a local, quarterly food drive. When I flip it over and see our address on the back a light kicks on in my head.

How did this fall out of the mailbox?

I spin and face the mailbox beside the door and lift the lid. Inside, a pile of mail sits waiting. I pull out the stack and walk back inside the house. For a moment, I fumble through the envelopes and advertisements, and weed out the crap. Almost to the bottom of the pile, I freeze.

An eight-by-eleven-inch piece of copy paper is folded in thirds, catching my eye as my jaw drops. I drop the other mail and unfold it, reading a note scribbled in black Sharpie.

We got your girl.
When you get this, text 555-876-3590.
Maybe we'll tell you where she is.
If you call the cops, she's as good as dead.

What. The. Fuck.

Why in the hell would someone abduct Christy? She is the sweetest person on the planet. Wouldn't hurt a goddamn fly. Behind my sternum, my heart thrashes like a wild beast for a new reason. Rage. Pure, undiluted rage. Whoever did this… Whoever took her… They are dead. Fucking dead.

I whip my phone back out of my pocket and start a fresh text message.

Rick: Who is this? And where the fuck is my girl?

Not up for any games, I get right to the point. Less than a minute later, my phone dings. When I glance down, I see an image of Christy strapped to a chair with a rope around her neck, head lulled to the side. From the picture, I have no way of telling if she is unconscious or worse.

Instantly, everything goes red.

Unknown: Come to the warehouse on 4th & Main. Look for her car. Come alone.

Rick: If you hurt her, I will fucking kill you.
Unknown: That's rich. You don't even know who I am. Good luck. Better hurry.

Before I bolt out the door, I run to the bedroom and grab the gun out of the safe tucked in our closet. Until now, the gun has never left the safe except for the occasional cleaning. When I purchased the gun years ago, I hoped to never use it. The same holds true now.

I check that the clip is loaded and lock it in the grip, pull back the slide, then tuck it in the back of my pants. Yanking my leather jacket off the hanger, I shoulder it on to conceal the gun in my waistband.

Bolting out the door, adrenaline surges through my veins as I speed down the highway. As I drive toward my girl, I pray this asshole hasn't hurt her in any way. If one goddamn hair is out of place… If there is even a scratch on her… There will be hell to pay.

In no time, I veer onto Main. Slowing down, I gaze up and down every side street. Still a few blocks from 4th street, I park my car and step out, opting to walk the rest of the way. I creep in the shadows along the street, most of the sidewalks dark or dimly lit. None of the businesses along here are currently open, so the whole street has this creepy movie vibe going on.

When I hit 4th street, I slowly peer around the corner. Fifty feet away, I spot Christy's car. In front of it, an old warehouse is lit up inside. Inhaling deeply, I close my eyes and pray to the universe that my girl is all in one piece and has no injuries.

A moment passes and I step out of the shadows then head for the door. As I twist the knob and crack the door open, a familiar head of brown hair comes into view. But that isn't what shocks me most. No, it's the person sitting across from her which has my jaw hitting the floor. The one with a big smile stretched across his face.

What. The. Fuck?

TWENTY-EIGHT

CHRISTY

DARKNESS BLANKETS EVERYTHING around me like eternal night. The air thick with mildew and stale cigarettes. I open my mouth and try to speak, but my tongue rests heavy and no words come out. No matter how much I beg my voice box to project—something, anything—it doesn't budge.

I need to get out of here. Wherever here is.

When I go to step forward, nothing happens. I glance down at my legs, and it is then I realize there is nothing there. No legs. No arms. And no body. As if I am a pair of eyes floating in the void. But would eyes have conscious thought? Honestly, I have no idea, but my first thought is no.

Maybe this is a dream. What a weird fucking dream.

What is the last thing I remember? I shuffle through my thoughts slower than dial-up internet and come up with nada. Why can't I remember anything?

"It's okay, Christy," I subconsciously whisper. "What *do* you remember?"

I stare into the darkness and dig deep into the corners of my mind, searching for clues. Who knows how much time passes—this place null of seconds or minutes or hours—before a speck of light appears. From where I stand—or am I floating?—it seems miles away. But I see it.

When I work to move closer to the speck, another appears. Then another. Soon, the specks form small clusters similar to constellations. I lose myself in the display, mesmerized by the illumination. Until it hits me. A memory.

At the end of my workday, I gathered up my things and headed to the wedding store for a planner.

One of the stars burns brighter in the darkness.

Inside the wedding store, I eventually asked one of the workers for help because I was so overwhelmed by all the options. She found exactly what I needed, rang me up, and then I left the shop.

Another star brightens.

Maybe these aren't stars. Maybe they are my memories. Memories of all the thoughts fogged over in my head right now. If a star burns brighter each time I remember, I need to try harder to conjure up what happened before I got here.

I pinch my eyes tightly and think, think, think. "Come on, come on."

When I open my eyes again, the star memories glow a brilliant white in the void surrounding me. Filling the dark space like pieces of an incomplete puzzle.

After the wedding shop, I went to the grocery store. There was a strange woman watching and following me. She freaked me out, but she disappeared after the deli. When I finished checking out, I bolted for the door and hauled ass to my car. I made it to my car and then… Nothing. As in I have no clue what happened after I reached my car.

The room around me slowly comes into view. My ankles and wrists are bound to the arms and legs of the chair I sit in. But it's as if I'm not in the chair. More like I'm hovering above it. When I glance down the length of my body, it feels as if I am staring into a mirror. Except the version of me in the chair isn't awake.

Am I dead?

Shit. Oh my god! Am I fucking dead?!

No way. No fucking way! There is no chance in hell I am fucking dead. Who the hell would strap a dead girl to a chair? Not anyone I know of. What would the point be?

I glance around the room and try to figure out where the hell I am. The space is huge. Maybe the size of two football fields. The exterior walls are concrete, as is the floor. Tall metal beams break up the space every hundred feet or so. Along the ceiling, water pipes with small sprinkler heads form a grid, occasionally dripping to mold-stained spots on the floor below. A single light fixture hangs from the ceiling where I sit, making it a central focal point, and it is sparse throughout the rest of the space.

Voices murmur around me, but I can't see anyone. I drift closer to myself.

How do I do this? How do I get back in my body and wake up?

This is the weirdest shit ever. Hovering inches from myself, I clamp my eyes shut and wish, over and over, to wake up. Whatever is happening, it cannot be good if I'm strapped to a chair.

"Please, please, please. Let me wake up," I mutter.

After a moment of pleading, a damp coolness pricks my lungs. Pain throbs at the back of my skull. Shrouded in darkness again, I crack my eyes open and the bright light stings my pupils. The mildew and stale cigarette smell is more pungent in my nose. Eager to get away from the unpleasant odor and this place, I go to stand. But a voice stops me.

A familiar voice. "He should be here any minute. You ready?" Who is that? And how do I know his voice?

Keeping my eyes shut, I jog through my memories and try to place the low timber of the man who just spoke. It isn't one I've heard much, but I swear it's familiar.

"More than ready." A woman's voice. And I have no idea who it belongs to.

Heavy boots clamber on the floor, quieting the more steps they take, and I assume the man walks away from me. "Go over there." He pauses. "Don't want him seeing you when he walks in. It'll ruin all the fun."

The boots trek back in my direction and panic inflates my lungs like helium. Is he going to hurt me? When I hear him settle not far from me, I breathe easier. *Just sit here and pretend you are still unconscious. Maybe they will leave you alone.*

Time ticks by in torturous silence. The man scrambles across from me, there is a faint crinkle before a scratching. Then, the faint odor of tobacco floats in my nose. I hold my breath and fight to not move as I inhale the unwanted smoke.

Another unfamiliar noise grabs my attention. *Splat. Flick. Splat. Flick.* Every part of me screams to open my eyes and bear witness to what the hell is happening. But a small voice in the back of my mind reminds me to remain quiet and stay put. I trust that small voice and don't move an inch.

I count another thirteen splats and flicks before a loud creak echoes behind me. Metal scraping metal. The clacking of shoes, growing louder and louder with each step in my direction. As badly as I want to spin around and learn where the sound came from, and who made it, I pretend to still be unconscious.

Then the room goes quiet again. Too quiet. The rapid beating of my pulse whooshes behind my ears and renders me deaf. Until I hear his voice.

"What. The. Fuck?" Heaven or hell. In life and death. I would recognize that voice anywhere. *Rick.* "Xander, what in the actual fuck?"

Shoes clack against the concrete floor again, louder

with each step, and I picture Rick in the dress shoes he wears to work. Then he stops. Too far back. I wish I wasn't so scared to just open my eyes. But it may make this whole situation worse if I do.

"Don't move another step." That must be Xander. "And it's Alex, actually."

I wrack my brain and try to place Xander or Alex—whichever the hell he is. *Think, think, think.* As I search my memory bank, a light kicks on. Xander—who is actually Alex—is the new bartender at Boundless.

What the hell?

"Why the fuck is my wife strapped to a fucking chair, *Alex*?" Rick seethes, his voice thick with venom.

For a split-second, I forget about everything happening around me. Rick just called me his wife. Behind my breastbone, the small, fist-shaped organ surges with new life and a tear slips from my closed eye.

"Since when is she your wife?" Alex roars. Wood scrapes against the floor a second before Alex's boots thump past me. Before Rick answers, Alex continues. "The price on her life just went up tenfold."

The price on my life? What the hell is going on?

On a whim, I crack my eyes open and hope Alex doesn't notice. The muscles in my neck are stiff as a board from hanging between my shoulders for so long. I angle my chin a little in the direction where I heard Rick, and peek at him and Alex.

"Who the fuck do you think you are? If you think you

can put a price on her" — Rick points at me and his eyes widen when he sees mine open — "you're stupider than I thought."

"Oh, there's a price. But you won't be paying it in cash."

Rick shakes his head ever so slightly and narrows his eyes at Alex. "Don't be cryptic, fucker."

Alex chuckles just as a new tip-tap enters the space. *Tip-tap, tip-tap, tip-tap.* Curious, I glance toward the sound and she catches me looking. The creepy bitch from the grocery store. I should have fucking guessed it.

"Look who's awake," she singsongs. Walking toward Alex and Rick, the woman exaggerates the sway of her hips. No clue who this woman is, but the way she carries herself indicates she thinks her shit doesn't stink. When I get out of this chair, I plan to show her how much it does.

At this point, I sit up straight and roll my neck until a rope tugs my windpipe. Not only am I tied to the damn chair, I'm completely bound.

The woman walks up to Rick and brushes her hands over his shoulders. Instantly, he steps out of her touch. "What's the matter, sugar? Gun shy now that the misses is here?"

"You're a sick bitch," Rick tells her. "What? I don't cave to your desires in the club, then I throw your ass on the street, and this is what you do? You bribe one of my employees and kidnap my wife? Really, you are a stupid cunt."

She waggles her finger in Rick's face. "Tsk, tsk. Might want to bite your tongue. Don't want me angry. Not when I control her fate." The stupid bitch points back in my direction.

"As I said earlier, you hurt her" —Rick glances over at me— "I will kill you."

The woman steps closer to Rick, and I want to scream for her to back the fuck up. But, right now, I sit helpless and at the mercy of Alex and this psychotic bitch, waiting to see what Rick will do next.

"I warned you," she hisses. A second later, she stands beside me and glances down. "Nice to meet you, *Christy*. I'm Lexi. Your replacement." Then she runs the end of a scalpel over my forearm and slices a four-inch wound in my flesh.

"Argh!" I scream. Bound to the chair, I have no way of adding pressure to the wound or covering it. "Bitch!"

Lexi laughs and the sound reminds me of the cackle of a witch in a movie. Maniacal and lifeless. A shiver slithers down my spine as bile threatens to come up. "You ain't seen nothing yet," she says, looking at me then Rick. And a huge part of me believes her. If this woman is as crazy as I think she is, she will kill me to get to Rick.

So, I play into her game. "Go ahead," I say, glancing over at Rick. "Take him." Rick's eyes on me, mine on his. The instant the psycho bitch shifts her gaze from me to him in my periphery, I widen my eyes at him. *Play along.*

It takes a beat, but when it clicks, Rick gives the slightest nod. He spins the ring on his thumb—our first bond exchange—with his index finger. When I spot the movement, I nod.

"Was ready for a change anyway," Rick says. He steps closer to me and Lexi, fixing his gaze on her. "But I'm not sure if you can handle me."

"Me?" Lexi points at her chest for emphasis. "I've done it all, baby. You want a real woman? Here I am." She lifts her hands over her head and spreads them wide. "But you need to prove you want me."

"Yeah? And how would I do that?" Rick steps up to her. If he moved two inches to his left, he would graze me.

"Fuck me," she says and Rick rolls his eyes. "In front of her. Now."

You have got to be fucking shitting me.

Rick lowers his eyes and studies me. The corner of his mouth twitches. His way of telling me he has a plan. Telling me not to worry. I swallow, drag in a deep breath, and close my eyes.

"Yeah, sure."

My eyes shut out the world as Rick's shoes tap a step closer to her. The contents of my stomach rise in my throat and the sudden urge to vomit creeps dangerously close. I refuse to open my eyes though. Refuse to watch what is about to happen. Might as well tear my heart out and stomp it into dust.

The room is quiet. More than quiet. And a sick part of my brain begs me to peek through the cracks of my lids and discover what the hell is actually going on. As peaceful as the darkness is, the unknown terrifies the hell out of me.

Just as I crack open my eyes, a hiss echoes through the air. A whoosh of air blows against the cut on my skin. Bodies shift beside me. Fast. Way too fast. And all I see is red.

TWENTY-NINE

RICK

My gorgeous girl. Her head bowed in fear of seeing what I may do with this woman. But my plan isn't what she thinks. Not by a long shot.

I step up to psycho bitch and plaster on an exaggerated smile. One she has no clue is as artificial as her tits. She smirks and tucks a strand of her bottle-dyed blonde hair behind her ear. When I'm as close to her as possible without gagging, I tip my head slowly her way and watch her eyes close.

Bingo, dumb bitch.

In a flash, I grip the hand with the scalpel and twist her wrist and arm, then pin it behind her back as I step behind her. The scalpel falls to the floor and I bend down, her wrist contorted in my grip, and pick it up from the floor.

"Ow! Ow! Ow!" she howls.

Xander or Alex—whatever the hell his name is—steps closer and I bring the scalpel to Lexi's throat. "Don't come any closer. I'll slit her throat," I warn.

His eyes dart from me to Lexi, again and again. Obviously, she means a lot to him. Otherwise, he would have already told me to kill her. His hands ball into fists at his sides as he scorches me with his stare. He has no idea what to do.

"Get her," Lexi hisses.

Alex shakes his head. "No, Lex. I can't. He'll kill you."

"I'm dead either way. Might as well not be for nothing," she demands.

I push the scalpel closer to her skin and a drop of blood trickles down her neck, below her jawline, and stops at her collarbone. "Alex, it's not worth it. Is your life worth what *she* wants?" I coax. "Is *she* risking her life for *you*? Or is she risking it for me?"

Alex pops his eyes up to mine. "She's my sister. I'd do anything for her." Although what he says may hold truth, there is a chink in his armor. Something underlying that has him doubting himself.

"Alex, I understand doing everything and anything for a sister. It's how things were with mine. But sometimes, we can't save everyone."

For so many years, I beat myself up over Harriett's death. Blamed myself for not being a better big brother. If I would have spent more time with her, talked to her more about what types of people to avoid, maybe she would still be alive today. For almost two decades, I blamed myself for her death and for my family falling apart. It wasn't until recently that it dawned on me how wrong I had been.

"But she's my sister," he whispers.

Just as I open my mouth to tell him he isn't responsible for her anymore, the door is kicked in and more than a dozen police officers run in with guns aimed our way. Immediately, I drop my arm from Lexi's neck and push her forward to Alex.

"That's them," I say to the officers as I point at Lexi and Alex.

"You'll pay for this," Lexi hisses at me and Christy.

"Shut the fuck up," Alex barks at her.

Officers cuff Lexi and Alex, pat them down and read them their rights. As Alex and Lexi are shoved out of the room, I cut the ropes binding Christy with the scalpel. As soon as all the binds are severed, she launches herself into my arms and suffocates me in hugs and kisses.

"God, I love you," she says, tightening her arms around my neck. "I love you, I love you, I love you."

I chuckle beneath her. "I love you too, gorgeous. And I hope you know I'd never let anything happen to you. Ever." She nods furiously in the crook of my neck.

"Excuse me, ma'am. Sir. We need to get a statement from you both."

An hour and a half later, Christy and I walk out of the warehouse. After giving the officers both of our sides of the story, letting them know how Alex and Lexi came to know who we were, then getting Christy's arm cleaned and bandaged, we are given permission to leave.

As we approach Christy's car, I tell her we will come back for it tomorrow. An officer overhears and offers to have it towed to the house at no cost to us. We accept the offer and tell them our address. Just as we walk off, Christy clutches my arm and stops me.

"The groceries are in the back."

Laughing for a beat, I say, "Just leave them. We'll grab them later."

Christy yanks on my arm harder. "No, there's perishables in there."

"Fine. I'll grab the bags."

Of all the things to worry about after being kidnapped, tied to a chair, and cut open. Leave it to my girl to worry more about the damn groceries.

After grabbing a quick bite to eat, followed by a hot shower, Christy and I climb into bed. Who the hell knows what time it is. And I refuse to check the clock. It's either really fucking late or super fucking early. Either way, I just want to lay in our bed and hold Christy in my arms for days.

She scoots back and molds her back to my front, clutching my arms as tight as they will go around her belly. In my arms, she trembles and I squeeze her impossibly tighter. "Thank you," she whispers into the dark comfort of our bedroom.

I kiss the back of her head and let my lips linger on the surface of her hair. The scent of her floral shampoo seeps into my senses and has me closing my eyes while my chest flutters. "You never have to thank me for saving you, gorgeous. It's my responsibility to keep you safe. And I will. Forever. Just wish I would've gotten to you sooner."

Christy slowly spins in my arms until she faces me. Her stormy blue eyes glisten with the threat of tears. Our room is blanketed in darkness, but enough light spills in from the streetlight outside to highlight the curves of her face. And without words so much is spoken between us in this quiet moment.

Fear and pain and so many unanswered "what if" questions. But most of all, it is her love that shines brightest. Love and trust and promise. My girl has been through so much in her life. So many highs and lows. And I consider myself a lucky son of a bitch to have her by my side.

No other woman seals the cracks in my heart like Christy. No other woman fulfills my desires and needs and life like Christy. Since the very beginning, she has been a bright burning star in my night sky. Navigating me to places I never knew existed. My compass.

"Sleep, gorgeous." I kiss her forehead and nose and lips. "I've got you."

Then she curls into my chest, kisses to the left of my sternum—just over my heart—and falls asleep in my arms. The only place she will ever be.

My eyes snap open and I take a deep breath, trying to calm my racing heart.

A week has passed since Alex and Lexi abducted me from the grocery store parking lot. And for the last seven nights, I've bolted awake with the smell of mildew and stale cigarettes lingering from my nightmare. Breaking out in a cold sweat when the flashes of Lexi cutting my skin appear behind my lids.

Lexi and Alex are sitting, uncomfortably I hope, in a jail cell while awaiting trial. Although I know this, it terrifies the hell out of me they could get out. The cops and our attorney have assured me, time and again, they won't be free anytime soon. Since both Alex and Lexi were involved with my kidnapping, they will each receive eight years. Add in Lexi cutting me and threatening to kill me, she may never leave the state penitentiary. Alex, on the other hand, will probably get parole, but not for more than a decade. Hopefully by then, he will have other things on his mind.

All in all, I truly believe Alex was a pawn in Lexi's grand scheme to get Rick. But just because someone you love asks you to do something heinous, doesn't mean you say yes. Life is a balance. Yin-yang. Black-white. Yes-no. Right-wrong. During childhood, most parents work to ingrain their morals on their children. Unfortunately, not all parents know good from evil. Even worse, not all parents care.

Yet another reason why I chose not to bring life into the world. Do I know right from wrong? Yes, I would like to say I do. But that doesn't mean shit nowadays. Too many outside forces clamber in and strip all the good away from young, impressionable minds, then fill them with lies and hate and greed. Not to say this happens with every child—because there are some really great humans in the world.

But it is a war I have no desire to fight.

Next to me, Rick stirs and tugs me closer to him. I rest a hand in the center of his chest and trail it down until I reach a few inches below his navel. Since the incident last week, sex has been absent from our life. Not because I don't want it. In actuality, I ache for it. But Rick is worried I want to use sex as an outlet instead of talking about my feelings.

My response… there isn't much to say. I may not be one-hundred percent comfortable walking or driving alone since everything happened, but fear *will not* hold me prisoner. I refuse to allow it.

"Morning, gorgeous." His voice is raspy and thick with sleep before he peppers kisses on my forehead. "You sleep okay?"

I drag my fingertip side to side an inch above his well-groomed pubic hair. "Yes and no," I answer, peering up into his lust drunk honey eyes. "Nothing to worry about. Promise." I zigzag my finger lower and graze the base of his dick. He shudders at the touch as his eyes roll back in his head.

"You should talk to me about it," he says, huskily. "Get it out in the open."

Leaning forward, I kiss along the dip above his collarbone as I skim my hand lower. "After," I say.

He growls beneath me. "You can't keep avoiding this, gorgeous." I bite my way down to his nipple. "We should talk about it."

I clamp onto his nipple. Hard. And he hisses loudly as I wrap my hand around his cock and yank. "I said, after. Please," I beg. "I need you."

Inching my hips closer to his, I rub the tip of his cock over my pussy. "Fuck, you're wet."

And within seconds, Rick brings me one step closer to paradise.

After we shower, Rick makes us breakfast and we talk. Mostly, I talk.

I tell him about my dreams since everything happened. Sometimes he wakes when I do, but most of the time he doesn't. I spill out every heart pounding, sweat inducing moment I have had since that night. And the great guy that Rick is, he sits there and listens to every word without interruption.

When I finish, he reassures me there is no more reason to worry. That Lexi and Alex will never bother us again. His certainty soothes any remaining panic and settles me in a way only Rick can.

After we finish washing the dishes, Rick spins to face me. "Why don't we go down to the courthouse today?"

I stare at him with narrowed eyes, thoroughly confused. Did I write down a wrong date for Alex and Lexi's hearing? Damnit. I swear I wrote them all down correctly.

When I don't say anything for several minutes, Rick brings both his hands to my face and cups my cheeks. "It's okay, gorgeous. Nothing to do with them. Alright?" I breathe deeply and nod. "I was thinking maybe we could go there and get married. Today. I have the band for your engagement ring set tucked away. And I may have already bought my band."

All the air gets sucked from my lungs. *Did he say what I think he said?* For us to get married today? "I… uh…" At a loss for words, I stand dumbfounded, blinking rapidly as the world around me turns fuzzy. He doesn't push me to answer. Just simply holds me and waits until I gather the courage to answer. A moment passes, then I snap out of my foggy state. "Yeah, okay," I whisper.

He squats down so we are eye to eye. "You sure? Don't say yes for me. Say it for you." I nod.

Although I wanted to spend some time planning out a wedding and deciding on small things like flowers and colors with Rick, going to the courthouse just feels *right*. On a later date, we can have the fancy party with our friends. And until then, the only people who need to know is Rick and me.

"I'm sure. Let's go."

We amble back to the bedroom, hand in hand. In the room, we break apart. Rick goes about dressing in black dress slacks and a black button-down shirt, leaving the top two buttons undone. I slip into a merlot red dress with three-quarter sleeves and the skirt ending just beneath my knees. The dress isn't as snug as others I own, but my curves are visible.

After I brush out my hair, I add a hint of product and leave it down. Once I add a light touch of makeup, I put my glasses back on and join Rick in the living room. When he glances up at me from the book in his hands, his eyes glaze over in a new light. Not lust or hunger or the urge to rip my dress off. No, a much stronger and deeper emotion blazes in his eyes. An emotion solely reserved for me. Call it love, if you will. But the way he looks at me, it is something so much greater than love.

He rises from the couch and saunters toward me. When he reaches me, he kisses each of my cheeks. "You look stunning. Ready?"

I nod. "Yes, more than ready."

The drive to the courthouse seems much quicker than any other drive in the city. Less than thirty minutes after we leave the house, Rick parks the car in the lot beside the courthouse. Rick gets out and comes around to open my door. When he offers me his elbow, I hook mine with his and we walk to the statuesque structure.

Ten minutes later, and we are sitting with a clerk, filling out the marriage license after providing our identification, and listening to her ramble on about marriage and divorce in the state of California. After we finish the license paperwork, she tells us to take a seat and we will be called in shortly for the ceremony.

We sit on a glossy oak bench in a long corridor. Other couples nearby chatter with one another while we sit in silence, cuddled close. Over the years, Rick and I developed our own language. One that requires no words. One based on trust and body language and expressions. With one slight change, Rick reads my every need, ache, desire, or pain. And it is moments like these—where we don't utter a single word—that the most thoughtful moments occur.

So while we sit in this chatter-filled space completely silent, Rick expresses how much he loves me, and I do the same. With light touches and occasional kisses and close proximity.

"Christy Nolan and Richard Matheson," a clerk yells from a room off to the right.

Inside the small room, a desk swallows up most of the space. The clerk tells us to stand on the side of the desk with no chairs. She verifies our identification once more and tells us the judge will be in momentarily.

When the door opens again, a rotund man wearing a black robe enters. "Ms. Nolan. Mr. Matheson. I'm Judge Jenkins. This is Clerks Roberta Johnson and James Townsend. They will be witnesses for the ceremony." He sits in the chair. "Let's begin."

The judge goes through a spiel that feels longer than it took us to drive here. When he finishes, he offers us a chance to say vows.

Taking a deep breath, I start. "Rick, for the rest of my life, I will honor and cherish you. I promise to take care of you, however necessary." I pause and waggle my eyebrows. Rick shakes his head and grins ear to ear. "But most of all, I promise to love you for eternity."

The judge nods, then waves his hand to Rick. "Mr. Matheson."

After a quick, rattled breath, Rick starts. "You are the most brilliant star in the night sky, Christy. A life without you isn't a life at all. I vow to protect and respect you.

Promise to keep you safe and hold you close. To love and worship you until my dying day, and every day after."

A moment later, we exchange our "I do's", slip on our wedding bands, and Rick kisses me as if no one else is in the room. After everyone has signed and notarized our marriage license, we leave the courthouse. Once my feet bounce off the bottom step, Rick hoists me up in his arms and spins me around like a teenager.

"Time to celebrate, wife."

This is the first time Rick has called me his wife… when we were actually married. I don't wish to rehash the first night I heard him say it. That night is tainted. But hearing it now, every molecule inside me bursts into flames.

"Yes, husband. Let's celebrate."

THIRTY-ONE

RICK

Christy and I step out of the shower and towel off. Five minutes ago, she screamed my name so loud, it wouldn't shock me if the neighbors three houses down heard. Once dry, I hang my towel and smack her ass as I step out of the bathroom. She doesn't yelp. Not my girl. She moans.

After I dress in jeans and a shirt, I leave her in the bedroom to get ready while I start dinner. In the kitchen, I take out all the ingredients for chicken cordon bleu, roasted root vegetables, and a side salad and get to work.

I chop all the vegetables first. Then toss the root vegetables in olive oil and herbs and put them in a roasting pan in the oven. Next, I assemble the chicken cordon bleu. Just as I pin the last one with a toothpick, Christy comes in and works beside me on the salad.

For a moment, I stare at my wife. *My wife.* Stunning in her sleek black maxi dress. Hair in a messy, wet bun on top of her head. If there weren't other things in life to do, I would get lost in her nonstop.

"Everything won't be ready on time if you keep staring at me like that," she teases.

I step up behind her, my hands pinned at my back, and whisper in her ear. "They would understand." Because it is true. Thomas and Ella wouldn't be upset if I told them I stopped cooking to fuck Christy against the countertop. If anything, they would tell me to turn the stove and oven off and continue.

Christy pauses her assembling of the salad and groans. The vibration as needy as her ass that grinds against my groin. I kiss the curve of her neck and back away. Dinner first. Then, no holds barred.

Shortly after I put the chicken in the oven with the vegetables, I clean the kitchen and wash up. As I'm pulling the food out of the oven, Christy walks in with Ella and Thomas on her heels. Smiles and hugs are exchanged before we head to the dining table and sit.

After the incident two months ago, I wasn't sure how Christy would handle being near other people for a while. For more than a week, she clung to my side. Her job had been generous and gave her time off to recuperate. During that time, she was never more than a few feet away. Also during that time, I worried the most. Worried that what happened to her at the hands of Alex and Lexi—which we later learned, during their hearings, were Alexander and Alexis, twins—tweaked something inside her. Similar to what happened to Sarah in Georgia. And every night I prayed my wife would heal from all of it.

Christy is so much stronger than I have ever given her credit for.

Within two weeks, she smiled and laughed and teased me like nothing ever happened. Just after she told me about every nightmare she'd had since the incident. Once she got it off her chest, it was as if she had permission to heal and be herself again.

And although she and I have had sex several times since everything happened, tonight is the first time Thomas and Ella have joined us since that night.

She hasn't told me, but my gut says Christy confided in Ella with some of what happened to her. And the idea of them discussing it makes me smile. Christy needs someone, besides me, that she can talk with and free her burdens. Thomas and I have somewhat done the same. The friendship and bond Christy and I have developed with Thomas and Ella is invaluable.

"Everyone up for dessert and a movie in the living room?" Christy asks as we clear the table.

While I finish loading the dishwasher, Christy takes the pan of cherry cobbler she made earlier, plates, and forks to the living room. As I'm putting the last of the dishes in, I hear the movie cue up in the living room.

Two portions of cherry cobbler and an hour of the movie later, Christy starts traipsing her fingertips up and down my thigh. Not something we set up, but it is sort of her cue she wants to play now.

I shift on the couch and face her, cupping her cheek and kissing the hell out of her. Her moan vibrates against my tongue and my eyes roll back in my head. Is it possible that making her my wife makes her that much more delectable? For me, it does.

When I open my eyes and peer over at Thomas and Ella, I see them kissing while Thomas strokes his fingers back and forth between Ella's thighs. My lips grow more urgent on Christy's as I slide her dress up, graze my fingers up her thigh, and dip them inside her hot, slick folds.

Tonight, Christy holds the reins. Until she signals she's ready to have another person touching her, only I touch her. Over the last few days, we discussed our comfort levels with Thomas and Ella. It is imperative Christy feels safe no matter what. So, when she told me she felt as at ease with them as she did me, I offered up something we had never done.

Going forward, Christy and Ella have free rein to kiss. If either of us had the urge, Thomas and I could as well. But I would still not kiss Ella, and the same held true for Christy and Thomas. The four of us are on the same page with that.

Christy whimpers in my ear. Her breath jagged, and her body begging for release. I slip the top of her dress down and expose her glorious breasts. Perfect lift. Plump. Firm. Nipples the color of summer licked skin. I take a taut bud into my mouth and suck and nip as my fingers slide in and out of her.

"Yes…" she moans as I grind my teeth over her nipple.

The moment she comes on my fingers, I slip them out and suck them off. So fucking delicious. Swear to God, she tastes better as my wife.

Once Ella comes beside her, Christy kisses her then lays her flat on the couch. In a blink, Christy and Ella are stripped bare and lapping the cum off of each other.

Unzipping my jeans, I drop them to the floor, followed by my shirt, and stroke my cock. Thomas follows suit as we watch our wives suck on each other.

Not that it has never happened, but it has been years —years before Christy—since I did anything with a man. But watching our wives. Seeing his arousal while I'm stroking mine in my clenched fist. I want more from this relationship we share with them.

In two short strides, I stand inches from Thomas. Both of us stroking ourselves. I glance down and watch his hand as he strokes up and down his cock. A hunger simmers low in my balls and trickles up my spine. With each pump of his shaft, greed licks a fire in my veins. But it isn't until Thomas reaches forward and lifts my chin that I see the ache inside him. An ache solely directed at me.

His jaw slackens and, in my periphery, his fist jerks harder. With hooded eyes, he steps into me, releases his cock, and slams his mouth onto mine. I open up and his tongue dives in, licking and sucking and mouth fucking mine.

There is something so completely different about kissing or touching a man than a woman. Kisses with either can be tender and sweet, or desperate and needy. A woman's lips are soft and supple, her jaw less rigid and angular, her skin smooth and scent sweet. Whereas a man's lips are firm and plump, his jawline sharp and strong, the skin of his neck and jaw gritty and rugged, his scent woodsy and rich.

Both divine. Both send a surge of white hot energy straight to my cock.

I break our kiss, slip my fingers into his hair and make a fist, and yank his head to the side. Running my tongue from the base of his ear to the curve where his neck meets his shoulder, I clamp down and suck the toned musculature beneath my lips.

"Fuck," he hisses. Against my hip, his cock jerks and I palm it.

My hand glides along his rock hard shaft—once, twice—before he inches back. For a moment, it crosses my mind that maybe Thomas doesn't want this side of the relationship and I overstepped my boundaries. I hadn't considered that maybe he had never been with another man before and only enjoyed the female aspect of our lifestyle.

But all thoughts go out the window the second he drops to his knees in front of me.

He reaches up, palms my balls, and rolls them in his hand like a pair of Chinese Baoding balls. I lean into his touch and hang my head, eyes fixated on his every move. After one, two, three rolls of my balls, he glances up at me with fire in his mossy green eyes. With his eyes locked on mine, hand massaging my sac, his tongue darts out and licks the crown of my cock. A shudder ripples out from his touch and spreads over every square inch of my body like an electrical grid.

Before I tell him how spectacular his hot tongue feels circling the head of my cock, he grips my hip and takes me in his mouth.

"Goddamn," I grunt out. Thomas massages the underside of my cock with his tongue as he goes from the root to the head. I grip his hair and hold him in place. "So. Fucking. Good."

Sucking cock has previously been added to his resume. No one sucks a man's dick like this without previous experience. While I hold his head in place, my hips piston and drive my cock in and out of his greedy mouth. As I thrust my cock to the back of his throat, I stare at his right hand as it pumps his own.

Fire licks hotter in my veins. Scorching me from head to toe. Sweat seeps from every pore. Building. Climbing. Winding around my spine and tightening. Before I explode in his mouth, I pull out and bring him to his feet. As much as I'd like to shoot cum down his throat, I'd much rather pump it into my wife's cunt.

Just as Thomas is about to question why I stopped, I grab hold of him and shove my tongue down his throat. After he strokes mine a few times, I lick and bite my way along his jaw, to the front of his throat, and down to his sternum. I pause my descent to give some appreciation to his lean, fit body. Drawing circles around each of his nipples with my tongue and then nipping the pert nubs.

As I run my lips and tongue over the ridged surface around his navel, I dig my hands into his ass cheeks. Below my chin, his dick jerks and grazes me. A wicked idea surfaces as lick over the shaved skin around the base of his cock.

I glance up at Thomas, my cheeks stinging from the wide grin plastered on my face. "Everything fair game?" I ask.

He cocks his head to the side and studies my face a beat. A moment passes before he nods, cups my jaw, and says, "Suck me."

Fisting his cock, I lift it and run my tongue from his balls to the tip before taking him deep in my throat. Thomas has the perfect dick. When aroused, his length easily hits the back of my throat with a couple inches to spare. And girth… just enough to stretch my lips tight, but not painfully so. For a woman, it may be a different experience. Not too veiny. Deep ridge lines around the crown —perfect for rubbing the elusive spot most men can't find in a woman's body.

Would it be odd to say I have cock envy?

As I bob up and down Thomas's cock, taking him all the way to the root, our wives cry out beside us. And for a split-second, we both forget about us and stare at how glorious they are on the couch. Currently, Ella lays on her back with one leg draped over the back of the couch while Christy rides her face and plays with Ella's clit. By now,

I'm certain they have both orgasmed several times. But Thomas and I have ignored their cries in an effort to chase our own.

Just as Christy bends back down and puts her mouth between Ella's thighs, Thomas continues to fuck my face. His hips jerk back and forth, and his groans grow louder with each lap of my tongue. And that's when I stop.

The moment he is no longer in my mouth, he glances down at me in question. I point to the ground beneath us. "Lay down," I tell him. Without hesitation, he drops and lies on the floor, resting his head on his hands.

I position myself between his thighs, spit onto my fingers, and watch him as I spread it between his ass cheeks. If possible, his mossy green eyes immediately shift to an almost black-green as his lids grow heavy.

"New territory?" I ask.

He nods. "Never been comfortable with anyone else there," he answers.

I jut my chin toward our wives. "Not even Ella?"

He shakes his head. "Never been brought up." His eyes roll back as I swirl my index finger over the tight hole and press slightly. Part of me relishes in the fact I will be the one to break this cherry. That I will claim his ass before anyone else.

I lower myself, hovering less than an inch above the tip of his cock, and take him back in my mouth as my finger slowly presses against the tight pucker of his ass. When I breach his body's initial resistance, his cock jerks in my mouth. "Holy fuck..." he hisses.

He fists my hair as I suck his cock in measured strokes and finger fuck his ass. As my pace picks up with my mouth, seconds later, it picks up with my fingers. Saliva coats his cock and rolls down his balls to his ass and lubricates my finger as it plunges in. His grip on my hair tightens with each tongue stroke up his shaft.

In my mouth, his cock grows impossibly thicker as his climax nears. Thomas's grunts and breathy cries come faster. And I know he is close. As if on cue, a hint of saltiness hits my tongue and I growl around him, picking up speed.

"Oh fuck. *Fuck, fuck, fuck…*" he hisses.

Then his hips press into the floor as he yanks my hair and holds me in place. Hot cum shoots to the back of my throat and I continue to suck him off as I withdraw my finger from his ass. When his orgasm calms, I climb up his body and kiss him roughly. Once our lips break apart, I rub the tip of my cock against his ass. "One day, it won't be my finger in your ass," I promise.

A wicked gleam lights his face. "Better be a man of your word." Something about the challenge in his words ignites me. "Let me finish you," he offers.

I glance over at our wives—our beautiful as fuck wives—and watch them a beat as they finger fuck each other, lips locked in a vicious battle of lust. As much as I would rather cum between Christy's legs, nights like this aren't just about the two of us. It's about all four of us. The bond we share. The connection we have developed that continues to flourish.

Scooting back to lean against the couch, I spread my legs, stroke my cock, and invite Thomas to finish what he started. And it doesn't take long before I spurt down his throat and taste my cum on his lips.

After hours of sucking and fucking, the four of us crash—Thomas and Ella staying at the house. Our sleep the best it had been in years. And an idea sparks when I wake in the next morning.

As everyone congregates in the kitchen for breakfast, I lure Thomas away from the girls. "You mind if I run an idea past you before mentioning it to the wives?"

He nods. "Shoot."

"What are your thoughts on the four of us living together?"

Ella and Thomas celebrated their ninth wedding anniversary November seventh—a little more than a month before the four of us met. They had been in a relationship for two years prior to marrying. When they first met, Ella was barely eighteen and Thomas seven years her senior. Of course Ella's family stirred up trouble, but as soon as she was able to leave home, she moved in with Thomas. The rest is history.

We may not know everything about one another, but both Christy and I are absolutely comfortable with the two of them. And my instincts tell me Thomas reciprocates.

The four of us living together probably seems odd to the outside world. The world of man-woman, single-partner relationship enthusiasts. But to us, living together is ultimate trust. Just as with a relationship with any two people, everything boils down to compatibility, trust, companionship, and desire.

Not every night would involve sexual acts with the four of us. Just as I want nights solely with my wife, Thomas and Ella will want the same. With cohabitation comes other factors. Safety and security. Stronger bonds—friendship and sexual. Companionship when others work odd hours.

Thomas rubs the tip of his finger over his lower lip. Eyes zoned out as they focus on something in the distance. "It would have its perks," he says. "Of course we'd need to sit down and hash out some things. With the four of us, rules, and where we'd live."

A smile kicks up my lips. "If you're good, we can talk logistics later. But first, let's see how our wives feel about the whole idea."

Three years later

ELLA WALKS into the open shower and steps under the second stream of hot spray. As her head tips back and the water trails down her body, I inch closer to her and trace my fingers from the top of her sternum to her pubic bone.

Although I have zero intention of fucking her in the shower right now, it is only natural to touch her every chance I get. Since we met Ella and Thomas, life has only gotten better.

Ella and I developed a fast friendship. Our bond rivals my other friendships, but each has their place in my life. Two and a half years ago, Ella, Thomas, Rick, and I moved in together. We found a house more suitable for all of our needs. One that gave us space, if we wanted to be with our respective spouses, but also brought us together when we so desired.

Shortly after we all moved in, I invited Liz and Tiffany over, as well as Sarah and Jackson. Having so many people who love me nearby grips my heart in unspeakable ways. But on that night, I fidgeted more than any other time in my life. It stirred up past memories of rejection and heartbreak.

In the end, everything worked out perfect.

"Thanks for coming over tonight," I say, my eyes bouncing between Sarah, Jackson, Liz, and Tiffany. "It means so much to me and Rick." At his name, Rick squeezes my thigh and presses a kiss to my shoulder. The perfect balm for my shaky nerves.

"I wouldn't miss a chance to spend time with you," Sarah tells me. "We're not as close, distance wise, as we were in Georgia, but it's not a hike to get here."

Nodding, I take a deep breath and remember one of the main reasons why I wanted everyone here tonight. Before everyone arrived, Rick and I asked Ella and Thomas if it was okay if we shared who we all were with my friends. Not that I needed the world to know I occasionally enjoyed the company of another woman or man, besides my husband. More like I didn't want to hide who I was from the people closest to my heart. And sharing who I am is important to me.

Acceptance is important. A peace of mind I have needed for years.

I swallow down the building lump in my throat, take a drink of water, then tell my two best friends about the side of my life I have never shared with them. "Sarah. Liz. Jackson. Tiffany. I introduced you to Ella and Thomas when you first got here." Their heads bob in acknowledgment. "What I didn't tell you is that the four of us live here. Together."

For a moment, Sarah and Liz stare at me in slight confusion. Certainly they are curious as to why we have "roommates" when we can afford to live on our own. And by Thomas and Ella's outward appearance, so can they.

"Okay…" Sarah says, judgment free but still unsure of where this will lead.

But when Liz's eyes light up, it is obvious she knows where this conversation is going. After all, I did mention Rick and I were kinkier than people realized. Perhaps she just couldn't grasp the gravity of it all.

"Ella and Thomas are married," I say. "And, occasionally, the four of us sleep together."

The room is so silent you can hear every breath I take. A voice screams in my head for someone to say something. Anything. For my friends to tell me they hate me. Or, hopefully, the opposite. When the silence stretches out and no one moves an inch, I pinch my eyes closed and mentally berate myself for this whole admission.

Stupid, stupid, stupid.

You should have just kept your mouth shut and left things as they were. Now you have probably lost more people you love. A boulder slowly crushes my soul.

"Well damn," Liz says. "You told me you were kinky, but hell." She glances between Rick, me, Ella, and Thomas and shakes her head. "This here." Liz waves her finger in front of us. "This is fucking hot."

I exhale the longest held breath on earth and laugh. Leave it to

Liz to turn a tense moment into the polar opposite. Bless Liz and her craziness. "Thanks, Lizzy. Can always count on you." I wink at her.

"Christy," Sarah speaks up. Her emerald green eyes study my stormy blues for a moment. Curiosity and sadness prick her expression. "Were you afraid to tell me — us — this?"

Sarah's genuine kindheartedness has always plucked my heartstrings. I shouldn't have been worried about her reaction — or Liz's — but I was. They are my sisters. The only two non-romantic family I have. Counting their significant others is off the shelf until they fully commit. And because of what happened with my flesh and blood family so many years ago, I lived in fear of receiving that rejection from Sarah and Liz.

I nod. "Yes."

Sarah reaches across the table and sets her hand down, palm up. After I place my hand in hers and she clutches mine with a strength I didn't know she possessed, she says, "Nothing you say or do will ever make me not love you. We are family. Jackson and I may not be as wild in the bedroom as you all" — a smile lights up her face — "but we are far from tame. If this is who you are, I'm happy you found Rick. And I'm also glad you both found Ella and Thomas."

My heart is a hot air balloon, inflating bigger and bigger, and soaring in the clouds. A tear rolls down my cheek as I stare at my best friend. The woman whose opinion means more to me than I fathomed. "Thank you."

After we finish washing up, I turn off the shower and we step out. As we towel off, I stare at us in the floor to ceiling mirror in the bathroom. Tonight, the four of us are going to a party hosted by another couple we met through Boundless. It is their third party, and each has been successful as far as attendees.

"What are you wearing?" Ella asks, snapping me out of my foggy trance.

I glance at her in the mirror. "Red lace. You?"

"Was thinking maybe I'd wear that black piece I got the other day when we were shopping."

That little black piece had my panties wet in the fitting room we shared. Ella stood five inches taller than me. Her tits more than a mouthful, and her hips curvy as hell. Not that I didn't have curves of my own, but hers were sinful. In the little black number she tried on... she was sin personified.

"Yes," I say all breathy. "Definitely the black."

She drops her towel to the floor and saunters over to me. Stopping in front of me, she swipes a finger between my legs and closes her eyes. "So fucking wet. Shall I clean you up before we finish getting ready?"

We shouldn't, but I want her tongue on my skin. Cleaning the juices between my legs. "Yes," I breathe.

Ella dips two fingers inside me and starts walking me backward toward the attached bedroom. When my knees hit the mattress, she slides her fingers out and pushes me onto the bed. Fifteen minutes and several orgasms later—for us both—we crawl off the bed and finish getting ready.

Ella and I get ready for the party in the joint bedroom and bathroom. When the four of us moved in together, it was key to find a house with adequate space for everyone.

We ended up with this magnificent three-story, five-bedroom house with a four-car garage, an oversized kitchen, and an open floor plan. The third level is intended to be attic space, but we converted it to office space for us all. Both couples have a bedroom. The third bedroom hosts a California king bed for nights when we all want to sleep in the same space. Most of our time together is spent in the third bedroom. Bedroom number four is the home gym. And bedroom five is a library—because that's what happens when one woman owns a bookstore and the other loves books.

All in all, this home is everything I dreamed of. Beautiful. Elegant. Comfortable.

Once we are dressed, Ella and I meet the guys in the living room. Rick and Thomas eye us up and down, and hunger floods my veins. Rick rises off the couch and walks toward us. Dressed in all black, I eat every inch of him up with my eyes.

When he reaches us, he wraps his hands around me, bends down, and kisses the spot beneath my ear. "You look delectable, gorgeous," he purrs. Glancing at Ella, he points at what she's wearing and says, "Love the new piece."

Thomas steps up to Ella and runs his hands down her sides. "Fuck, baby. Not sure this will stay intact on the way there."

I glance over at Ella and mouth, "Told you."

After Ella and I slip on our coats, we pile into the car. Rick drives and I sit up front with him. During the forty-five minute drive, Thomas and Ella explore each other in the backseat and I turn sideways in the seat to watch them. Legs spread as wide as possible, I play with my clit while Thomas devours Ella's pussy. On occasion, Rick reaches across the console and dips his finger in me.

When we pull up to the party, we park along the street and head inside.

These parties are strictly invitation only. For the most part, the number of people here is limited as well. Less crowded and more enjoyable.

Once the front door closes, Rick removes my coat. Beneath the red trench coat, equally vibrant red lace hugs my body like a second skin. The strapless piece has a straight bustline at the start of my cleavage, while the bottom hem sits an inch below the apex of my thighs. There is no underlay. The simple piece is just lace and a zipper at the back. Every inch of my skin is on display beneath the soft material.

"Stunning," Rick says as he traces up the inside of my thigh.

Beside me, Thomas removes Ella's coat. The second it's off, my mouth waters and I want to lick every dip and curve of her body.

That little black piece has me chomping at the bit. Honestly, there is almost no fabric in the first place. Just a web of one-inch strips of leather joined with rivets and rings. It starts and ends in almost the same places as the dress I'm wearing, with the exception of the crotch. Which is exposed.

We meander through the party, grab some wine and hors d'oeuvres, chat with other couples while music plays low in the background. The hosts—husband and wife—walk around and chat with everyone before everything begins. They're such a fascinating couple—and how they met even more intriguing—and the six of us have recently bonded. But they have a strict rule. They don't join other couples. Just watch.

A few minutes later, the music pours louder from the speakers. The signal that everyone has arrived and the party can begin.

Rick, me, Ella, and Thomas wander over to a puffy cloud of large pillows on the floor. After Ella and I step onto the makeshift lounge area, I spin and face her. "Time for me to repay the favor from earlier." I drop to my knees, spread her legs and lick the length of her slit.

Rick steps behind Ella and fondles her tits while kissing the curve of her neck. Thomas squats down behind me, scoots my feet further apart, and drags his finger over my slit before dipping it inside me.

It doesn't take long before Ella and I lay completely exposed. Rick and Thomas slowly peel off their clothes and join us on the fluffy pillows. We watch other couples in the house lick and suck and fuck. Something each of us gets off on seeing.

Over the last three years, some rules each of us established has fallen away. Some still hold true. The husbands don't fuck the other's wife unless all are present. That is a hard rule we all agreed will never change. But kissing is the one that has relaxed the most.

Since the four of us started living together, and, for all intents and purposes, are bound to each other, it is only natural for us to exchange that simple intimacy. Thomas's kiss will never light my soul on fire like Rick's does, but it fulfills the bond we share. The same for Ella and Rick when they kiss. And the four of us stated in the beginning how important it is to have an open line of communication. We have no room for insecurity or jealousy in our relationship.

Thomas lines his cock up between my legs and strokes himself along my slit. "You ready, kitten?" he whispers in my ear.

Something else we all share... pet names. Ella and Thomas never exchanged pet names before us. Both men now answer to daddy, and Ella and I respond to kitten. At first, it turned my stomach, but then it dawned on me that it's just a name. Roleplay. It doesn't define who I am, just the role I play.

"Yes, daddy."

Thomas rubs the head of his cock up and down my slit again, slow and steady, then thrusts inside me. "So fucking tight, kitten."

He pumps his hips as I clutch his ass. Thomas has a magnificent cock. Nothing gets me off better than Rick, but Thomas is a close contender. As if the universe knew Ella and I needed more to be thoroughly satisfied in life.

"Fuck me harder, daddy," I moan.

Thomas hikes my legs over his shoulders and drives into me harder. Beside us, Ella rides Rick's cock like a rodeo champion. As I watch her grind on top of my husband, a molten heat boils in my core. Her eyes glance my way and we stare at one another. And for a beat, it is me and Ella.

Seconds later, I come on Thomas's cock and Ella shudders over Rick.

When we float down from the clouds, Thomas goes to his wife and Rick joins me. As I mount Rick, I moan at the pressure of his girth stretching my walls. Thomas may have a magnificent cock, he may be able to make me come undone, but nothing will supersede the way Rick feels inside me. As if he was made specifically for me. Thomas and Ella lay on their side facing us as he props her leg up and enters her from behind. Such a sight to behold.

As I claw Rick's pecs and grind my hips over his pelvis, he sits up and kisses up my neck. When he reaches my ear, he whispers, "Remember who you belong to, gorgeous." His hand trails up my spine, grips the hair at the base of my skull, wraps it around his wrist and tugs.

"Always," I answer.

"Remember who I belong to."

"Yes."

No matter who enters our lives, one factor holds true. Rick Matheson belongs to me. And I belong to him. Until my dying day, regardless of whatever challenges life throws at us, he will always have my undying devotion.

BONUS CONTENT

ELLA

Never did I think Thomas and I would ever find another couple like us. Two people who enjoy exploring their sexual fantasies the way we do. A couple so open and compassionate and generous. No one Thomas and I have been with compares to Christy and Rick. Chloe and Dominic were close, but our connection with them was strictly primal.

Before Thomas and I met, I had been with my fair share of people. Men and women both. I started exploring my sexuality at the ripe age of eleven. I remember my first experience was with my best friend at the time. Brianna and I were both curious about what we had heard some of our older friends talking about. Sex and masturbating. Although we were young and inexperienced, we wanted to see what the big deal was.

. . .

One day after school, Brianna and I walked home to my house. My parents wouldn't be home from work for hours. At first, we had no clue what to do. So, we listened to music and sat on my bed like we normally did.

"Are you nervous?" I asked her.

"A little," she told me.

Slowly, we inched closer and closer to each other. A few songs played before her arm brushed against mine. Another song ends and my fingers traced over her denim-covered thigh. As each song started and ended, we made another move.

Excitement flashed in my veins as her fingertips explored my small breasts through the cotton fabric of my t-shirt. No one had ever touched me like this. And no one made me tingle the way Brianna did.

Thirty minutes in, I experienced my first kiss. It was wet and sloppy and exhilarating. I didn't want to stop kissing her. So we kept kissing.

Ten minutes later, I ran my fingers through another person's pubic hair for the first time. Although it was soft and curly like mine, I enjoyed the texture of it so much more than my own. Course and velvety at the same time.

Another ten minutes later and I dipped my fingers inside a girl for the first time. Slipped my fingers in and out. Memorized the ridges inside her walls. Gloried in the warm wetness dripping from her core. And relished the taste of her on my tongue.

After that day, Brianna and I remained friends. But we were never anything else. Exploring my sexuality with my friend first is something I will never forget. When we started high school and Naomi stepped into the picture, I saw less of Brianna. From time to time, we still catch up, calls or texts, but not much else. A few years back, she married a guy she met in college. A month ago, they welcomed their first child into the world.

Brianna was my first sexual experience. Before I met Thomas, there were easily dozens more. I never kept track. But after learning what sex tasted like and how my body reacted to it, I hungered for it. It didn't bother me that guys in the school told other guys I was a freak in the bedroom. Nor did it bother me that girls either hated or envied me.

But the day I met Thomas is one I will never forget.

Naomi and I just graduated high school. To celebrate, she wanted to go out and party.

Going to clubs or bars was nothing new for us. A guy she dated a couple years back made us fake IDs and we'd been getting past bouncers for two years. We never drank, just had a good time.

That's what I thought we were doing tonight. Going to a night club.

This was a club alright. Just not the typical places we went. Nope, this one is packed wall to wall with varying degrees of nudity and lots of sex. I am far from a prude, but this… I wasn't prepared.

After giving Naomi the third degree, she swore to stick by my side. That lasted all of five minutes. Naomi, my best friend, ditched me in an underground sex party. She texted her apology and I replied with how much she sucked.

I bought a drink, found an empty couch and watch a woman give oral to a man. It wasn't long before some old pervert sat next to me and tried to cop a feel. Across the couch circle, Thomas saw my discomfort and swooped in for the rescue.

He asked my name and I'd given him my fake name. He pinned the lie immediately. Minutes passed as we chatted. Our attraction was immediate and irresistible. In no time, he'd peeled my clothes from my skin and took me in that grungy warehouse.

I'd had sex in front of others before, but not people I didn't know. It was awkward and liberating. When we left the party, Thomas invited me to his place. Reluctant as I was, I caved. Best decision I ever made. Because after that night, and some tense moments with my parents, Thomas and I were inseparable.

We fucked like fiends every chance we got. And two years later, Thomas asked me to be his wife. Saying yes was as easy as breathing. Saying I do on our wedding day had been even easier.

The rest, as they say, is history.

I walk into the third bedroom in our house —the joint bedroom. Christy lays naked, sprawled across the sheets on the bed built for all four of us. Her legs spread wide, her fingers circling the bud between her thighs. Majority of the time spent in our house is without clothes on, and we all love the freedom.

Crawling onto the bed, I go straight to her and kiss my way up the inside of her leg. When I reach her apex, she lifts her hand away and I eat her pussy like it's my last meal. Christy tastes divine. Like no other woman I've had my mouth on. Sweet as berries with a hint of salt.

As I lick her clit and finger her cunt, the light padding of two sets of feet enter the room. I peek up over Christy's shaved mound and watch her tweak her nipples. Her lusty eyes look over my shoulders at the two men who entered the room. Our husbands.

I spread my legs farther apart and push my ass into the air as I finger fuck my girl. 'Cause that's what Christy is — my girl. Just as I am her girl. Her walls clamp around my fingers and I lick her faster. As she comes, I withdraw my fingers and suck her folds.

Behind me, the mattress dips. I lift my ass as high as it will go and wait. When I finish sucking Christy off, she shifts position and slides down beside me.

With my face pressed into the mattress, Christy traces a line from my neck to the end of my spine, down my ass crack — where she stops and teases my hole for a moment — and along my slit. I haven't determined if it's Rick or Thomas behind me yet. They're just out of my line of sight.

Christy continues to run her finger over my folds for one, two, three strokes before she dips inside. She finger fucks me slow and steady for a minute before running her fingers back up to my tight ass. Painting circles around the hole, she slowly pushes inside and I gasp.

Once she finds a rhythm, she kicks her legs back and

is on her knees and one hand. With her finger pumping in and out of my ass, a cock slides inside my pussy.

"Fuck, you're wet," Rick groans.

I push up onto all fours and repeat the same Christy just did with me. Soon, we are ass fucking each other while we both have cocks filling us.

No possible way life could get any better.

THOMAS

Ella's finger pumps in and out of Christy's ass as I fuck the shit out of her pussy. Honestly, I want my dick in her ass. I tap Ella's hand and she peeks up at me. I jerk my chin to the side, silently asking my wife to remove her finger. When she does, Christy's hole stays open a beat as I spread her cheeks wide.

I grab the bottle of lube we keep near the bed and squirt some down her crack. It slides down and I smear it around her hole.

Christy sucks in a breath and peeks over her shoulder. "Fuck my ass, daddy," she purrs.

She always called Rick daddy when they played, but Ella never called me anything and I only called her pet. The first time we allowed the pet name exchange between us all, I wasn't sure how I would feel about it. The first time it fell from her lips, my cock got a new surge of life. Has happened every time since. Occasionally, Ella calls me daddy, but it has a different effect than when Christy does it. For Ella, the term daddy has a dark history. Her saying it shocks me. But Christy truly is a kitten when she begs for daddy.

"You want daddy's fat cock in your tight ass, kitten?"

"Please, daddy. I need your fat cock deep in my ass."

Fuck my life.

Since Ella and I met Rick and Christy, I have never fucked so many times in my life. Ella and I went at it like rabbits before, or so I thought. But with Ella's and Christy's appetites under one roof, we fuck several times a day.

Rick pounds into Ella while I fuck Christy's tight, plump ass. Our women scream and cry out in pleasure. The salty scent of sex fills the spacious room. After Christy's third orgasm, I spurt into her ass. Ella begs for it harder, coming on Rick a moment later for the second time and he releases inside her.

After cleaning up, we all collapse on the bed and pass out for a time.

When I wake, the room is dark. Everyone still in the bed, but I hear Ella and Christy kissing and playing with each other. Rick lies behind me, but from what I can tell, he is still asleep. I slowly stroke myself in the dark under the comforter. The more I stroke my cock, the more my hips rock and my ass bumps Rick.

Quickly, I learn he is far from asleep. And his cock is hard as steel.

I inch my ass closer to him, rocking back and forth as I stroke myself. When the head of his cock grazes my ass crack, I clench my cheeks and pinch the head slightly. With each rock of my hips, I bring myself closer to him. He doesn't move, but his hand runs up and down his shaft. Every few trips up, his fingers run up the length of my crack.

A few more rocks back and the head of Rick's cock presses firmly against my ass. My back to his chest. He wraps his arm around my waist and grabs my cock in his hand. "You want this?" He whispers in my ear.

I push my ass into him farther as my answer.

Ten minutes and a shit ton of lube later, and I have never come so hard in my life. Beside us, the girls lay quiet, eyes locked on us.

If it wasn't official before, it is now. We are one. And fuck if I have ever been happier.

Ella wakes me the next morning. "Hey, sleepyhead. Time to get up. Big day ahead of us." I groan and roll out of bed. We have been planning this day for months, best not to ruin it by oversleeping.

After a quick bite to eat, I shower and get dressed.

When I come down the stairs, Ella, Christy, and Rick wait near the door. Our wives both radiant as ever. Ella wears a sage green backless dress that ties at her neck. Christy in her classic red, the dress the same style. Rick clad in his typical all black, same as me.

We all hop into the car and Rick drives us to Boundless. Today, the club is closed for our gathering. A small intimate get together to celebrate us. We invited our closest friends to join us. On the way there, the girls discuss how excited they are about sharing tonight with whom we consider to be family.

Once Rick parks the car, we head inside and go downstairs. In the bright lights, the club is a whole new place. The walls still ooze sex, but it is less in your face. Either way, I love this place. It is where the next chapter of our lives began. For me, Ella, Rick, and Christy.

One after another, slowly our friends make their way inside. Light chatter fills the open space as soft music plays in the background. After everyone arrives, Rick signals for Elizabeth to start.

"Can I have everyone's attention, please," Elizabeth shouts. After everyone quiets, she continues. "Thank you for being here today. And for honoring Rick, Christy, Thomas, and Ella."

Elizabeth waves us to the front of the room. Everyone else sits on couches or chairs positioned to face the front of the room. Ella and I stand on one side of Elizabeth while Christy and Rick stand on the other. Once we all stand in the right place, Elizabeth faces our friends and family then begins.

"Today, Rick, Christy, Thomas, and Ella have asked you all here to witness their special day. Although under the eyes of the law, this ceremony is not recognized, it holds significance for them and their future together. Today, we join these two couples—Rick and Christy Matheson and Thomas and Ella Reynolds. Call it a marriage of sorts. Between them, they vow to uphold all the promises they exchanged before arriving here today. The same that holds true in any bond formed. Safety. Love. Honor. Commitment. Devotion."

Elizabeth pauses and I glance down at Ella. Her smile brighter than the summer sun. Since the heated start of our relationship, I never imagined we would be standing here today. Utterly devoted to each other. Both of us in love with the couple across from us.

When I gaze at Rick and Christy, two of the most beautiful souls stare back at me. Two souls who mimic mine and Ella's. Two souls who love fiercely and give completely. Luck is the only word I can use to describe the chances of our finding each other.

"Today, Rick, Christy, Thomas, and Ella make an unbreakable promise before the people who matter most in their lives. The promise of loyalty to each other." Elizabeth hands us each a box. We open them and each slip out a ring. Christy and I have our rings, and Rick and Ella have their rings. As we exchange rings, placing them on our right ring fingers, I kiss Christy, and Rick kisses Ella.

After I kiss Ella while Rick kisses Christy, then me and Rick and Christy and Ella. "Before your loved ones, I now pronounce you husbands and wives."

After Elizabeth announces the final declaration, my heart jackhammers between my lungs. For the first time ever, a sense of absoluteness fills me. Similar to what I felt when I found Ella. She filled in all my missing parts. But once we found Rick and Christy, it was as if they sealed our hearts and gave us new life.

A new life we will all enjoy together. Always.

Want more steamy goodness, grab Ella and Thomas's steamy prequel novelette, Darkest Devotion, and prepare to binge this short.

Happy reading! xoxo

Darkest Devotion

At an underground rave, the last thing either plans is a hook up. When he takes her home the next day, an unexpected confrontation threatens to keep them apart.

Distorted Devotion

Free-spirited Sarah lives life to the fullest. When a new love interest enters her life, she starts receiving strange gifts and letters. She doesn't want to relinquish her freedom or new love, but fears the consequences.

Beloved Devotion

Liz asks the love of her life, Tiffany, to marry her. When Tiffany hesitates, but says yes, Liz is determined to learn why. As the pieces start to fall in place, Liz discovers she doesn't know her fiancée at all.

The Insomniac Duet

He was her high school bully. She was the outcast that secretly crushed on him. More than ten years later, he's her boss, completely oblivious to their shared past, and wants no one but her. More importantly, he doesn't understand her animosity toward him.

Depths Awakened

A small town romance which captivates you from the start. Mags and Geoff are two broken souls who have sworn off love. Vowed to never lose anyone else. But their undeniable attraction brings them together and refuses to let go.

The Click Duet

High school sweethearts torn apart. When fate gives them a second chance, one doesn't trust they won't be hurt again. Through the Lens (Click Duet #1) and Time Exposure (Click Duet #2) is an angsty, second chance, friends to lovers romance with all the feels.

The Inked Duet

A man with a broken heart and a woman scared to put herself out there. Love is never easy. Sometimes love rips you apart. Fine Line (Inked Duet #1) and Love Buzz (Inked Duet #2) is a second chance at love, single parent romance with a pinch of angst and dash of suspense.

Thank you so much for reading **Undying Devotion**, book two in the **Devotion Series**. If you wouldn't mind taking a moment to leave a review on the retailer site where you made your purchase, Goodreads and/or BookBub, it would mean the world to me.

Reviews help other readers find and enjoy the book as well.

Much love,
Persephone

Here are some of the songs from the **Undying Devotion** playlist. You can find and listen to the entire playlist on Spotify!

Wallflower | Kimberly August
What You Need | The Weeknd
The Wall | PatrickReza
Lover. Fighter. | SVRCINA
Holocene | Bon Iver
Voyeur Girl | Stephen
Do It For Me | Rosenfeld
All I Ever Need | Austin Mahone
Forever Ain't Enough | J. Holiday
BBY | Two Feet

ACKNOWLEDGMENTS

Readers are the best humans! Thank you to each and every one of you for reading my words. It still blows my mind that I'm publishing. Thank you times a million. If I could hug you all, my tentacle arms would squeeze you tight.

Bloggers!! I would be nowhere without you! Thank you for reading my words and promoting my books all over the internet. YOU ROCK!!

To my ARC review team! Thank you for taking a chance on me. Thank you for wanting to read my books and supporting me. And thank you for every review—they are GOLD! Without any of you, things would be so much different.

Abi... Thank you for this steamy as fuck cover! It's so perfect for this story.

Ellie and Rosa at *My Brother's Editor*! Thank you for editing and proofing this book. Thank you for making my manuscript better than it was before I sent it to you. Your input is priceless!

To every author I have bugged with questions. It amazes me how wonderful the writing community is. To belong to a community where every person wants everyone to thrive and succeed… I love it and you!

WIFE!! Thanks for being my alpha reader. Thank you for sharing your brutal honesty and cheering me on. And thanks for never getting aggravated over my non-stop schedule.

To my family who supports and roots me on! It freaks me out when I hand a copy of my book to my dad or daughter. Although I'm proud of my accomplishment, it's strange to have someone so close to you reading your work. Especially this book… eek!

ABOUT THE AUTHOR

Persephone Autumn lives in Florida with her wife, crazy dog, and two lover-boy cats. A proud mom with a cuckoo grandpup. An ethnic food enthusiast who has fun discovering ways to veganize her favorite non-vegan foods. If given the opportunity, she would intentionally get lost in nature.

For years, Persephone did some form of writing; mostly journaling or poetry. After pairing her poetry with images and posting them online, she began the journey of writing her first novel.

She mainly writes romance and poetry, but on occasion dips her toes in other works. Look for her non-romance publications under P. Autumn.